LAST FIRST LOVE

TATIANA GÓMEZ

To my wife. I love you so much.

Mom, if you somehow found this book and decide to read it, I'm sorry, I told you not to!

LAST FIRST LOVE

TATIANA GÓMEZ

1

LILY

It's hard to believe it's been ten years since I left Stanwood because honestly, not much has changed. There's a few new shops lining the main street downtown but for the most part, I see the same quirky mom-and-pop shops and the same tall evergreens—firs, cedars, and spruces —peeking through the edges of town.

I roll the window down and almost immediately I'm welcomed by the smell of fresh pine and recent rain. I take a deep breath, filling my lungs with.... cow manure. *Gross...* The stench hits me like a slap, and I gag. I roll my window up as quickly as possible, grab the perfume in my bag, and spray it all over myself. I'd forgotten Stanwood consists mainly of farmland, making the town sometimes have this nasty smell.

Moving back here after a decade away feels almost surreal. When I left home to go to college, I was sure I'd never move back. I was set on building a life in Portland, so after graduating with a BFA in Creative Writing, I threw myself into my dream of becoming a writer, and I did! It's been six years since I self-published my debut novel, and

I've written four more since then. Thankfully, they're selling, but it's just not enough to cover all my expenses anymore. And as much as I wish I could handle two jobs at once, I absolutely can't. So, I'm starting to think traditional publishing is the only way I'll be successful.

I'm working on another book now, that I'm hoping to query soon. But I'm more stuck than I ever thought possible. So here I am, moving into the cottage in my mom's backyard, hoping that a little peace and quiet—and a much-needed break from the endless bills—will give me the focus I need to finish the book I've been chipping away at for the past year.

After almost a decade of the city's constant noise and chaos, coming back to Stanwood feels weird, but good—like the weight I've been carrying is finally starting to lift, which is surprising because I half-expected the sight of the "Welcome to Stanwood" sign to make me second-guess everything. Maybe even trigger some dramatic U-turn moment, sending me into a hasty 180 in my trusty Subaru (because, yes, lesbian cliché—Subarus are basically in the contract. But also, they're ridiculously reliable and, let's face it, kind of adorable, thank you very much).

My phone rings and I glance at the screen. It's my mom. Of course. It's like she has a sixth sense of knowing the exact moment I cross into town.

"Hey, Mom," I answer.

"Hey, bug! Are you almost here?" she chirps, her excitement crackling through the phone.

"Yep, just about to turn onto your street now."

"Good, good!" I can hear her clapping on the other end. "I can't wait to see you. Drive safe!"

"I will," I say before hanging up.

It's been about a year since I last saw my mom at Christmas, and the thought of finally seeing her again fills me with pure joy. I know everyone says their mom's the best, but mine actually is. And that's all I'll say on the matter, thank you very much.

I pull into the driveway and relief immediately washes over me as I cut the engine. After hitting the road at 5 a.m., the three-and-a-half-hour drive is finally behind me. The dark, empty roads at that hour made for an eerie—but traffic-free—drive, and now, with the sun finally starting to rise over the gray sky above, I'm just itching to get out of the car take in some fresh air, and stretch my legs.

Pickles, my cat, has been surprisingly patient the whole ride, but I can tell her limit is nearing. Her soft black fur is ruffled from the drive, and her big yellow eyes are narrowed in silent protest. If I don't get her onto solid ground soon, I know she's going to unleash her fury in a way only a cat can —which is bound to be utterly chaotic.

I scoop her up and pop her into the cat carrier before stepping out of the car to take in our new home.

The cottage stands before me, smaller than I remember, but it gives off a cozy feeling—like slipping into one of my favorite sweaters.

I step inside and am greeted by soft cream-colored walls bathed in the early morning sunlight, casting a warm, golden glow across the hardwood floors. Every creaky step I take makes me smile; it's as if the house itself is saying, "Welcome home."

I quickly put Pickles down, and she immediately starts to explore. I wander from room to room, a bubbling excitement rising inside me. I can already see it all—the way I'll arrange the small living room, the cozy reading nook I'll make by the big window. My room will be cozy, with soft linens, and warm lights. The perfect place to unwind. My office will be my creative zone, packed with books, plants (definitely lots of plants), and a big desk where I can get lost in my writing, and hopefully soon because the book I've been working on has been on hold for far too long and my deadlines are fast approaching. The kitchen is small but I can already see myself cooking up something delicious, the smell of fresh herbs and spices filling the air as I finally (finally!) learn to cook. Yup, I'll be canceling that Uber One subscription in no time!

"Hey stranger!" a warm voice calls out from behind me.

I spin around, and my heart swells the moment I spot my mom by the front door, smiling from ear to ear, her deep brown eyes glassed over.

She's holding a few boxes—my old high school keep-sakes. Of course she still has them, she's the queen of holding onto all my things. Seriously, she never throws anything away. You'd think she'd want to toss a few maca-roni necklaces into the compost bin, but nope! She's kept every single one. Honestly, it's kind of adorable.

Seeing her there, with that same bright smile, instantly melts all the ache of missing her. It's always been just the two of us—I'm an only child, and my bio-dad disappeared the moment he found out my mom was pregnant. So Mom and I have always been super close (think Lorelai and Rory from the Gilmore Girls). She was devastated when I decided to go to the University of Oregon, five hours away. So I know she's happy to have me just outside her door for a bit.

I sprint over to her and wrap her in the tightest hug I can manage.

"Hi Mom," I murmur as I lean into her further. Her signature perfume—a blend of rose and sandalwood—fills my senses and grounds me in this moment. Hugging her feels like sinking into the safest place in the world and I can't help but melt into her.

When I finally let go, I take the boxes from her hands.

"Come on in!" I say, leading her through the front door.

I set the keepsake boxes down on the kitchen counter and we start walking through each room. Mom points out all the things that still need fixing—small touch-ups on the paint, replacing the carpet in a few places nothing major, mostly cosmetic fixes.

The cottage is tucked away from the main house, deep in the backyard, surrounded by trees so thick that it's easy to forget you're in someone's backyard. She used to rent this place out but the tenants she had before were a total nightmare. The kids would paint and draw all over the walls, the entire family would leave trash all over her property along with dog poop they never bothered to pick up. Their poor dog had separation anxiety so he would chew up the carpet whenever he was alone—which was every day since the kids were at school and his owners had on-site jobs.

Somehow I convinced my mom to tell them they had to go. She's been chipping away at repairs for a few months now, slowly making it livable again.

After showing me around, Mom and I head back to the U-Haul to start unloading. The afternoon slips away in a blur of boxes and packing paper.

"Did you hit much traffic?" Mom asks as she unwraps my collection of spatulas all resembling a veggie or fruit (carrot, celery, rhubarb, etc.) She laughs clearly amused by my eclectic taste in utensils.

"Not really. Just a few slow patches in the last hour, but nothing too bad," I reply, as I try to figure out how to build the bookshelves I refused to toss, even though I lost the assembly instructions years ago. "How about you? How's the garden?" I ask, even though I already know the answer. Mom has the greenest thumbs I've ever seen.

"Oh, it's thriving! I've got carrots coming out of my ears," she chuckles. "You know I always plant too many."

I laugh, picturing her buried under a mountain of carrots.

"Are you planning to see the girls soon?"

"We haven't made any plans yet, but I'm sure I'll see them soon," I say, as I try to fit two pieces of the bookshelf together, but they stubbornly refuse to cooperate

"Great!" Mom says brightly. "Just let me know before you do—I'll give you some carrots to share with them. I'm sure they'll love them!"

When mom mentions "the girls," she's referring to Valeria, Alejandra, and Clara—my best friends since middle school. We were the only Latinas in our town so we kind of stuck together and never let go. Even after graduating high school and going off to different colleges, the four of us have stayed incredibly close. There used to be a fifth member in our group, someone I've known since pre-K—Isabella. But things with her took a different turn. The summer before our first semester of college, everything went downhill. She was my closest friend, but obviously, that's no longer the case.

Thankfully, at the time, Mom didn't push for details— one of the many things I love about her. When she heard about my falling out with Isabella, she didn't press for answers or try to make me talk before I was ready—and still hasn't. Even after all these years, she still doesn't know what happened between Isabella and me, but let's be honest, do moms ever truly know the full story behind their kid's first heartbreak?

As twilight sets in, Mom decides she's done enough

unpacking for the day. "I'll let you get some rest and we can finish unpacking tomorrow," she says.

I struggle to my feet, untangling the pretzel I've made of myself and my legs on the floor, and walk over to her.

"Thank you for everything," I say before giving her a peck on the cheek. "I couldn't have done this without you."

She beams at me and pulls me in for a quick hug before I walk her to the door.

"Shout if you need anything, okay?" she says, her hand lingering on my arm, giving it a gentle squeeze. "I'm so glad you're back home, Lilybug," she adds. The crow's feet at the corners of her eyes deepen as she smiles. It's a look filled with warmth and so much love that it makes my heart feel three times its size.

With one last hug, she steps out into the cool night, her footsteps gradually fading into the quiet as she makes her way to the main house.

I click the door shut behind me, and just like that, it's just me and the quiet of my new place. I look around at the half-open boxes scattered across the living room and the—still—unassembled bookshelf waiting patiently on the floor. With a dramatic roll of my eyes and a resigned sigh, I head to my bedroom grabbing my phone from the kitchen counter on the way. I hate moving.

A quick few taps on my phone and my favorite true crime podcast kicks in. "Hi weirdos... I'm..." echoes in my room, but I let it fade into the background as I survey the mess in front of me. Unlabeled boxes everywhere, my mattress is still rolled up in the corner, and the unassembled bed frame lies awkwardly on the floor.

I roll up my sleeves, ready to tackle the chaos in front of me, but the doorbell rings. I shuffle to the door, half-expecting it to be my mom dropping by to grab something she forgot. But when I open it, there's Valeria, grinning from ear to ear.

"I hope it's okay. I showed up unannounced," she says almost shyly. "I just couldn't wait to see you!"

"Oh my God, of course, it's okay!" I pull her into a hug and wrap around her as tightly as I did my mom. When I finally let go a wave of warmth washes over me as I take her in. Her hair is shorter than the last time I saw her. Her usual long, messy blond curls are now styled into a cute pixie cut that frames her face and highlights her smile beautifully.

"Wow, you cut your hair! It looks great."

"Thank you!" She says as her fingers fidget with the ends of her hair. "I did it this morning. I was nervous at first, but I love how easy it'll be to style now."

I step aside to let her in and I guide her further into the house.

"Let's go to my room," I say, gesturing for her to follow me. "If I don't get this bed frame sorted, I'll be sleeping on the floor tonight, and I don't think my back can handle that." I laugh.

"Uh oh, I won't be much help with that, but I'll give it a shot."

"Noted," I say as Valeria and I walk to my room.

"Here she is," I say with a sigh, pointing at the pile of metal that used to be my bed frame.

Valeria kneels, and tries to fit a few pieces together but after a few futile attempts and some awkward twisting and turning, she sits back on her heels, shaking her head. "This is going nowhere fast."

I chuckle.

"You should call Clara tomorrow. She'll have this up in no time," Valeria says.

Defeated, I lean against the wall and cross my arms.

"Looks like I'll be on the floor after all. Let's have some wine. I don't want to look at the mess in this room right now."

Valeria stands and follows after me. As soon as we're in the kitchen, she notices the boxes my mom brought over earlier.

"Are those your keepsakes from high school?" she asks, her voice going a little higher than normal. That's how I know she's excited. Valeria is usually the more reserved one in our group.

"Yeah, my mom brought them over earlier. I'd honestly forgotten I had them," I laugh.

"Let's open them," she says as she walks faster towards them.

"You're on!" I say. At this point, I'll do anything to distract myself from the mess waiting in my room.

I walk towards my purse, pull out a bottle of wine—because priorities—and grab a couple of mugs from one of the unpacked boxes my mom left open in the kitchen. I tuck the three small boxes under my arm and guide us into the living room. With no furniture until tomorrow, it's looking like tonight is shaping up to be a classic wine-on-the-floor type of night for us.

As I scan the boxes, one catches my eye—worn at the corners, labeled "Keepsakes" in faded, barely legible marker. I pause, a mix of curiosity and hesitation creeps in. I haven't touched these boxes in years, not since I stashed them in my mom's attic after graduation. I can't even remember what's in them.

"Let's do this one first," I say to Valeria, who is looking increasingly excited.

With a deep breath, I gently lift the lid of the box. The smell of old paper wafts up alongside faint traces of my mom's perfume. Inside, fragments of my senior year of high school are tucked away.

"Look at this," I say, pulling out a yearbook filled with scribbled messages with a few ticket stubs tucked away between the pages.

I pull one out, my fingers tracing the edge of a stub from a concert where my friends and I danced like fools, lost in the music and each other's company. As we continue to sift through the box, I find a collection of notes rubber-banded together, notes exchanged in class between Valeria, Alejandra, Clara, and...

"Oh wow, is that... Isabella's handwriting?" Valeria asks and my stomach drops.

I grab the bulk of Isabella's notes and stare at them, each loop and swirl of ink like a ghost from the past. They're held together by one of our friendship bracelets, its vibrant colors now faded. A wave of sadness hits me as I realize that even after all these years, echoes of my friendship with Isabella are still here, carefully preserved. Each folded note a reminder of the person who had once meant everything to me.

"Yeah," I say softly, feeling the ache in my chest coil around and solidify, making it hard for me to breathe. I take a big gulp of my wine hoping that will ease the tension.

As I set the notes aside, something nestled at the bottom of the box catches Valeria's eye. She reaches down and pulls out a folded piece of paper, slightly yellowed with age.

She hands it to me, and I carefully unfold it, the paper crackles in protest. At the top of the page, in my teenage handwriting, are the words "Summer Bucket List."

I can't help but smile. Excitedly, I turn the paper over and show it to Valeria.

"Do you remember this?" I ask, holding the paper a

little too close to her face. Valeria scoots back, and together, we scan the page.

Immediately that summer comes alive in my mind. Each completed item a snapshot—the night we spent in an abandoned barn by the woods, making up ridiculous stories 'till Alejandra got too scared of the dark and forced us to go home. The night we snuck into the community pool after one too many rounds of drink or dare.

As we read through the list, we notice that some of the items were left unfinished.

1 Sunrise hike to our secret spot
2 Nighttime swim under the stars
3 Cabin weekend getaway

A wistful smile tugs at my lips, but it quickly fades as my eyes land on the last unchecked item.

4 Go to Isabella's art show.

Regret settles in my chest as I think about that night. I had gone to Isabella's show, but instead of going inside to talk with her proud parents and teachers like I should have, I stayed outside in the cold. When it started to rain, I leaned fully into my sad girl moment, standing there as the droplets soaked through my coat, watching the girl I loved through the big gym windows.

She looked towards the door a few times, probably wondering if I'd show. And each time, the guilt got heavier and I felt like I was sinking into the pavement. I know I should've gone inside, I should've been there like I said I would to support her and tell her how amazing I thought she was. But I just couldn't do it—not with how broken I was. So, I stayed outside, letting the moment slip away. I've regretted it ever since.

"I can't believe we never finished it," Valeria says, oblivious to the storm brewing in my mind.

"Yeah, well... Isabella and I had our falling out so I think we all just kind of forgot about it."

Valeria's expression softens. "Yeah, I guess so," she says, her tone thoughtful. "We all kind of let it slip, didn't we?" She pauses. "But... I remember how much we cared about finishing it. Maybe it just wasn't the right time back then..." She glances up at me with a mischievous shimmer in her deep brown eyes. "You know we could finish it now!"

I blink, surprised and a little confused by her suggestion.

"Finish the list?" I say, the words feeling foreign on my tongue.

"Yeah, why not?" Valeria nudges me with her elbow, grinning. "We may not be those carefree kids anymore, but who says we can't relive a little of it? I'm sure everyone would be up for it."

For a moment, the idea doesn't seem so crazy. But then my eyes drift back to the last item—Isabella's art show—and just like that, all the optimism in me drains. That one feels impossible.

"I don't know, Val," I reply, my voice barely above a whisper.

Valeria's smile wavers, her brows knitting together as she follows my gaze.

"Isabella," she murmurs, and suddenly the mood shifts.

"I don't think we can do the list without her," I admit. "And she still refuses to talk to me, so... I just don't think we should do it. Not without her. It wouldn't feel right."

She shrugs, a playful grin creeping back onto her face.

"She's hardheaded," Valeria says, her voice gentle. "She's had too much time to stew in whatever she's feeling. I have no idea if she'll want to join, but what's the harm in asking? Worst case, she says no and we pack up the list." She says as she shrugs and pretends to dust off her hands. "But honestly, I'm pretty sure Alejandra and Clara will annoy her so much about joining that she'll probably give in just to shut them up." That thought makes her giggle and I can't help but smile.

Clara, Alejandra, and Valeria have spent the last ten years trying to get Isabella and me to talk, but it's been no use. I've reached out to Isabella a few times, sent texts, and left her voicemails, but she never replies. The girls have even tried to get her to talk to me when I Facetime them and she's around but she would just walk out the room till I hung up. It's beyond frustrating, especially because I want to fix things, but she won't give me the chance—despite the fact that she's the one who broke my heart. I've never really understood her anger, to be honest. I made everything easier for her, even when it hurt me.

Before I can say anything, my phone buzzes in my back pocket. I pull it out and glance at the preview. It's a message from my mom, wishing me good night. I'm about to open it and reply but my eyes catch something else—an old group chat with Valeria, Clara, Alejandra, and Isabella. The chat has been quiet for months now, with only the occasional birthday message or holiday greeting breaking the silence. A stark contrast to the lively group chat I have with Valeria, Alejandra, and Clara.

Reviving the old chat feels nerve-wracking, and a sure way to let myself down again. I stare at my phone for what feels like hours. Thinking up all the reasons why I should just do it, why this is a good idea but I can't think of a single one.

"I don't think I can," I say looking up at Valeria.

"What's the worst that can happen? She ignores you? She's already doing that," Valeria says. And she's right—but that doesn't make this any easier.

I rub at my forehead trying to gather up enough courage to type up the message. I try and I try but when I can't, I blow out a raspberry and set my phone down.

"May I?" Valeria asks reaching for my phone. I nod and watch as she types something up and takes a picture of the list. "There, when you're ready just hit send," she says.

I take the phone back, my thumb hovering over the send button for an eternity.

Just hit send. One little click, you can do one click. I repeat to myself over and over, and over.

"Just do it!" Valeria says and before I lose my nerve completely... I do.

> Lily 7:00 p.m.: Hey, guess what Val and I found while unpacking.
>
> Lily 7:00 p.m.: Attachment: 1 image
>
> Lily 7:00 p.m.: Remember this?

A few minutes pass without a single reply, and I'm just sitting there, staring between Valeria and my phone, willing someone—anyone—to respond. The longer the silence drags on, the more convinced I am that I've completely messed up and that I should never ever listen to Valeria again!

My phone buzzes, and it's a private message from Clara.

Clara 7:08 p.m.: Did you mean to send that to THAT thread? 👀

Lily 7:08 p.m.: Yeah, Val said I should send it to see if Isabella wants to finish the list with us.

Clara 7:09 p.m.: That messy girl. Tell her I love her.

Clara then replies in the group chat, and soon, everyone's texts start to trickle in.

Clara 7:10 p.m.: OMG, no way

Alejandra 7:10 p.m.: I haven't thought about this in years 😍

Valeria 7:10 p.m.: I told Lily we should complete it even if it's fall.

Alejandra 7:11 p.m.: 💯 that would be so fun! Plus, there's not much left!

Valeria 7:12 p.m.: Let's meet up in a couple of days once Lily gets all settled. Maybe at The Owl Coffee at 11 on Thursday. Work for everyone?

Clara 7:12 p.m.: Works for me

Alejandra 7:12 p.m.: Yes!

"See, I told you they'd love the idea," Valeria says, giving herself a self-satisfied pat on the back.

I shake my head at her and smile. I set my phone down, and excitement bubbles within me. But as the initial rush of emotion fades, sadness settles in as I realize Isabella didn't reply... and to think I let myself believe she would.

I try to focus on seeing the girls. But the silence from Isabella lingers in the back of my mind, making my heart ache a little more. Her silence is like an annoying itch I can't scratch. You'd think I'd be used to it by now. After all, I've spent the last ten years being ignored by her, even though she broke my heart. Saying that relationship messed me up would be an understatement—I haven't been able to maintain a long-term—or even a short-term—relationship since. Even when I meet someone I really like, I always feel like I'm not enough, like I'll never measure up and that they'll just end up leaving me anyway so why get close? Every time something starts to feel right, I'm just waiting for it to fall apart. It's like I'm stuck in this loop, expecting things to go wrong before they even have a chance to go right.

I know better than to wish for Isabella to show up because I know she absolutely won't, but the thought of not seeing her makes me feel a bit sad.

"Well, love, I should probably head out. Brooke will be home soon, and if I'm not there, she might actually kill me," Valeria says with a tight smile.

"How are things with you and Brooke?" I ask.

Valeria doesn't say anything for a few seconds. Her eyes fixed on her fingers as she spins the ring around her thumb. "They're... not great, but we're working on it. Sometimes, it feels like we're just hanging on by a thread."

Valeria and Brooke have been together for four years, and it's been a complete mess the entire time. Brooke is incredibly controlling, and Val just goes along with whatever she says. Alejandra, Clara, and I have had endless conversations with her about how Brooke's behavior is incredibly toxic, but Val just doesn't see it. Or at least does a great job at ignoring it. I want to bring up how weird it is that she needs to be home to greet Brooke but I know better than to bring it up right now. So instead I reach for her arm and give it a tight squeeze.

"I'm sorry, Val,"

"It is what it is," she replies as she straightens her posture and gives me a tiny smile.

"Let me walk you out," I say, closing the box and setting it aside. I struggle to get myself off the floor, letting out a grunt as I stand up and stretch. My muscles protest and I can feel each bone in my body settle back into place. I guess this is late twenties for you.

"I'll see you in a couple of days!" Valeria shouts back as she walks out the door and down the front door steps.

"Text me when you're home," I yell back as I watch her get into her car.

When her car is out of sight, I close the door and lean back against it. My eyes drift to the dark window across from me. The quiet outside feels almost eerie after being so used to the constant hum of the city, but it's a welcome change. I'd forgotten what true stillness sounds like.

My eyes glance at the remaining boxes scattered around the living room, but the thought of tackling them tonight feels exhausting. Tomorrow, I tell myself. Right now, a hot shower and some sleep are the only things I have the energy for.

I stroll down the hallway to the bathroom and turn the shower on, watching as steam starts to fill the room and fog up the mirror. I step inside the shower and let the warm water cascade over my skin, soothing away the tension in my body. As I wash away the long day, my thoughts kept drifting back to the list, to my friends, and—unsurprisingly —to Isabella.

Isabella. The name alone sends a jolt through me. It's strange, the way memories of her can resurface so easily. The Isabella-shaped hole in my life hasn't fully healed, and being back in Stanwood is like poking at a half-closed wound. She had been my best friend, my confidante, my... everything.

I try to shake off thoughts of her as I step out of the shower—there's no use in obsessing over the past. Still, my mind won't let go of the idea of seeing her again, of trying to repair our friendship. I tried for years, and now I've just kind of given up but maybe if she agrees to do the list I can try again.

I slip into some mismatched pajamas and unroll my mattress. Not waiting for it to fully expand, I crawl onto it, letting it settle beneath me. My back will definitely feel this tomorrow.

My phone buzzes beside me—there's a new message in the group chat. My heart freezes, and I shoot up, hope surging through me before I can stop it. For a second, I think it's Isabella. My fingers hover over the screen, anticipation building in my chest, but when I open the message, it's not her.

> Alejandra 9:55 p.m.: Can't wait to see you all!

The wave of disappointment hits hard, and I sink back into my mattress, trying to push down the ache that lingers in the back of my mind.

Of course, it wasn't her.

2

ISABELLA

To say I am tired would be a severe understatement. I am a living zombie. I got maybe two hours of sleep last night and if that wasn't enough now there's an obnoxious blare cutting through the quiet of my house...the door buzzer. I squint at the clock on the nightstand. It's 7 a.m., who the fuck is here so early? I'm tempted to just let it ring until whoever is at my door gives up but the buzz only grows more insistent and now my dogs are barking. I groan and drag myself out of bed.

I grab the first things within reach—a worn graphic tee draped over the bed frame and a pair of black sweats I'd left on the floor. I quickly put them on, not caring about the wrinkles. I hear the buzzer ring again, followed by Alejandra's voice slicing through. "Wake up, Isabella! I brought you coffee!"

Great... Alejandra is at my door at the ass crack of dawn... Don't get me wrong, I absolutely adore her, but it's just too fucking early, and I can already feel her high energy vibrating through the door.

I swing the door open just as Alejandra's fist freezes

mid-knock. She tumbles inside, a tray of coffee in one hand and a couple of pastry bags in the other, teetering on the edge of spilling everything. My arm shoots out instinctively, but she catches herself at the last second, flashing me a grin as the coffee sloshes dangerously close to the edge.

"Ale, what the fuck are you doing here so early?" I grumble as she barges in, her cheerful energy practically shoving its way into my house alongside her.

"I noticed you didn't reply to the group chat yesterday," she chirps, as she plops on the couch making herself at home. "So, I figured I'd stop by and check on you before heading to the studio. I can only imagine what kind of night you had."

And as we all know, she's dead right. My night had been a complete disaster—tossing and turning, unable to shut my brain off, thanks to Lily's stupid message. The notification had thrown me into a full-blown nervous spiral, pacing around the living room like some deranged animal. My two dogs watched me aimlessly walk around my house for hours. I could almost hear their thoughts: Is she okay? Should we bark for help?

It's not that I didn't know Lily was moving back to Stanwood; Valeria, Alejandra, and Clara have made sure to keep me annoyingly up to date on Lily's life through the years. But the thought of seeing her again is something else entirely. And now they're all giddy about jumping right back into the bucket list—a list that used to mean something but now just feels like a reminder of the summer when everything went to shit.

My legs eventually gave out, and I collapsed onto the couch, burying my face in the cushions. Lily just waltzes back into town, no big deal, like she didn't leave a trail of chaos in her wake? It's maddening. And now I'm supposed to smile and play nice while she gets a clean slate? Please.

Lily wrecked me beyond repair, and that says a lot, considering I was in the most toxic on-and-off relationship imaginable for three years before her. But even that doesn't compare to what happened with Lily. Since her, I haven't dated. I've had a few situationships here and there, but nothing serious. After all I've been through, I've mastered the art of casual.

I take a small cup of coffee from Alejandra, muttering a groggy "Thanks" as I collapse onto the couch.

"So," Alejandra starts, as she looks around my living room, taking in the half-finished canvases and scattered art supplies. "Are you going with us to the coffee shop tomorrow?" Her tone is annoyingly casual.

I take a slow sip of coffee, letting the warmth seep into my bones before grumbling, "Absolutely not."

Alejandra raises an eyebrow, clearly expecting more. I sigh, setting the cup down, and run a hand through my tangled hair. "We haven't had a real conversation in, what, ten years? I'm not exactly excited to dive back into this whole bucket list thing with you all. Especially not when Lily and I still haven't hashed things out. It'll just make everything more... awkward, and honestly, I'm not in the mood to pretend like it won't."

"I get it. It's been a long time. But you two were so close. Maybe this is your chance to, I don't know, clear the air."

"Yeah, maybe," I mutter, but the words feel hollow. "But honestly, I don't want to get into it with her right now, so I don't think I'll go. It's just not worth the headache." The thought of her stirs up way too many memories—good and bad—that I have zero interest in unpacking right now.

Alejandra leans in, her voice softer. "Are you ever going to tell us what happened between you two?"

I look away, staring out the window as old memories churn in my mind, burning like acid. The girls have asked so many times over the years, but I have always just left it at: we had a big argument. I'm not even sure you could call it that but regardless, I never went into detail, never told them the real reason—just that I knew it was something we'd never be able to fix.

What they don't know is that that summer, Lily and I hooked up. But "hooked up" doesn't really cover it—we'd spent the better part of a month tangled up in each other, full of—what is to this day—the best sex I've ever had and so much laughter I swore I'd have a six-pack by the time school started in the fall. It felt electric as if we were the only two people that existed. I believed her when she said she wanted something more. It wasn't just the sex that had me hooked it was all the corny shit. It was the stolen moments, the gifts, the deep talks about our future. The way we would lie under the stars, dreaming of what our life together could be. She sold me a dream—made me think we were real, that we'd head off to college as a couple and I bought it. But by the end of Summer, Lily made it abundantly clear I had been way off. She disappeared. No goodbye, no text, no explanation, not even a post-it. She ghosted me like I didn't matter at all.

After weeks of trying to get ahold of her and getting nothing, my sadness turned into anger. And the anger that flooded through me was so intense, I was sure I was about to develop magical powers and accidentally set everything on fire. Once that switch happened, I swore I'd never speak to her again. So, when she finally reached out months later, I couldn't bring myself to read her messages, let alone respond. Eventually, she got the hint and stopped trying. And now, here we are—ten years later.

I turn back to look at Alejandra, her usually bright eyes full of concern. And as much as I want to lay it all out, I can't do it.

I shake my head slightly, feeling that tight, nagging knot in my chest. "Not right now."

She sighs, her eyes lingering on me, lips pressed tightly together. "Do you think, now that Lily's back in town, you two might finally talk things through?"

I let out a sharp, humorless laugh. "Doubt it. It's been too long, and I don't care enough to dig it all up."

Alejandra raises an eyebrow at me, her eyes piercing as she slowly narrows them. "Stop pretending like none of it matters when we both know it does. I remember how broken you were when she left. You can't just shut off your feelings and act like you don't have a heart, Isabella."

Her words hit me like a splash of cold water, and I can't stop thinking about the countless nights I wasted drowning in confusion. I'd stare at my phone, desperate for a message that never came, only to get one when it didn't matter anymore—because what doesn't kill you texts you a few months later. Every time my friends mentioned her name over the years, my stupid heart would sink to my stomach, that same old ache in my chest resurfacing, never fully fading.

The day Clara texted me that Lily was moving back, it felt like the pit I'd buried deep inside me clawed its way to the surface, choking the breath out of me. All the anger I thought I'd buried came roaring back. I huff and lean back, trying to brush off the wave of discomfort that hits me. "Yeah, well, things change. People change. I'm over it."

"Sure. Keep telling yourself that," she says as she pats my knee.

I clench my jaw, my voice dropping to a near whisper. "Please, just drop it."

"You're so stubborn."

I let out a frustrated huff. "Maybe."

"Anyways, I hope you change your mind," she says with a smile. "We kind of need you for the last item on the list. Can't exactly go to an Isabella art show without Isabella!" She sings.

I know the girls are excited about all of us getting together again, but the last thing I want is awkward small talk with Lily. I know it's only a matter of time before I'm forced into a hangout with her. I can't avoid her forever— thanks to my annoyingly over-involved best friends—but I just don't want to do any of this right now. I'm still so hurt and so mad.

Alejandra looks down at her watch. "Shit, I've got to get to work. We'll talk more later, okay?" She says as she flashes a quick smile.

I nod, managing a tight smile as she gathers her things.

"I love you," she says, kissing my cheek before walking toward the door.

The moment her footsteps fade down the hallway, the silence in my house closes in on me. The half-painted canvases scattered across my living room stare back at me, judging me.

For hours, I drift through the mess of half-finished projects, pacing from one distraction to the next, but nothing sticks. Every thought pulls me back to Lily, the group chat, and the fucking bucket list looming over me like a storm cloud. The urge to paint has completely dried up for the day, replaced by a persistent heaviness in my chest.

And it couldn't have come at a worse time, since I have a commissioned piece due in three days, and all I've managed to complete is the outline.

Unfortunately for me, painting is tied to my emotions in a way I can't escape. I can't simply push through the creative process when I'm struggling—my art is more than just a career. It's my therapy, my silent confidant, the one constant in the storm that is my life. When my dad passed, it was the only thing that kept me tethered to reality. And when Lily left, it was the only thing that held me together, piece by fragile piece. For as long as I can remember, it's been the only thing I've ever truly needed, the only thing that truly understands me.

My phone pings on the coffee table and when I reach for it I see there's a new message in the group chat and I freeze. I hesitantly open it but It's just Clara sending the location for tomorrow. *I need to change my text preview settings so I can see who's texting me before I give myself a heart attack.*

I stare at the picture of the bucket list, my fingers hovering above the keyboard, unable to commit to going. The longer I stare at the list, the heavier the weight in my chest grows. Memories of Lily and me flash through my mind, and my blood boils just as it had all those years ago.

My phone pings again and it's a private message from Clara.

> Clara 4:00 p.m.: Alejandra and I are heading to Shorty's near your place for a drink in a bit. Want to join us?

> Isabella 4:02 p.m.: what time?

> Clara 4:02 p.m.: Meet you there at 5?

> Isabella 4:02 p.m.: 👍

I run a hand through my hair, frustration eating away at me, because I already know what they're going to say. Man... I need a drink. I decide to go to the bar now and wait for Clara and Alejandra to show up.

But before I head out I text Myra. I need all the distraction I can get.

> Isabella 4:14 p.m.: meet at shorty's in 5?

> Myra 4:14 p.m.: Sure, but I can't stay for long

> Isabella 4:17 p.m.: that's fine, meeting with ale and clara in a bit

Myra is someone I've been seeing very, very casually. Neither of us is into the whole dating or commitment thing, but we're both big fans of sex, so it works perfectly. Plus, she's fun to be around. She's easygoing, laid-back, and doesn't try to complicate things, which is honestly all I need.

———— ♥ ♥ ♥ ————

Once I'm at the bar, I settle into a stool and order a whiskey on the rocks. The clink of glasses and low murmur of conversation, are a very welcome distraction from the chaos in my head.

The bartender places my drink in front of me, and as I take my first sip, Myra walks through the doors and immediately my eyes sweep over her body. She's wearing a knee-length black dress that hugs her curves just right. Her dark hair falling straight and smooth, down to her shoulders and her bright green eyes sparkle even in the dim light. She's absolutely stunning. If I were into dating she's exactly the type of girl I'd go for. Myra catches my eye and smiles.

I smile back before turning to my drink, finishing it just as she reaches me.

"Hi," she says, sliding into the stool next to me.

"Hey."

"You ok?" she asks, as she kisses me on the cheek.

"Yeah, just needed a distraction."

"From?" She asks, raising an eyebrow.

"Lily's back in town."

"Oh?" She leans in, intrigued.

Myra went to school with us, so she knows Lily. She doesn't know all the details of what happened between us— but she knows more than the girls do. She knows Lily and I hooked up but she doesn't know much past that. Just that it didn't end well.

"Yeah, and I guess she found this bucket list from our senior year. Now everyone's all excited about completing it, but honestly, I'm not into it. Alejandra already came by trying to talk me into joining, and I'm pretty sure that's exactly what she and Clara are going to want to talk about when I see them in a bit."

"Sounds like a lot," she says, her jaw tightening as she shifts around on her stool.

"You good?" I ask, feeling a switch in her energy, not entirely sure why.

"Mhmm," she replies. Her lips pressed tightly together. A flash of irritation flying through her eyes.

"Okay..." I laugh not knowing what else to say. I reach for my drink to take a sip, but it's still empty.

"Let me get you a drink," she says, as she turns to flag down the bartender.

"Thanks," I say, as I swirl the ice around in my empty cup.

"Well, what can I do?" she asks, leaning in slightly.

"Mmm... Nothing, unless you know a way to keep my mind from spinning,"

She raises an eyebrow, her lips curling into a playful smile. "Oh, I think I know a way or two," she says in a sultry voice.

"Do you now?" I say, a teasing grin creeping onto my face as I turn to face her.

Myra doesn't say a word. Instead, she stands, her smile widening as she turns and starts walking toward the bathroom. Just before disappearing from view, she looks over her shoulder and gives me a small nod.

And that's all I need. I push off the stool and follow after her.

The moment the bathroom door closes behind me, she pulls me close, and her lips slam into mine. Myra's hands find their way into my hair, and she pulls hard, exposing my neck. She buries her mouth against my skin, igniting a whirlwind of desire that pools beneath my belly button.

I walk her towards a wall, my hand desperately fisting and bunching her dress. I'm not usually this rushed but I need to drown out Alejandra's voice reminding me of how broken I was when Lily left, to erase everything to do with the list and push aside every thought circling my mind about Lily and me even if it's just for a second. And hearing Myra moan, my name as I slip my hand into her underwear, and circle her clit is doing just that. Her panting drowns out everything in my mind. The world outside fades away, and all that matters is her and the need I have to make her cum.

Myra is so wet I easily slide two fingers inside her, thrusting in and out of her. Losing myself in the slick sounds coming from between her thighs. Her hands find their way inside my shirt and her nails dig into my back as I feel her wrap around my fingers. I push deeper into her, curling my fingers and she moans. The sounds she makes make me go faster and harder until she's wrapped so tightly around me that I can barely move my finger. I kiss her hard, ready to feel her cum, when the bathroom door swings open.

Myra drops her head on my shoulder as she murmurs a low "fuck."

Neither of us moves, my hand still buried between her thighs.

"Oh... um, sorry," a familiar voice says from behind me. I turn quickly and see... Lily. My stomach drops and I don't know if it's the alcohol or the fact that Lily is right in front of me that makes me want to puke.

Fuck. Fuck. Fuck

Lily's eyes widen as she realizes it's me and all the color drains from her face. Her big brown eyes dart back and forth between my hand and Myra and I feel like I'm watching her brain reboot in real-time.

I slide my hand out from between Myra's thighs and watch as Lily's eyes gloss over. Her eyes linger on Myra for a little too long. A pink flush starts to creep up her neck, and I can see the heat rise to her cheeks.

"I'm so... I didn't mean to. I... I'll... Sorry," Lily finally says as she turns and closes the door behind her.

"I'm sorry," I say, as I turn to Myra, trying to gulp down the nervous laughter bubbling up in my throat. "Next time, let's make it into a stall," I joke.

"What is Lily doing here?" Myra asks as she cocks her hip and crosses her arms over her chest.

"How should I know?" I say defensively.

She doesn't say anything else, just narrows her eyes at me.

We busy ourselves, smoothing out our clothes. I recoil a few messy strands in my hair, trying to regain some semblance of composure but all my movements feel foreign and unnatural. My brain stuck on Lily's shocked face. The knot at the base of my throat makes swallowing nearly impossible. I don't know if I'm going to cry, scream, or throw up, but one of the three needs to happen because I feel like I'm about to explode.

I take a few deep breaths trying to get my heartbeat under control before leaving the bathroom. When I finally feel like I've got it under control I swing the door open and find Lily standing near the door with her head buried in her hands. Fucking great...

"What are you doing here?" Myra asks, her tone sharp enough that Lily flinches.

"Oh, um... Clara and Alejandra asked me to come," she replies, barely able to look at me.

"They didn't tell me you were coming," I say, my heart racing.

I'm going to kill them...

"Yeah, well, surprise!" Lily says as she forces a laugh.

I do my best not to roll my eyes and instead turn to look at Myra. Her brows are knit together, her nose is slightly flared and that's when I realize I need to get us both away from Lily.

I grab Myra's hand, and we awkwardly squeeze past her without another word.

When we make it back to the bar my brain is still trying to process what the fuck just happened. My last few brain cells doing their very fucking best to figure out how to feel or act. Myra doesn't say anything when we take our seats and I can't decide if that's a good thing or a bad thing. We sit in silence for a few minutes until I can't take the quiet anymore.

"Are you ok?" I ask reaching for Myra's hand.

Myra turns to look at me a whisper of a smile on her face. "Yeah... that was just not very fun," she says looking down at my hand around hers.

"I know... I'm—."

"Are you going to hang out with her when I leave?" she asks cutting me off.

I close my eyes and pinch the bridge of my nose. "I don't know," I say honestly. Part of me wants to show Lily her presence has no effect on me but the other part just wants to go home and try to ignore all of this.

"Well, I don't think you should," Myra says as she lets out a sigh pulling her hand from under mine. "Ale and Clara shouldn't have sprung this on you."

I know she's right. But I was almost expecting something like this to happen, so it's hard for me to get mad at them about it—granted, I wasn't expecting them to try and force us into a hangout so soon after Lily got into town but clearly I underestimated them.

"Anyway, I need to head out, but text me and let me know how this all goes," she says as she points her finger at the ceiling, drawing lazy circles in the air.

"Yeah, sure," I say, but I already know how this is going to go. Spoiler alert: not good.

As Myra stands she rolls her eyes so subtly at something behind me that I almost miss it. Before I can ask her about it she leans in to kiss me goodbye. Which catches me off guard because she's never done that before. She usually gives me a peck on the cheek, but I kiss her back anyway and watch her walk out the door. When she's out of view I turn to try and find Clara and Alejandra, only to find Lily talking to them. Her cheeks crimson red, and their eyes wide. I can't deal with this right now, so I quickly text Clara and Alejandra to let them know I'm leaving.

I can't fucking believe them.

------- ♥ ♥ ♥ -------

Once I'm home, frustration and disappointment finally start to settle in. Clara and Alejandra know things between Lily and I are shit, but they still invited her without saying a word to me. I knew this was coming, but a heads-up would've been nice. Disappointed but not surprised is bound to be the theme these next few weeks, and I already can't fucking stand it.

I start walking around my room, trying to give my restless legs some kind of outlet. My feet tracing a path from my bed to the door and back, over and over. And then, it hits me: they're not going to stop doing this... They're going to keep inviting her to everything, acting like it's no big deal, and hoping we'll just "work it out."

The more I think about it, the more I realize there's only one way to go about this—just lean into it, join the group, and finish this stupid bucket list.

I let out a heavy sigh and sit on the edge of my bed. If I go along with the list, at least I'll be in on the plan and won't be caught off guard.

But if I'm going to do this, I need a little backup of my own. Immediately I think of Myra. She's easygoing, and fun and I know she likes me so I'm sure she'd do it. Plus, I could use a buffer, if Myra is around the girls won't be so fucking pushy, making everything a lot more manageable for me.

I grab my phone and start typing a message, hoping it doesn't sound too weird.

> Isabella 6:13 p.m.: any chance you'd want to join me for this bucket list meeting at the coffee shop tomorrow? I need a buffer

My thumb hovers over the 'send' button, and I feel a little ridiculous for even asking, but if she's down, it could make this whole thing a lot easier.

> Myra 6:22 p.m.: I don't know if that's a good idea

> Isabella 6:22 p.m.: PLEAAASE!

> Myra 6:22 p.m.: You don't think it'll make it extra weird? your old hook up hanging out with your new one?

> Isabella 6:23 p.m.: why would it? I doubt she'll care

> Myra 6:24 p.m.: Fine. what time were you thinking?

> Isabella 6:24 p.m.: atta girl! we're meeting at 11

> Myra 6:25 p.m.: I can't at 11 but I can meet you at 12? do a little vent sesh after?

> Isabella 6:26 p.m.: sounds good, thanks for doing this

> Myra 6:28 p.m.: Already regretting it!

With Myra onboard I quickly type up a message and send it to the group chat, letting them know I'll be there tomorrow. Once I hit send, I turn my phone off, trying to block out whatever cheerful texts the girls are bound to send next. I set it down on my nightstand and head to the bathroom.

I look at myself in the mirror and I'm a fucking mess—tired eyes, messy hair, smudged mascara, and red stain all over my lips from Myra's lipstick. I stand there for a second, just letting the silence sink in before I start brushing my teeth. I change into the comfiest pajamas I own and crawl into bed even though it's barely 7 p.m. I'm hoping to catch up on at least a few hours of sleep so I'm not extra grumpy tomorrow, but as soon as my head hits the pillow, my mind kicks into overdrive. Thoughts of Lily keep circling, along with the mess I'm about to walk into. I try to focus on the quiet, but all I can hear is my heart pounding in my ears.

I pull the blanket up tighter, wishing sleep would just come, but I know it's not going to happen anytime soon.

Why did I agree to this?

3

LILY

I make it to the coffee shop a little earlier than planned. My nerves have been all over the place since last night, and I'm hoping for a moment to calm down before Isabella shows up.

The thought of seeing her today twists my stomach into tight, painful knots. I'm still trying to piece together everything that happened last night. I hated seeing Isabella with someone else, and the fact that it was with someone I knew made it even worse.

A twinge of jealousy was coursing through me all night, which was odd because that's not something I usually feel—hell, it's something I've never felt—or at least not since Isabella and I had our falling out. So the fact that she—of all people—can draw it out of me so easily... is unsettling. Frustrating even. It's been ten years. Ten years, and somehow, she can still push all the right buttons, and make me feel things I thought I was done with.

I barely slept last night. My mind was stuck on the image of Isabella elbow-deep in Myra. *Ugh...*

I walk up to the counter and order a black drip coffee

with a shot of espresso. I usually order sweet drinks, but today I need all the caffeine I can get. The barista almost immediately hands me a warm to-go cup with a kind smile, and I cradle it in my hands, letting the heat seep into my palms.

I sit near the window, hoping the view outside will somehow steady my nerves. I tap my fingers on the table, trying to focus on the smell of fresh coffee beans, the soft murmur of other customers talking, and the world moving outside. I watch people pass by, cars rolling down the street, raindrops lightly dotting the window. I'm doing everything I can to stay grounded, to slow the racing thoughts spinning in my mind. But deep down, I know the moment Isabella walks through that door, it'll all come rushing back. I set my coffee down, reach into my bag, and pull out my deep calm essential oil roll-on. I gently roll it onto my temples and dab each wrist, rubbing them together before bringing them to my nose. I close my eyes and inhale deeply, letting the smell of lavender, petitgrain, and orange fill my senses, hoping it will guide me into a calm state as I settle deeper into the booth.

Just as I open my eyes, my phone buzzes. I reach into my bag and pull it out.

> Alejandra 11:01 a.m.: Clara and I are running a bit late. Leaving our house soon!

> Valeria 11:02 a.m.: Me too, sorry!

I sigh.

Just as I bring the cup of coffee to my lips, the bell above the door jingles. I look up, half-expecting to see a stranger walk in, but instead, Isabella walks through. I freeze, my breath catching as I watch her scan the screen of her phone.

She furrows her brows slightly, fingers tapping rapidly before I see her mouth the word "fuck."

When she finally looks up and sees me sitting here alone, something flickers across her face. Surprise? Maybe confusion? It's hard to tell, but for a brief second, her usual confidence falters.

Seeing her again hits me like a tidal wave of emotions I wasn't ready for. She's wearing a sleek leather jacket, her short brown curls spilling perfectly over her shoulders, still exuding that effortless coolness that always drew me to her. She's as beautiful now as she was all those years ago. I'd like to say last night, but honestly, I hadn't spent much time looking at her then—I was too preoccupied with Isabella's hand buried between Myra's thighs to pay much attention. Now, though, it's like all those missed glances come rushing back at once, and I feel completely thrown off balance.

Neither of us moves. The bustling noise of the coffee shop fades into a distant hum as my heart pounds louder and louder, echoing in my ears.

I grip my coffee cup a little too tightly and pop! The lid flies off, and hot coffee splashes everywhere.

Great.

I fumble for napkins, trying to contain the coffee that's now dripping off the table and onto the floor. My stomach twists, and I can't help but wish for a hole to open up right under me so it could swallow me whole and I could just disappear. Because that sounds much better than what's happening right now.

I look up and watch as Isabella hesitates, her hand tightening around her phone before slowly moving toward me. My heart pounds in my chest, and I'm almost glad for this mess so I don't have to watch her walk toward me—funny how things change.

When she finally reaches the table, she hands me a few napkins with a calmness I definitely don't feel. I flash her a small, awkward smile—or at least, I think it's a smile, but honestly, it probably looks more like a grimace. My face feels like it's doing weird things, and I've never felt more awkward in my life.

"Thanks," I say, my voice trembling a little.

"No problem," Isabella replies, her tone calm and controlled.

She takes a seat across from me and starts helping me clean up. Honestly, it's impressive how this whole awkward situation isn't phasing her in the slightest.

Once I'm done cleaning the floor I see Isabella standing by the counter, filling a cup with water. When she makes her way back, she hands me a wet napkin. "You've got coffee all over your shirt."

I look down, and I'm immediately irritated with myself. My favorite white silky button-down shirt is speckled with dark coffee stains. I grab the napkin from Isabella and start to pat it down, hoping against hope that I haven't ruined it for good. But my heart sinks as the coffee spreads.

"Damn, I just bought this shirt," I say, as I throw my hands up. Finally giving up the fight against the coffee stains. Frustrated, I reach for my jacket and throw it on. I can feel Isabella's gaze on me, her eyes studying my every move. I look at her, half-expecting her to say something, but she pulls out her phone instead.

"Thanks for helping me clean up. You didn't have to," I say, my voice cracking as I force a smile.

"Mhm," she replies, her eyes flickering to me for only a second before they drop back to her phone. She taps at the screen, clearly more invested in whatever's happening in there.

Memories of the voicemails she left me years ago flood my mind, overwhelming and vivid. "You couldn't even say goodbye? Lily, what the fuck?" echoes in my head, her voice from all those years ago slicing through the present like a knife. The pain in those messages feels as raw and fresh now as it did a decade ago, and my heart tightens as I remember the anger that filled her words.

I trace the rim of my coffee cup with my fingers, trying to steady my racing thoughts, but the past feels like it's pressing in on me as if everything I left unsaid back then is demanding to be spoken right now.

"Isabella," I finally say, my voice breaking as I feel a big ball of nerves jump to my throat.

Isabella looks up at me, her big brown eyes searching mine. And my mind goes blank. Everything I want to say on the tip of my tongue. "I..." I say but nothing comes out. What I want to say is: I never meant to disappear, I'm so sorry, I miss you, but the words get lodged in my throat.

My silence stretches on way too long, and Isabella stares at me with that icy look of hers. Just as I feel like the silence is going to swallow me whole, Valeria, Clara, and Alejandra burst in, their laughter slicing through the tension like a knife.

I let out a breath.

"Sorry I'm late!" Valeria says as she hugs me. "Brooke insisted on dropping me off."

"Sorry we're late, too. Traffic was a nightmare!" Alejandra sings as she pulls out a chair and drops into it with an exasperated sigh.

"By 'traffic,' she means she couldn't decide which shoes to wear, and we ended up leaving the house way later than we should have," Clara clarifies, shaking her head at Alejandra, her blue hair swaying back and forth. Then she glances between Isabella and me. She wiggles her eyebrows and teases, "Well, look at that! You two haven't killed each other yet, impressive!"

I shoot a nervous glance at Isabella who just rolls her eyes dramatically, a smirk tugging at her lips.

"Fuck you," she mutters lightheartedly.

For a moment, that familiar playfulness flickers back into Isabella's eyes, and it stings. A painful reminder of what I've lost. I've missed that playful banter dearly, and seeing her offer it so easily to Clara while I can't get more than a forced 'hello' feels like a painful reminder of the space between us.

"Ignore her," Alejandra says, swatting her hand at Clara as she stands. "You have no idea how much we have missed you!" Alejandra beams, pulling me into a tight hug as she bounces up and down. "It's about time you returned to save us from our boring lives!"

"Speak for yourself. I have a pretty damn adventurous life," Clara exclaims as she throws me a wink.

Once Alejandra lets go Clara wraps me in a bear hug that almost lifts me off my feet.

Valeria laughs and gives my hand a little squeeze before taking a seat.

"Seriously, though, you can't leave us again!" Alejandra says.

"Don't worry. I doubt my mom will be letting me leave anytime soon!" I reply, grinning as I try to match her enthusiasm.

As we all settle in, the energy in the room lifts. And I think the essential oils are finally working because I feel a little more at ease, but the tension with Isabella doesn't budge—it's there, simmering just below the surface, like a coiled spring ready to snap.

"So, what's the plan?" Alejandra asks. "I vote we start with something easy."

"Easy is good," I say, my voice coming out a bit too bright.

Isabella looks up, her eyes locking with mine, as a slow smirk spreads across her lips. My pulse quickens, and my eyes involuntarily fixate on the curve of her lips, making it hard to think about anything other than her.

"Do you have the list?" Valeria asks quietly. I hear her, but it doesn't click that she's talking to me.

Silence falls over the group, and I look around, trying to piece together what I missed, but all I can focus on is Isabella, her eyes locked onto mine, intense and unyielding.

"The list?" Clara says, with a teasing tone as she glances between Isabella and me.

"What about it?"

"Do you have it?" Clara laughs.

"Oh, um... yes, yeah. It's in my bag," I reply, fumbling to pull it out. Get it together, I tell myself, trying to get a grip on my nerves.

Isabella's attention is entirely on me now, and I can't shake the feeling that every move I make is under her scrutiny. The weight of her stare makes my hands tremble slightly.

"Honey, are you okay?" Valeria asks concerned.

I give her a small nod. "Yeah, sorry, I didn't sleep well last night," I say, which is true, but far from why I can't seem to follow what's going on right now.

I finally pull the list from my purse and the paper crackles as I smooth it out on the table before handing it to Alejandra.

"Thank you," she sings before she starts to read off the unchecked items on the list.

"Sunrise hike to our secret spot, nighttime swim under the stars, cabin weekend getaway, go to Isabella's art show. Easy enough," she says as she sets the list down on the table and looks around.

Clara, Valeria, and Alejandra lean in and start discussing which item to tackle first.

I try to focus on the conversation, but my eyes keep drifting toward Isabella, drawn to her despite my best efforts. Why does she have this kind of power over me after all this time? Every glance I take makes it harder to concentrate. Meanwhile, she's glued to her phone, her face unreadable, as if the conversation around her is just white noise.

Isabella has always been good at hiding her feelings. A skill I never mastered, unfortunately. While I'm the kind of person who wears their heart on their sleeve, she's like a fortress, guarded and impenetrable. It's frustrating and fascinating, and I can't help but wonder what's going on behind that composed exterior. It's like trying to solve a puzzle with half the pieces missing.

"The hike could be a good choice," Clara says, pulling me from my thoughts. "It's something we can do this weekend."

"Let's do it this Saturday," Alejandra chirps.

Valeria nods. "Yes, plus, the weather is supposed to be nice. I think it'll be the last day we hit 67."

"Perfect!" Alejandra agrees, her big hazel eyes lighting up as she claps excitedly. "Who wants to drive?"

"I don't trust any of you to drive. So Alejandra and I can pick you all up," Clara says, almost cutting Alejandra off.

"I'll meet you guys there... Brooke will probably want to drop me off," Valeria says, her voice soft, her gaze fixed on her hands, fingers nervously twisting together.

"That works," Clara replies, her eyes scanning our faces trying to catch a glimpse of everyone's reaction.

The silence that follows is almost uncomfortable. Thankfully Clara clears her throat and asks, "Isa, when's your art exhibit? Don't you have one coming up?" Clearly trying to steer the conversation away from the awkwardness that's settled.

Isabella—finally—looks up from her phone. "Yeah, I do."

"We could count that as the 'Go to Isabella's art show.'" Alejandra chimes in.

Isabella glances at Alejandra, her expression neutral. "Yeah, that works. It's at the end of October," she says before looking back down at her phone.

"Great, that gives us a couple of weeks to wrap everything else up!" Alejandra exclaims, her excitement infectious. It makes me smile without thinking. Alejandra's the smallest of us all, but her energy feels like it belongs in the body of a seventy-foot giant. I have no idea where she stores it all, but it's impossible not to get caught up in it.

I turn my gaze towards Isabella and when she catches my eye, her frosty gaze greets me like an old, unwelcome friend. It's a look I've come to know well over the years but it stings regardless. And I feel the smile on my face fade.

"I hate to cut this short, but I need to get going," Valeria says as she looks down at her watch.

"Yeah, I've got a meeting in a few minutes, so I should probably head out and pretend I've been working this whole time," Clara says as she wags her eyebrows.

"Well, I came with you, so I guess I'm leaving too," Alejandra adds with a frown.

"No worries, I've got plenty of boxes waiting for me at home anyway."

Isabella doesn't say anything, she just gives us a thumbs-up and a small, half-hearted smile.

Valeria, Clara, and Alejandra stand up, and each one leans in to kiss Isabella and me goodbye on the cheek before heading out the door.

Isabella and I stay behind. I stare at her unsure of how to say goodbye. Finally, she stands and offers me a quick, impersonal smile and a casual "See ya." Which I honestly hate more than her just ignoring me.

As she starts to turn away, a woman approaches, wedging herself between Isabella and the wall, effectively trapping me, and the sight sends my heart racing. I watch, frozen, as I realize it's Myra.

She leans in and kisses Isabella, her lips brushing against hers with an intimacy that feels like a punch to the gut. A sharp pang of jealousy stabs through me—something I haven't felt in ages, and somehow, Isabella has managed to stir it within me twice in less than twenty-four hours. I hate this...

My blood boils as tension coils tightly in my shoulders. The world around me fades, and all I can focus on is the two of them together.

Before I can stop myself, I shout, "Can you move!" My voice breaks halfway through, and Isabella turns to look at me, her eyes searching, curious. But just as quickly as that flicker of curiosity appeared, it vanished.

She brushes me off without a second thought, turning away as her gaze finds Myra again, locking onto her like I was never even there. There's a warmth and ease in her expression that I haven't seen in ages, a stark contrast to the distant coldness she has shown me for so long. This isn't just a random hook-up at the bar; the thought that Myra could be someone she's dating makes me want to scream.

Myra doesn't say anything. She simply steps to the side and motions for me to pass. Her annoyance is so obvious it makes me want to shove past her but as much as I want to... my feet feel like they're cemented to the ground and I can't. Instead, I just stand there, frozen, until Myra rolls her eyes and pulls Isabella away, their hands intertwined. With each step they take, my heart twists itself into a million more knots.

When I finally get my feet moving again. I rush out of the coffee shop and into the crisp air, the breeze hits my skin, sharp and refreshing. I inhale deeply, hoping to shake off the tension that still clings to me. I didn't think Isabella could still affect me this way, and I'm left grappling with a longing that I thought I had buried long ago. *What the heck is wrong with me?*

I want to believe this is a fluke that I can just walk away and forget. But the walk home is brutal... each step I take is heavier than the last, and I can't help but replay the way Isabella's face lit up when she saw Myra, and how quickly the warmth in her eyes vanished when they turned to me. I don't understand why she's still angry. Why, after all this time, she's the one shutting me out?

Once I'm back home, I toss my keys on the kitchen counter and collapse onto the couch, replaying my interaction with Isabella over and over. The jealousy I felt earlier is still alive and rampant, coursing through me like it's part of my bloodstream.

I sigh, frustrated with myself because I like to think I have a shred of common sense. But when it comes to Isabella, my heart always seems to take over. I've spent nearly ten years trying to move on, trying to give someone else a real chance, but I keep finding myself looking for traces of her in them.

And now that I'm close to her again, it's like my heart is in overdrive, desperate to be near her. Every glance, every smile—even the half-hearted ones— pull me in deeper, and all those feelings I tried to bury are now front and center, impossible to ignore.

The thought of anyone else making her laugh or smile makes my heart hurt. I know, if anyone were reading a book about my life, they'd be thinking, "Lily, you're an idiot." But luckily, these are just my private thoughts.

I get up and move to the window, watching the rustling of the trees. Maybe it was foolish to hope that something had changed just because she was willing to meet at the coffee shop today.

I pour myself another cup of coffee and head to my office. I pass the mirror in the living room and realize I'm still wearing the coffee-stained shirt. In a rush to take it off, I accidentally spill even more coffee onto the fabric. Just my luck.

I spend an hour scouring YouTube and TikTok for every cleaning tip known to man, even calling my mom for advice, but nothing works. I spend the next thirty minutes scrubbing away, hoping the weird mix of dish soap and vinegar I found on Pinterest will finally do the trick, but the stain's only getting worse, and now the fabric is ruined. Finally, I give up and toss it in the trash.

I change into a thick sweater and head into my office. Ready to lose myself in some writing. I open my laptop, determined to get some writing done, but my brain has other plans and proceeds to send me into an Isabella-induced frenzy. Playing and replaying the moments, it was me on the tip of Isabella's tongue instead of Myra.

Day one of being around Isabella, and this is where I'm at already? I'm so screwed.

4

ISABELLA

I'd be lying if I said the way Lily kept—not so subtly—sneaking looks at me yesterday didn't send a thrill through me.

And I'd be lying even more if I didn't say I was definitely checking her out—probably more than I should have if I'm being honest.

Seeing her up close and outside the dim lights of the bar was something else entirely. Fuck, she looked as beautiful as she had the last time I'd seen her... hell, maybe even more so now. Her once short hair is now a cascade of brown, falling in soft waves down her back, but everything else is still the same. Same full lips, same button nose, and dark brown eyes. I might not like her, but I'm not blind. Anyone can see Lily is absolutely beautiful.

My phone pings loudly, cutting through the quiet of the gallery, jolting me out of my thoughts. I grab it and look at the screen—it's a message from Myra.

Myra 2:55 p.m.: Are we still hiking on Saturday?

> Isabella 2:56 p.m.: yeah, but you should stay over tonight, clara is driving us up there

> Myra 2:55 p.m.: Cool! Just text me when you're home.

Clara, Alejandra, and Valeria weren't exactly thrilled when I told them I'd invited Myra to come hiking with us, but I told them this was the only way I was doing it. And I'm glad they didn't put up much of a fight. Maybe they just knew I'd bring her along anyway and decided to give up.

I slip my phone back into my pocket and start wandering through the gallery, straightening frames, adjusting the lighting, and wiping away smudges on the glass. Why people feel the need to put their nasty fingers on the glass is beyond me. It drives me insane. I move slowly through the space, looking for anything else that needs tweaking, when I spot a flickering lightbulb above a painting. I reach up and twist it tighter, and just as the flickering stops, I hear the soft creak of a door, which startles me, and I lose the sweet spot on the light. I drop my head and try to conjure up enough patience to try again when a familiar voice calls out. "Hello?"

I turn slowly hoping I'm wrong... but I'm not, it's Lily. Just my fucking luck...

Her head pokes through the door, her eyes scanning the room. When her eyes finally land on me she freezes and her eyes go wide. We're both locked in place awkwardly staring at each other as a pretty pink creeps up her cheeks.

She looks like a deer caught in headlights, and I can't help but think it's kinda cute. But whatever possessed me to think that is quickly vanquished, and now I'm a little annoyed that she seems to be surprised to find me at my own fucking gallery. *What the fuck was she expecting?*

"Oh," she says, her voice strained. "I didn't know you would be here today. I'm so sorry."

She starts to back away slowly, her movements almost comical, but before Lily can make her grand escape, Sarah— my art director, who also runs the store—yells out, "Hi, come in come in."

Today is not my day.

Lily turns to me eyes wide.

"It's fine," I say. I can't exactly tell her to leave without having to explain to Sarah why. So I just awkwardly stare at Lily and do my best to smile.

Lily hesitates and bites her lip, and even though I hate her, watching her do that makes me wish I were the one doing it instead, which is absolutely insane. Whatever demon took over my body earlier is back.

"You sure?" she asks, her face scrunched up.

"Yeah," I reply, as I force a smile that I hope comes across warmer than it feels.

With a hesitant nod, Lily steps back into the gallery, her footsteps quiet on the smooth concrete floor.

The gallery is modern and minimal—white walls, bold abstract paintings, and a few sculptures by other local artists scattered around.

Lily stops in front of a huge canvas, the messy brush-strokes and vivid colors pulling her in. Watching her get into the painting is nerve-wracking. Then again, I feel that way whenever anyone gets lost in them. After a few minutes, her attention drifts to something else and my eyes follow her.

My mind stuck on one thing: what the hell she's doing here?

I walk towards her trying to keep the mood light. Lily and I barely talked yesterday, and I don't want her to think I'm just being nice to sell her something but given how awkward she's made this day for me, maybe I should... might as well get something out of this, but first answers.

"You called to make sure I wouldn't be here today?" I ask.

"Oh... yeah, I've been wanting to see your gallery for a while but I didn't want to make you uncomfortable so I figured I should come while you weren't here." She says apologetically.

I nod. Well, that explains why she looked surprised to see me. I tilt my head slightly, and the scent of her coconut shampoo drifts past me, soft and sweet. Why does she have to smell so fucking good?

Lily looks around the gallery, her fingers nervously tugging at each other. "I can go if you want... I don't want to bother."

"You're not," I say even though she very much is "It's been a slow day, and I don't think it'll pick up so we might close soon but feel free to wander around." She looks at me, and I can see the hesitation. "I mean it," I say trying to reassure her even though I most definitely don't. Honestly, I'd love for her to leave. But seeing as we're going to be around each other a lot these next couple of weeks, I might as well start getting used to being around her without wanting to scream. And what better place to start than here, where I'm most comfortable?

She gives me a small, relieved smile. "Thanks. I won't be long."

I nod, letting my eyes trace the familiar curve of her body as she walks further into the gallery, her footsteps light, stopping in front of every painting and tilting her head back and forth.

There was a time when this was exactly what I wanted, what I dreamed of—for Lily to be here. For her to get lost in the paintings, to wander from room to room doing exactly what she's doing right now. But at this moment I want the opposite. I don't want her here. I want her to leave and never look at my work again. Something about her dissecting them feels wrong. I can't watch her anymore, so instead, I head back to the register.

I start to close the register down as Sarah turns off the lights, wipes down the counter, and organizes a few stray magazines. Every now and then, I catch myself looking at Lily, watching her move so comfortably between the paintings, her fingers lightly brushing the edges of the frames. I roll my eyes because, of course, she's one of those people who press their fingers on the glass.

I look down at the till, counting the cash in the register to make sure everything's set for tomorrow's opener when I see Lily walk toward Sarah.

"Hey, do you happen to have that abstract painting with the blue and gold swirls? I saw it online, and I can't stop thinking about it. I was hoping to buy it."

I pause for a second, making a mental note of what she just said so I can dissect it later. Then my mind runs through the gallery's recent sales.

"I think we just sold it," I say. Almost immediately.

Lily's face turns to me as it falls. "Oh, bummer."

"But we've got some pieces in the back that are pretty similar. Isabella can show you if you want." Sarah offers and I wish I would have sent her home early...

"Yeah, sure, I'd love that," Lily replies, tucking a loose

strand of hair behind her ear, a tiny smile appearing on her face again.

"Cool, let me just finish this up and I'll take you."

"Oh, don't worry about it I can close the register," Sarah offers. I give her a tight-lipped smile.

I set the cash down, straighten my blouse, and lead Lily toward the back. As we inch closer and closer to the back-room my heart hammers in my chest so loud it drowns out everything. My hands are slick with sweat, trembling slightly no matter how hard I try to steady them. I've done this a million times with a million other customers, why am I so nervous about Lily being back here? She's no one.

I unlock the door and Lily follows me in, her steps slowing as she takes in the space. Watching her get starry-eyed makes the pit in my stomach grow even deeper like it's been replaced by a black hole.

The room is filled with old paintings stacked neatly against the walls, some leaning and others arranged in orderly rows but all of them tucked in protective mirror boxes, keeping them safe from dust. Shelves line the back wall with art supplies—brushes, tubes of paint, and sketch-books—neatly organized and ready to be used. Canvases stacked in one corner, some blank, others partially worked on.

I crouch down, pulling a few canvases from a stack. I grab a few that are pretty similar to the one Lily was looking for—same style, same series, just different colors.

The one she was asking about was part of my Pride series. I made six variations of it, each using different colors from the pride flag. Originally, I wanted to sell them as one big piece, but Sarah talked me out of it. Said I'd probably end up sitting on them for way longer than I'd like if I tried to sell them all together. And maybe she was right because the blue one barely sold last week and they all went up for sale four months ago.

I place the canvases against the wall, arranging them carefully so Lily can get a good look. "Here you go," I say, stepping back.

Lily walks over and crouches next to the canvases, her eyes scanning each piece. "Wow, these are amazing."

I smile. A small—very small, subatomic almost—part of me loves hearing that from her. But hearing that also stirs something else in me... anger. Anger for all she took from us. Anger for all the times I wished she'd been there when I loved a piece and wanted to share it with her. I know *I know* it's been years, and I should be over it, but I'm not. No matter what happened between us, even if she regretted it, she should've talked to me. She shouldn't have disappeared without a word because who fucking does that?

A sudden clatter snaps me back to the present, and I watch as a few of my paintbrushes and half-finished sketchpads tumble to the floor. Lily's eyes go wide before she scrunches her face, bracing for the pang as everything hits the ground.

"Oh my gosh, I'm so sorry!" she says, dropping to her knees to pick up everything.

I quickly crouch down beside her, reaching for the brushes that have rolled out of sight beneath one of the shelves.

"It's okay," I say, as I scoop up the last of the scattered brushes. How did this even happen? But I don't think about it long, Lily is easily the clumsiest human on Earth she probably lost her footing getting up or something.

Lily laughs softly as she hands me what she's gathered, a strand of hair slipping loose. She tucks it shyly behind her ear, her smile warm and a little embarrassed.

We both stand and Lily knocks into me nearly losing her footing but I grab her just in time and pull her against me to leverage my weight against hers hoping she won't drop us both to the floor or worse, destroy my paintings.

"Thanks," she says, leaning into my chest as she tries to steady herself.

"Mhm," I reply, feeling her heart pounding against mine. Holding her should feel foreign, wrong... but it doesn't it feels kind of nice. And that thought makes me so uncomfortable that I jump back, practically shoving Lily's hands back at her. *Smooth. Real fucking smooth.*

"We should," I mumble, pointing awkwardly over my shoulder at the door.

It takes Lily a few seconds to say or do anything but eventually, she nods and follows me out.

We make our way back toward the front office, and after a few steps, she looks up at me. "Isabella... you think we can talk?" she asks, her voice a little quieter than usual.

"What's up?"

"I've been thinking about what happened between us..."

I step a little closer to her, hoping to cut off the conversation before it spirals. I look around me trying to figure out where Sarah is but I don't see her. She must be back in her office.

"Lily, don't," I say before she can finish her sentence.

"I just thought—"

"It's fine. It's been ten years—let's just, I don't know, move on?" The words spill out before I can stop them, but I hardly want to have this conversation now. What the fuck is she thinking? Why would she just spring this on me? It's not that I don't want answers. I do. I just don't know if I'm ready to handle them. Not yet at least. I've barely wrapped my head around the fact that she's back in my life at all—or

54

at least will be for the next couple of weeks. I've managed to make some kind of peace with that, but diving back into everything that happened... Well, I'm not quite there yet.

"Look, it's in the past. We were young, and things happened... whatever. It shouldn't have happened." I say before I can think about what I'm saying, and I see the moment they land.

Fuck... I don't mean it, of course I don't mean it. It hadn't been a mistake; it had been the happiest I'd ever felt. But I don't want to lay all that out right now because it'll throw us into a conversation I'm not ready to have. So, I just let the words hang between us.

Lily looks down at her shoes and nods.

I take a deep breath. "Look, Lily, I'm sorry that things went down the way they did... but you're back in town now. Let's just try to be friends." I don't mean it but now I'm in clean-up mode because if things go south the girls will just assume it's because of me. And I don't feel like arguing with them about my attitude towards Lily again.

She doesn't say anything right away, just keeps her eyes on the ground.

"Isabella..." Lily starts but pauses for a few seconds, chewing the inside of her cheek. "I appreciate you saying that. I really do... I've missed you, and I'd like to try to be friends too," she says as her eyes meet mine, but there's a shimmer in them that wasn't there before, and my heart twists itself into so many knots I don't even know what the name of the number would be.

I should have taken it back. She wasn't a mistake, and I'm letting her believe she was. But even if I take it back now, she'll think I'm only saying it because she's teary-eyed, but if I'm being perfectly honest with myself... I also don't want to. In the most fucked up way possible, seeing her sad about it makes me almost feel... vindicated, like maybe I wasn't alone in my pain.

"I'm sorry I left, I just—" she starts, but I cut her off... again...

"Lily, it's fine. We don't have to get into it now. Let's just finish the bucket list. The girls are excited about it, and I don't want to be the one to mess it up." I say, trying to sound as sincere as possible.

I stare at Lily, trying to figure out what could be going on in her head.

"I get it," she says quietly. "I don't want to mess it up for the girls either."

She takes a step closer, stopping just inches from my face. Her eyes search mine like she's looking for something —what, I don't know.

"I'm willing to try if you are," she says, her breath shaky as she sticks her hand out.

I look down, and I hesitate. Watching her hand hover in the air.

"You want to shake on it?" I ask, my voice a little more playful than I mean. Lily nods and smiles at the floor.

"I am if you are," I reply. Slowly reaching out to give her hand a little shake.

"Good," she says, her smile getting bigger. "Thanks for taking me back there," she adds pointing toward the room.

I nod, "Sorry, I don't have the painting you were looking for anymore."

"Oh, it's ok. I'm sure I'll find something at your exhibit in a few weeks." She looks down, and that's when we both realize our hands are still clasped together. We quickly let go, and I watch as Lily flexes her fingers, like she's shaking something off.

"Let me walk you out," I add quickly.

She smiles and we turn toward the front of the gallery. When we reach the door Lily turns back to me and my body crashes into her. She grabs my waist to steady herself, and her eyes lock on mine for what feels like far too long. I suck in a breath but don't move. Paralyzed by her touch. I don't know what I'm feeling but I don't like it. It's a little too pink and soft.

"Thanks again," She says as she clears her throat and lets go of me.

I nod, reaching past her to unlock the door.

"I'll see you tomorrow," she says as she turns and walks out.

I hear the door click shut behind me and roll my head around, trying to loosen the knots forming on my shoulders. I head back to my office and grab my jacket.

On my way out, I do a quick scan of the gallery, making sure we haven't left anything for the openers to deal with in the morning, but everything looks good.

Outside the gallery, I crouch down to lock the gate, trying to distract myself from the nervous energy that's clinging to me, but it's completely taken over, I stand a little too quickly, lose my footing, and bump straight into Sarah, dropping us both to the ground, accidentally making her spill coffee all over herself. I wince at the sight of the coffee cascading down her pristine white shirt. I guess Lily's clumsiness rubbed off on me today.

"Fuck, I'm sorry about that," I say, rushing to help her up.

"It's okay! It's just coffee," she replies, looking down at her stained shirt. I try to pay her for the coffee and the shirt but she won't take it.

"I promise it's fine."

"I'll buy you coffee tomorrow. I'm so sorry. If you

change your mind let me know. I'll give you money for a new shirt."

She swats me away and ignores me.

"Bye Isabella," She says and turns to walk to her car.

I can't help but think of Lily's white shirt getting ruined at the coffee shop, and an idea pops into my head. Maybe I should buy her a new shirt to replace the one she probably had to toss. It would show her that we're good and I need to make up for what I said... Of course, the shirt won't magically make her forget that I called her a mistake but it would make my guilt a little lighter. Lily also loves gifts, so maybe it will help her forget what I said.

I get in my car and head towards the mall a town over. It has more stores, and I'm more likely to find a similar shirt there than at one of the boutique stores in town.

The mall parking lot is mostly empty by the time I pull in. So I get premium parking right by the entrance. I get out and head inside, the mall's fluorescent lights almost too harsh after the cool darkness outside. It's quiet this late, with only a few stragglers wandering between stores.

I wander past shop windows, scanning the displays, not seeing anything that's even remotely similar to the shirt Lily was wearing. I've been walking around the mall for nearly an hour and I'm almost ready to give up and leave when I stop dead in my tracks. In the next window, I spot a shirt—almost identical to the one Lily was wearing.

I walk into the store, grab the shirt—in what I guess is her size—and pay for it. I make my way back to my car, practically buzzing with excitement. I was not expecting to find it!

Once I'm home, I sink into the comfort of my couch, eyeing the shopping bag resting beside me. A wave of satisfaction washes over me; I can already picture Lily's face lighting up when she sees the shirt. I think this is the perfect first step to make sure we can complete this list without a major argument and ruining it for the girls.

Feeling a surge of energy, I get up and start tidying my living room. There are art supplies scattered everywhere so I start organizing, putting brushes back in jars, stacking canvases into a neat pile, and capping paint tubes.

My phone pings on the coffee table startling me and of course, dirty paint water splashes all over me. *Wonderful.*

Clara 7:01 p.m.: Hey wanna go to beauty bar and have a drink?

Isabella 7:02 p.m.: depends. who else did you invite?

Clara 7:02 p.m.: Fair enough... No one, just you and me

Isabella 7:02 p.m.: what time?

Clara 7:02 p.m.: Gonna head out in 15

Isabella 7:04 p.m.: see you there

I toss the last dried-up paintbrush into the trash and head toward my room. I need to get out of this shirt.

I spot my favorite graphic tee hanging out on the clean laundry bin and throw it on along with some basic black straight pants and a green pair of sneakers. I head to the bathroom, catching a glimpse of myself in the mirror, and immediately notice my smudged eyeliner. My wing is practically gone, and my blush has faded. I dig through my makeup bag, pull out my eyeliner, and blush. Carefully, I fix my liner, restoring the sharp wing, and then reapply a touch of blush to bring some color back to my cheeks. Feeling a bit more like myself, I give my reflection a final check before I head toward my car and make my way to the bar.

I park and head inside.

The moment I cross the door, the smell of hair dye and styling products hits me like a wave. Beauty Bar is a hair salon by day and a bar by night. I have no idea where they keep everything, but by the time it's set up, it looks just like any old dive bar. I scan the room, looking for Clara and I finally spot her sitting at our usual corner table. She waves me over, her newly dyed pink curls bouncing around as she does. She must have been here earlier 'cause I swear she had blue hair yesterday. Next week it might be green. You never know with Clara, she loves to change her hair color.

"Looking sharp as always, Clara! I like the hair and your jacket," I say, sliding into the seat across from her.

"Thanks," she replies, looking down at her denim jacket.

"Sorry, I'm late. You wouldn't believe the mess in my living room," I say as I grab the bar menu, quickly scanning through their cocktails.

Clara laughs. "Painting at home? Who are you painting this time, the girl from the bathroom?"

I roll my eyes. I wish she was wrong, but I have a really bad habit of painting my more spicy pieces at home rather than at the gallery, and it is almost always inspired by my latest hookup.

"You know what they say, 'Never date an artist; you'll end up as their muse.'"

"Oh, come on!" Clara says as she gently punches my arm.

"I can't help but admire the female form so much that I feel the need to immortalize it," I joke.

Clara rolls her eyes at me. "Seriously though, you good?

Can't imagine that little bathroom reunion was very comfortable."

Before I can answer, the bartender comes by our table and takes our order. Both Clara and I opt for a glass of their house red. Once she's gone, Clara leans in, clearly still waiting for an answer, which I don't want to give her. If I did, I'd have to explain everything that happened between Lily and me in high school, and I simply don't want to.

So instead, I deflect. "You know, her running into me in the bathroom wouldn't have happened if you hadn't invited her."

Clara leans back on her chair and frowns. Nothing like a little guilt trip to derail the conversation.

"I know, that was shitty of me. I'm sorry," she says. "But in my defense, it was all Ale's idea."

Of course, it was.

"It's okay," I say, as the bartender drops off our wine. I take my glass from her before she's even had a chance to set it down and take a big gulp.

"How are you feeling about tomorrow?" Clara asks.

I set my—now empty—glass of wine on the table and stare at it. Trying to figure out how I feel, but I honestly have no fucking clue. I wish I wasn't going, that's for sure. But aside from that, blank.

"I don't know. I'm indifferent," I say.

"You guys still haven't talked about whatever happened?"

I pick up the glass again, even though it's empty, just to have something to do with my hands.

"Kinda, she stopped by the gallery today. We got as close as we probably ever will."

Clara's eyebrows shoot up to her hairline, and I can tell

she wants to ask more but doesn't know if she should, so she just stares at me. I roll my eyes.

"It's not like it'll change anything but at least we're on friendly terms for now."

"Well that's good?" she says, narrowing her eyes at me.

I shrug. "I guess we'll see tomorrow."

"Is Myra still coming then"

"Yeah," I say reaching for her glass of wine but she slaps my hand. I turn to the bartender and somehow manage to signal for another round.

"Why is she coming again?"

"Because I don't trust you guys."

Clara rolls her eyes. "Seriously?"

"Seriously, you guys haven't let go of the idea of Lily and me fixing everything that happened between us even after ten years, so now that she's around, I don't know what you're capable of."

"And what did happen between you guys?" Clara asks, leaning in and resting her head on her hand, batting her eyelashes at me.

I look at her with a straight face and shake my head. She and Alejandra are relentless.

"Fine," Clara says, letting it go for now. She knows me too well to keep asking. "At least I can tell Alejandra I tried."

We spend the next hour talking about the fifty different girls Clara is seeing, the upcoming exhibit at the gallery, and her promotion to Marketing Director.

It's only 9 p.m. but the bar starts to quiet down, and the crowd begins to thin. The joys of living in a small town I guess.

"I'm gonna go meet some friends in Seattle, want to come?"

"Nah, I should get home. Myra will be over soon."

Clara wags her eyebrows at me but I ignore her.

I hug her and watch her walk off, her hair swaying with every step. I finish my drink and head home.

━━━━━━ ♥ ♥ ♥ ━━━━━━

As soon as I step through the door, Porter and Shadow come running toward me, tails wagging furiously.

"Hey, you two!" I laugh, dropping to my knees to greet them as they nudge against me with such force I nearly topple over.

"Alright, calm down," I say as I stand. I fish my phone from my back pocket and text Myra.

> Isabella 9:12 p.m.: I'm home

> Myra 9:12 p.m.: I'll be over in a bit I'm on a
> date now. But I'll come over once
> we're done

> Isabella 9:12 p.m.: 👍

This is honestly why this thing between Myra and I works. We don't expect anything from each other other than a good fuck.

I probably have an hour 'till she gets here, which is plenty of time to get some painting done, so I head straight for my office. Canvases lean against the walls, half-finished paintings clutter the room, and the smell of paint and turpentine fills the air. I flip on the light, grab a brush, and focus on finishing the half-outlined torso in front of me.

I work for about an hour and then there's a knock at my door. I set the brush down, hands streaked with paint as I head to the door.

When I open it Myra's leaning against the frame with a smirk. I don't have the chance to say a word before her mouth crashes into mine, warm and insistent, tasting faintly of tequila. She pushes us past the door, guiding us both inside, her hands already on my hips, sliding under my shirt.

She kicks the door shut, walking us toward the living room couch. We fall onto it, her weight settling over me, her fingers threading into my hair as she pulls me close. Her kiss is urgent, and there's no hesitation, no holding back—just heat and desperate need.

5

LILY

I've spent all day replaying my conversation with Isabella over and over. Each word, each pause, looped in my mind.

I can't stop thinking about her—her voice, her eyes, the way she looked when she said, "It shouldn't have happened." The words keep echoing in my head, and no matter how hard I try, I can't shake the sting. She saw our time together as a mistake, something to erase—a footnote in her life that she barely acknowledged. Her words hit like a punch to the gut, and it shattered my heart into a thousand pieces all over again. To think that the most profound and beautiful time of my life could be dismissed so easily is unbearable.

Has she really spent the last ten years thinking that? The thought alone makes me sick and I feel like I'm going to pass out. I need to talk to someone. My first instinct is to call my mom, but it's near midnight and I know she's sleeping. So I call the next best thing... Valeria.

"Hello?" Valeria answers with a groggy voice.

"Hey, I'm sorry... Did I wake you?" I ask, feeling even worse.

"No, no, I wasn't sleeping. I was reading, what's up?"

I take a deep breath and try to organize my thoughts. "I saw Isabella today," is all I manage to say.

"Oh! How was that?"

I sigh into the phone, unable to speak for what feels like an eternity. My throat tightens, and I blink away the tears that suddenly threaten to spill.

"Not good," I finally say, my voice breaking.

"Oh, honey... What happened?" Valeria asks, her voice full of concern. I hear a ruffle of sheets, and I know for sure I woke her up.

I try to think of how to even start telling this story because in order for her to understand what I'm feeling, she needs full context, but the words are tangled in my throat, and I have no idea where to begin.

Do I start by telling her about how during our junior year of high school I realized my need to be around Isabella was maybe more than friendly that she had been the mystery girl that helped me realize I was a lesbian or do I go even further back and tell her that when Isabella first mentioned Resy—her first girlfriend—I felt like my world was crashing, or do I tell her about the moment during senior year where I realized I'd fallen impossibly in love with Isabella, my classic, cliché "baby gay" moment of falling for my best friend.

But I don't say anything, because Isabella's voice echoes in my head: "Let's just finish the bucket list. The girls are excited about it, and I don't want to be the one to mess it up." I hate her for planting that thought in my head because I don't want to mess it up either and if I tell Valeria any of this it might... My chest feels even tighter than before because I can't do this... I can't tell her... not now, not when we're hours away from jumping into the first item on the bucket list.

"Nothing," I finally say, wiping the tears from my face. "I just went to her gallery today, and she was there. It was a little awkward for me."

"That's all?" Valeria asks suspiciously. "I don't want to sound mean but you're telling me you're crying because it was a little awkward?"

"I'm not crying," I lie, sniffing and wiping at my face.

"Uh-huh."

"I promise. This whole move has just been a lot and small things feel big," I say. I want more than anything to spill the tangled mess of my feelings, the memories, the guilt —but I can't. Not yet. "I'm sorry I called so late for nothing. Now I feel silly."

Valeria doesn't say anything for a few seconds, and the silence stretches so long that I look at my phone to make sure the call didn't drop.

"You know I'm here," she finally says. "Always. No matter what. You can tell me anything."

"I know," I whisper.

There's another pause, and I know she's waiting for me to say more. When I don't, she lets out a quiet sigh.

"Okay," she says, and I can hear the worry in her tone. "Goodnight, honey. Get some rest, alright?"

"Goodnight," I reply, the lump in my throat making it hard to speak.

I hang up, staring at my phone before letting out a long, shaky sigh. I set it down on the nightstand and collapse back onto the bed. Almost instantly, my mind swells with everything that happened between Isabella and me.

A soft meow pulls me from the spiral. Pickles is perched on the edge of the bed, her big green eyes watching me.

"Hey," I murmur, reaching out to scratch behind her ears. She hops onto my chest and settles there, purring softly.

"Have I ever told you about Isabella?" I say, my voice breaking. "Isabella... God, where do I even start? She was my best friend, and I—" I stop, choking on the words. Pickles blinks at me, her calm presence somehow making it easier to keep talking. I tell her about how I'd spent about a year pining over Isabella. How she had been in an on-and-off relationship with a girl from school named Resy for about three years.

"I almost threw Isabella a party when she finally decided she'd had enough and she said they'd broken up for good. And then, instead of focusing on piecing my best friend back together. I spent the next six months worrying about how to make my first move and when to make it I'd finally come up with a plan, but in true Isabella fashion, she turned my world upside down. She kissed me during one of our sleepovers and everything came together. We spent the next month in a little world of our own making." I say almost giddy.

Pickles lets out a soft meow, as if responding, and I can't help but smile. I know it might seem silly to some but at this moment it's all I need.

"Those four weeks with Isabella were nothing short of magical, or at least, they were for me. But clearly, I'd been alone in that. Now, it all makes sense...why it had been so easy for her to brush me aside and run back to her ex... she thought we were a fluke. A mistake." I say and the tears start rolling down my cheeks.

I remember hearing Isabella talk to Valeria about it like

it was yesterday. They were sitting on the bleachers, chatting like they always did. I snuck into the gym and crawled inside, fully planning to grab one of their ankles and give them a good scare. But as I reached out, I froze when Isabella mentioned she'd bumped into her ex during a teen night she and Clara had gone to.

At first, I brushed it off—people run into their exes all the time, right? But then she talked about how it messed with her head, how seeing her ex again stirred up doubts. The moment those words left her mouth, it felt like the ground beneath me crumbled, and every magical memory felt tainted as if it had never been real and I started to question everything—had I just been a placeholder until Resy found her way back? Had I ever really mattered to her?

I wanted to barge in, to confront her, and make her understand how much those weeks had meant to me. But instead, I stayed hidden, my heart breaking as her words sunk in. I didn't stay to hear more. I couldn't bear to hear about how I wasn't enough. I thought we were building something special, something real. But hearing her talk about her ex as if she were the unfinished business of her life made me realize I'd been living in a fantasy.

So I left, disappearing without making our goodbye a big deal. I made her choice easier. There was no reason for me to stick around to hear Isabella's excuses on why we wouldn't work out. Now that I'm older I know I messed up. I should have talked to her but I really had a flare for the dramatic back then and I had some serious self-esteem issues.

When I heard she never got back with her ex, I hoped that we had meant something to her. But Isabella never replied to my messages, and every time I tried to bring it up, she'd sidestep the conversation or ignore me. Today had been the first time she'd ever let me say anything and I guess, I got my answer. I promised myself I'd move on once I had it, and that's exactly what I'm going to do. I can finally let go of the last piece that tethered me to her and focus on rebuilding our friendship instead of trying to fix whatever we had because now I know our time together didn't matter to her like it did to me and while I cherished every moment, she didn't, and that's ok—or at least it will be.

Tomorrow, we're tackling the first bucket list item and going hiking, and I'm determined to stay focused on moving forward.

By the time we've checked off everything on this list, Isabella and I will be well on our way back to where we were before feelings got involved—or at least that's the goal.

This list is the perfect excuse to spend time with her again, to get to know her again, and I'm not going to waste it. It's the chance I've been waiting for to rebuild the friend-ship we lost, and that's exactly what I plan on doing.

6

ISABELLA

I've been awake since 4 a.m. but I just couldn't bring myself to get out of bed partly because I don't want to wake Myra, but mainly because I'm not looking forward to today.

When I finally manage to get myself up, it's already 5:30 a.m.

I nudge Myra awake, and she blinks slowly, trying to figure out what's going on.

"Time to wake up," I say, trying to keep my voice low so I don't scare her.

"Mm... what time is it?" she mumbles.

I look up at the clock on my nightstand. "It's 5:32. The girls will be here soon. We need to get ready," I reply, nudging her a bit more. Not wanting to get up in case she falls back asleep. After a few minutes, she groans, sits up, and rubs her eyes.

"Alright, alright, I'm up," she says.

I laugh and head towards my closet. I keep my look simple and throw on a pair of black leggings and a black hoodie. I try to tie my shoulder-length hair back in a pony-tail, but everything I do looks ridiculous, so I just leave it.

My phone pings and it's Clara letting me know they're almost here.

I walk towards my bedroom to tell Myra to hurry, but she's already dressed and ready to go. We're basically wearing the same thing, but she added a thick, long jacket on top. Seeing her layered up makes me second-guess my outfit, so I pull my favorite leather jacket off the hanger and throw it on.

"Ready?"

"Ready!" Myra says, pressing a quick kiss to my lips before we head out the door.

Just as I'm locking the front door, Clara pulls into the driveway.

I climb in first, sliding into the middle seat next to Lily, muttering a quick, "Morning," to everyone. When Myra and I settle in our seats, I catch Lily looking between us, her eyes hovering over Myra's hand on my knee and my skin prickles under her stare. I have to fight the sudden, irrational urge to move Myra's hand. Something about the way Lily is looking at it makes it feel... wrong.

"It's nice to see you again, Myra," Lily says, her voice overly polite, like she's trying too hard to sound happy.

"Is it?" Myra shoots back with one eyebrow raised.

I turn my head toward Myra so fast I'm worried I just gave myself whiplash. I stare at her like she's just grown a second head, wondering what the fuck could have possibly possessed her to say that. My eyes search her face for some kind of explanation or even the smallest sign she's joking, but all I see is her staring back at Lily with that same raised eyebrow and an unrelenting glare.

Maybe this was a bad idea after all... but not in the way I was expecting.

I turn back towards Lily, my mouth opening and closing trying to figure out what to say to make this better, but nothing comes out.

Thankfully, Lily ignores Myra and Myra doesn't say another word.

"Okay?" Clara says, dragging out the 'A'.

"Are you guys ready for a hike?" Alejandra asks cheerfully as Clara pulls out of my driveway.

"Mhm," I mutter.

Clara looks at me through the rearview mirror, her eyes throwing a million questions my way—questions I don't have the answers to because I have no idea what's going on.

The drive is quiet. Everyone is either too sleepy or too afraid to talk. Myra keeps trying to hold my hand no matter how many times I let go and Lily's eyes are practically glued to her, tracking every time her hands land on me. It's like she's cataloging every touch, and it's driving me insane. Controlling my facial expressions around Lily will be the toughest thing I do today.

My phone pings in my jacket and when I reach for it it's a message from Myra.

> Myra 6:06 a.m.: Is it just me or this is very awkward?

> Isabella 6:06 a.m.: nope it is...

I kind of regret roping her into this, had I known Lily would be so weird about it I wouldn't have brought her. I reach for Myra's hand and bring it to my lips giving her knuckles a quick peck. Hoping it'll somehow translate that I'm sorry I'm putting her through this.

Out of the corner of my eye, I see Lily turn her head, her eyes locking on me just as I kiss Myra's hand. She freezes but her eyes follow me as I straighten, sharp and disapproving, and then she quickly looks away, almost annoyed. I'm about to ask her what the hell her deal is when Clara asks us a question. *Probably for the best.*

"Do you guys remember our sophomore year when we all came up here in matching neon onesies and got lost trying to find Bigfoot?"

Alejandra groans. "How could we forget? You screamed so loud when you thought you saw Bigfoot that the Park Rangers thought there was an emergency!"

Laughter erupts from Lily, Alejandra, and Clara.

"There *was* an emergency! I slipped off a tree and got stuck on a branch trying to get a better look at Bigfoot!" Clara says defending herself as she throws her hands up.

"Keep your hands on the wheel!" Alejandra shouts.

Clara laughs but immediately grabs a hold of the wheel.

"We were about five minutes away from calling the fire department," Lily adds

Alejandra laughs, wiping away a fake tear. "I can't believe you even considered it. Imagine explaining that one —'Excuse me, sir, we need help. Our friend got stuck in a tree looking for Bigfoot.'"

"A conversation I'm sure they have on the daily in the Pacific Northwest." I joke.

Everyone bursts out laughing and can't stop for at least a minute. These girls feed my ego. That wasn't that funny.

"Whatever," Clara says, shrugging as she fights to keep a straight face.

"I missed this. All of us together." Alejandra says reaching over the center console to grab my hand and Lily's.

I turn to Lily, narrow my eyes at her, and smile, knowing it's her fault we haven't all hung out.

"It's been ages since we've done something like this. We need to make this a tradition again."

"Count me in," Lily says with the biggest smile ever.

Clara agrees but I say nothing. They're lucky I'm here now. I will not be here next time.

The girls start talking about all the trails "we're" going to hike but I tune them out and instead try to remember the last time we were all up here together—maybe it was the summer before our senior year? Yeah... it was. Lily had just got her driver's license, and she insisted on driving us up here. The whole drive up was a mess, all of us screaming and laughing as we realized Lily had no idea how to drive and probably cheated on her driver's test. I can almost feel the warmth of that sun-soaked day on my face.

Before I know it, we pull up to the trailhead where Valeria and Brooke are already waiting for us.

We all pile out of the car and head straight over to give Valeria a big hug. Brooke doesn't say a word to any of us, even though we all greet her. She just turns to Valeria and says, "I'll pick you up when you're done—text me when you're heading back down." Without another word, she gets in her car and drives off. *Fuck ass.*

"Don't mind her," Valeria says with a small shrug. "She's just in one of those moods today."

I raise an eyebrow at her but don't push it. Brooke's been in "one of those moods" for weeks now and I'm so sick of it.

"Right," Clara says, dragging out the 'I'. "Well, let's hit the trail before we miss the sunrise."

We all turn to follow her and start walking.

We don't usually talk on the way up and this time isn't

any different. The only sound around us is the crunch of our shoes and the rustling of birds moving from tree to tree.

The trail is steeper than I remember—or maybe I'm just more out of shape than I'd like to admit—I have to keep reminding myself to breathe in through my nose and out through my mouth but I'm not getting enough air and my mouth already tastes like blood. I've been so busy stressing about being stuck on a hike with Lily that I forgot how much I hate hiking.

After about an hour we—finally—reach the top and the view of the sunrise spreads out before us, but none of us bother looking at it—we're too busy trying not to pass out. Alejandra drops to her knees heaving, Clara flops onto her back, gasping for air, Valeria and Lily cling to a tree for support and I double over onto a massive rock. Myra seems to be the only one not dying.

Once the burning in my chest eases and the taste of blood is no longer on my tongue, I walk to the edge of the cliff and stand next to Valeria.

"Wow," Valeria whispers as she leans her head on my shoulder. "This was worth every blister."

We all laugh.

"It feels like we're standing on top of the world," Lily says, her eyes fixed on the horizon. "I'd forgotten how beautiful the view is from up here."

"Yeah," Valeria and I say at the same time.

"First bucket list item, officially checked." Alejandra sings as she throws her arms up in the air, spinning in a slow circle like she's absorbing every last bit of the sun. "But next time, someone else carries the snacks."

"I told you not to bring the family-size bag of trail mix." Clara laughs.

Alejandra sticks her tongue out at Clara.

We all sit at the edge of the cliff, looking out at the horizon as we pass around Alejandra's massive bag of trail mix.

I pass it to Lily, who's sitting next to me, and she gives me a small smile in return. And in this moment, I forget the awkwardness in the car. It's almost nice to be sitting here with her. But that cozy, warm feeling fades the second I turn back to look at the horizon. Myra lays her head on my shoulder, and I can feel the intensity of Lily's stare switch from relaxed and inviting to sharp and intense, like she's trying to burn a hole through the side of my head. *What could I or Myra have possibly done to make her this mad?*

And that's when it hits me... she probably didn't know Myra was coming and now, she's mad, it isn't just the five of us. Fuck. I probably should have told her at the gallery, but I kind of thought Clara and Alejandra would tell her. Of course, the one time I want them to tell her something they don't. I need to find a moment to talk to her, or my temporary truce will be shot.

"Alright, what's the plan? I'm bored," Clara says, stretching out.

"I know it's early, but I think we've earned a little treat," Alejandra says, grinning.

And I immediately know what she means. When we were teenagers, we made up a rule—every hike ends with pizza, no exceptions. There's something about those greasy slices that tastes so much better after a hike.

"Pizza?" Lily says, her eyes lighting up.

"Pizza," everyone agrees as we stand.

Which is perfect because then I can talk to Lily on the way down. But Myra will not leave my side, and I'm starting to feel claustrophobic and annoyed.

Finally, someone talks to her and I slip away.

I start trailing behind since Lily is a lot further back, but it's harder than it sounds. She's easily distracted by everything around her and stops to take pictures every two steps. I stop dead in my tracks, right in the middle of the trail, and wait for her to catch up to me instead. Looks like it's going to take a while, so I use the time to figure out what I'm going to say. I want to explain that I thought the girls would tell her Myra was coming and apologize—not that I think I need to because I haven't done anything wrong but because the last thing I need is for the girls to see us fighting and blame me for upsetting Lily—I also want to figure out what is going on with her. She's been in a terrible mood all day and it can't just be about Myra. Maybe she's still mad at me for what I said yesterday.

"Hey," I say, startling Lily.

She turns, a hand over her chest. "You scared me."

"Sorry," I reply. "I was just waiting for you to come down."

"Oh? Won't Myra care?"

"I don't see why she would." I shrug.

Lily nods, and we walk in silence for a few minutes. I'm not entirely sure how to bring this conversation up, so we just keep walking quietly. I stop whenever she does and watch as she contorts herself into a pretzel to get "the right angle." I haven't seen her do this in years, and honestly, I kind of like seeing it now. It's like I'm getting to know her all over again, and it's nice to see some things haven't changed. It takes me a second to realize I'm smiling at her. I quickly force my expression back to neutral, hoping she didn't see. Luckily, Lily doesn't seem to notice. She's in another impossibly uncomfortable position trying to get a picture of a frog. I shift my weight as the awkwardness sneaks back in, crawling under my skin. I hate this feeling—I'm not the awkward type, but when I'm around Lily it's my default. I try to shake it off and roll my shoulders back trying to walk a little straighter.

"Look at this," Lily says holding her camera up at me. I crouch next to her and I lean in to see the picture she took.

"Cute."

Lily smiles confidently.

We both go to stand but when she turns her foot slips on a loose rock and Lily tumbles forward, reaching out instinctively to catch herself. But instead of steady ground, Lily finds me right in her path.

We collide in a chaotic tangle of limbs, tumbling down the hill. Lily screams bloody murder, and I can't help but burst into laughter. Thinking we probably look like those cartoon characters that turn into a snowball, just a tangle of limbs tumbling downhill. When we land on the ground, her camera swings safely away, and she ends up right on top of me, her legs straddling my sides.

It's only when I feel the weight of her press down on me that I fully realize she's on top of me, and my heart starts racing. My mind goes fuzzy and I gulp, the sound of it somehow louder than I thought possible. The laughter dies in my throat, and suddenly, everything feels way too close—too intimate. I try to breathe normally, but it's hard with her so close to my face. My eyes land on her lips and a breath catches in my throat. I force myself to look away, but my eyes keep getting pulled back to her mouth, just inches away from mine.

Lily's cheeks flush pink and everything south of my belly button is warm, making it hard to focus on anything but the weight of her body and how good it feels on top of mine. I must've hit my head or something because this isn't right.

"Will you... uh..." I say, awkwardly gesturing for her to get off me.

Her eyes widen and she quickly looks away. "I... I didn't mean to, I'm—" she stammers, her words tumbling out in a rush. She shifts her weight and rests her hands on my shoulders as she lifts herself off me.

She reaches for her camera and begins adjusting the strap nervously.

I stand and start brushing a few blades of grass from my jacket. Trying to ignore the intrusive thoughts circling in my head. It's been years since I thought about Lily and me together and I'd like to keep that going but my brain seems to have other plans.

Alejandra, Valeria, and Myra poke out from around the trees, concern plastered across their faces.

"What's going on here? We heard someone scream," Alejandra says as she steps into the clearing.

Lily's cheeks flare a deeper shade of red, and she quickly takes my hand, standing up as she shoots Alejandra a pout. "I fell over."

Alejandra lets out a relieved sigh. "Is that all? I thought something serious happened." She steps closer, eyeing Lily.

"Yeah, I lost my balance, but I'm fine! Just a little slip," she says, as she brushes off some dead leaves from her pants.

"Well, I'm glad you're both okay," Alejandra says.

Myra steps closer to me and begins plucking dead leaves from my hair.

"You're a mess," she says with a half-smile.

"Thanks," I say, letting out a chuckle as I roll my eyes.

When she's all done, Myra gives my ass a playful slap. "All good," she says with a wink.

I automatically look at Lily, when her eyes meet mine,

her lips press into a tight smile before quickly looking away. A cloud settles over my chest, heavy and uncomfortable.

"Come on, slowpokes!" Clara calls from a distance.

Lily and Alejandra both shake their heads and smile.

"We're coming!" Alejandra calls back.

As Lily starts to walk, there's a tug at my hand, and when I look down, I realize neither of us has let go of the other's hand. We must've both noticed at the same time because we both quickly pull our hands apart. I don't even have a moment to think about what I'm feeling or what it means before Myra slips her hand into mine. All the tingles Lily left behind are now gone, and I'm a little disappointed.

"Sorry," Lily blurts out looking at Myra before running ahead of us.

"What are you doing," Myra scowls.

"What do you mean?"

"You're flirting with Lily."

"What? I am not, I'm just being nice."

"Well, stop," Myra says as she lets go of my hand and speeds past everyone.

I think about running after her, but I don't want to feed into whatever's going on with her, so I let her go. She probably needs the space to cool off, anyway.

———— ♥♥♥ ————

We walk into the pizzeria, and it looks the same. I haven't been back here since our last group hike—the same one where Lily almost killed us with her bad driving—and it's been hard to stay away, especially since our town only has one other pizzeria, and this one is, hands down the best.

When the waiter finally sets the mac and cheese pizza

we ordered in front of us, I swear I hear angels sing. I quickly grab a piece and bite down.

"Mmm," I moan.

When I open my eyes, Lily is staring at me, wide-eyed. She quickly looks away and starts picking at the noodles in her pizza, her cheeks crimson red. Myra, on the other hand, looks like she's about to kill me but I grin, completely unapologetic. The pizza slices are even better than I remembered.

After we polish off the last slice, Clara stretches in her chair. "So, what's next? Do you guys want to go home, or do something else?"

"Let's head back to our place, make some mimosas, and just hang out for a while," Alejandra says, as she turns to Clara.

"I'm in," Valeria says. "But I'll meet you guys there. Brooke is picking me up soon. I have to drop something off at my parents' before noon."

Alejandra and Clara nod.

"Lily? Bel? Myra?" Clara asks.

"Count me in," Lily says.

My first instinct is to say yes, because I love hanging out with the girls, but with Lily going, I kind of want to say no. The hike was fine and all, but I don't know if I want to spend the whole day with her. But if I say no, they'll know it's because of Lily and will make me go, anyway. Clara and Alejandra are not above kidnapping me. I look over at Myra, hoping she can somehow get me out of this.

"I can't today. I have a lunch date," she says.

"With Isabella?" Alejandra asks.

I widen my eyes, silently begging Myra to say yes, but my face must be saying something completely different because she narrows her eyes and says, "No?"

Fuck.

"Alright, well, we can drop you off at home."

"Yeah, that'd be great, thanks."

"I guess you're free then," Alejandra says, looking straight at me. "You're coming with us," she chirps before I can come up with a good enough reason to say no.

We clean up our table and head out.

As soon as we drop Myra off at her apartment, Lily visibly relaxes. And again I feel bad for not telling her Myra was coming, but it's too late now, so I just let it be.

When we get to Alejandra and Clara's house we all slip off our shoes, lining them up neatly by the door. Alejandra's a bit of a germaphobe so the no-shoes in the house rule is strict. Their place is spotless, not a single bit of clutter anywhere but it's still surprisingly homey. Clara's room, though—that's a different story. I've lost count of how many times I've heard Clara and Alejandra go back and forth about the random stuff Clara leaves lying around. Why these two ever thought being roommates was a good idea is beyond me.

We make our way to the kitchen and watch as Clara whips up some mimosas. When she's done we carry the pitcher out to the screened-in porch, settle into the cozy chairs, and end up staying out there for hours, sipping on our drinks, playing UNO and Go Fish, but what starts as a casual hangout quickly turns into an impromptu house party. When it gets too cold to be outside we all head in and Clara puts music on, and before we know it, the living room becomes a makeshift dance floor just as Valeria gets here. Clara's gone full DJ mode pretending to spin records on some pots and pans she grabbed from the kitchen, looking absolutely ridiculous. Alejandra plugs in some strobe lights from an old photoshoot she used them for, and Lily is already dancing around the living room like she's at some underground rave.

"You guys are too much!" Valeria laughs, dropping her bag by the door as she kicks off her shoes.

Clara turns up the music, and Alejandra pulls me and Valeria into the center of the "dance floor." The room pulses with the beat of the music as the strobe lights flicker and I swear I'm in that one SpongeBob episode where his house shakes to the music and jellyfish are dancing all around.

We're all taking back shot after shot drinking more than we should. I've lost count of how many shots I've taken but my body feels looser, my thoughts fuzzier, even Lily's presence isn't really bothering me anymore, so I'd say I'm at the perfect amount.

"Let's tango," Lily shouts.

She takes hold of my hand and pulls me in close before I get the chance to dodge her.

I fight the need I have to shove her off me because I don't want to make a scene right now. So I go along with it.

She pulls me even closer, and the smell of her shampoo hits me, suddenly, I have this ridiculous urge to bury my face in her hair. With her body pressed so tightly against mine the intrusive thoughts from earlier come flooding back only now I can't seem to push them back because the alcohol is messing with my head making my entire body feel like it's buzzing. *It's the drinks*, I say over and over because nothing else makes sense.

"I need some water," I say to Lily, as I untangle myself from her.

"Me too, let's go," Lily says as she slips her hand right back into mine.

I freeze and look down. Her hand fits so easily into mine. I try not to memorize the way her hand feels, but my brain captures every detail, pressing it into my memory whether I like it or not.

The kitchen is dimly lit and quieter, a much-needed rest for my eardrums.

I open the fridge and grab two bottles of water. When I turn back I'm surprised to find her just inches from my face. And I hate that her being this close makes my stomach flutter but it does. Why can't my body get on fucking board with my brain?

"Here," I say, stepping back.

"Thanks" she mutters as she takes the bottle.

"So, um..." Lily says, her voice trailing off as she looks around the room.

I lean against the counter and raise an eyebrow, waiting for her to say something, but the silence just stretches out uncomfortably.

"Myra, she's uh... very pretty." Lily finally says.

I narrow my eyes. Where is this going?

"Um.. yeah, I guess she is."

"Does she... um... does she know about... us?"

"There is no us."

"Well, yeah... not now but... there... was," Lily says playing with the sleeve of her shirt.

And yeah there was a time when the idea of "us" felt so solid. But now, when I think about "us," it feels like a word from a made-up language.

I chew on on my bottom lip not sure what to say. I could be an ass about this because she's the reason there is no "us" —granted I risk Alejandra, Clara, and Valeria getting mad at me—or I could stick to my truce.

"She knows we hooked up, but that's it," I end up saying. Fighting with her doesn't sound like a good idea right now.

Lily nods and she looks almost sad. Which makes me regret my decision. Because what right does she have to be sad?

"Oh, good, you're together! We're all heading outside to make some s'mores!" Alejandra announces her words a little slurred.

Lily and I nod and I follow after her.

We all collapse onto the soft grass, forming a loose circle with our heads touching, limbs sprawled, lying on our backs. As I look up at the stars, the girls start debating birth charts and which planet is causing the most chaos in their lives. I opt out of the conversation, tuning in and out. I hate astrology, but the stars above twinkle brighter, almost as if they're amused by the conversation happening below.

Even if I wanted to join in I couldn't. My thoughts are stuck on Lily—on us, on everything we used to be. And my brain keeps pulling out memories I rather not relive like the way her eyes crinkle when she smiles big, the way she kisses, the way she says my name when she—I shake my head, trying to push those thoughts back where they belong, buried and forgotten. But the harder I try, the more they come rushing in.

Fuck, I hate this.

7

LILY

I wake up at Alejandra's house with a dull ache in my head and the realization that I am definitely not in my bed. The living room is littered with empty bottles, half-eaten pizza slices, and a random sock that has somehow found its way onto the coffee table. *Typical.*

Just as I'm trying to recall how the sock got there, I see Isabella tiptoeing toward the door. She's moving slowly, clearly trying not to wake anyone.

Isabella and I ended up crashing on the couch last night. Clara and Alejandra were too drunk to drive us home, and leaving with Valeria wasn't an option.

"Morning." I groggily call out, interrupting her stealthy escape.

She jumps slightly, then turns around, her eyes still half-closed and heavy with sleep, and her hair is a frizzy halo. That just-woke-up look of hers is both messy and ridiculously sexy. I can't help but stare, mesmerized by the sight of her.

"Sorry, did I wake you? I was trying to be quiet," she whispers, her voice low and groggy.

"No, you didn't," I say, forcing myself to look at anything but her. "Are you leaving? I can give you a ride home. We just have to walk to my house first and it's just up the street."

Isabella stares at me and chews on the inside of her cheek. "No. I'm good."

"You sure?"

"Yup."

I sigh. If Isabella won't even let me take her home, we're never going to get back on track.

"I'll walk out with you. I should get going anyway. Alejandra's couch is not doing my back any favors," I say, forcing a smile.

I slowly peel myself off the couch, my head throbbing as I try to stand upright. The room spins for a second, but I manage to grab my things and stumble to the door without tripping over anything. Small victories.

Once we step outside, I instantly regret it. The sun is shining way too brightly for my fragile state, and I squint against the light, trying to figure out why it has to be so obnoxiously sunny today—the one day I need Washington to be gloomy...

"Alright, well, I'll see ya," Isabella says, walking ahead without waiting for me to respond.

I shuffle along behind her, not because I want to, but because, unfortunately, we're headed in the same direction.

After an uncomfortable few minutes, she spins around. "Are you following me?" she snarls.

"What? No!" I yell a bit too loud. A few people walking down the street turn to look at me and my face heats. "I'm just, uh... going to get coffee before I go home," I say, pointing down the hill.

"Oh." She pauses, glancing down the street. "Me too."

"Well, then let's walk together so I don't feel like a stalker." I joke.

Isabella nods and we start walking side by side.

Her pace is unhurried, hands tucked into the pockets of her jacket, and I can't help but steal a glance at her—it's completely unfair how effortlessly beautiful she looks, even this early. I watch the breeze play with a few loose strands of her hair. There's something calm and effortless about the way she moves. I must have stared at her the entire walk because before I know it, we're at the café.

As soon as we step inside the smell of fresh coffee instantly lifts my spirit. Isabella orders before me and I see she ordered her drink in a mug so I do too—now I'm being a stalker but only because I need to show her we can hang out without it being awkward. Isabella's coffee is ready first, she grabs it and walks off sitting on a stool near a window. When my drink is ready, I grab my cup and follow after her.

"What are you doing, Lily?" Isabella asks rubbing her forehead as I sit on the stool next to her.

I don't answer her. I just smile and shimmy around trying to get comfy on the stool. Isabella shakes her head but I ignore her annoyance. I am on a mission and I can't let her derail me.

Once we take a seat I sip my coffee, sighing and moaning contently. "This is heaven."

"Mhm."

"You ok?" I ask as I watch Isabella close her eyes, and rub her temples.

"Yeah, just regretting yesterday's drinks," She says as she opens her eyes and blinks hard.

"Yeah, same," I say feeling the pressure behind my eyes intensify. "Oh, but I have just the thing." I reach for my purse and pull out my migraine ward essential oil roll-on.

"This isn't exactly for hangovers but I've used it before and it's worked like a charm," I say handing it to Isabella.

She grabs it and inspects it.

"What am I supposed to do with this? Drink it?"

I laugh.

"No, you roll it on your temples, wrist, and chest. Here," I say grabbing it from her.

I uncap it and reach for her hand. Isabella pulls back.

"Come on, it's not going to do anything but make you feel better and smell good."

She hesitantly places her right wrist in front of me and I roll a little bit of the oil on her skin. Without thinking I grab her wrist and rub the oil in with my thumb. But as soon as my fingers make contact on her skin I swallow nervously, feeling a tingle dance at my fingertips. I try to ignore it but my heart is beating faster.

"There, just like that," I say struggling to speak as I hand her back the tube. My hand trembling slightly.

I couldn't tell you if or where Isabella put the oil on because I didn't look back up at her. My eyes too focused on the heartbeat on my thumb.

"How's your mom?" I ask, eager to shift my focus.

Isabella is quiet for a few seconds.

"Um... my mom's doing well. Loving retirement," she replies as she shifts in her seat.

"I didn't know she'd retired."

"Yeah," she nods. Bitting on her bottom lip.

I stare at her, waiting for her to say something else, but she doesn't. So I turn back to my coffee, idly playing with the spoon.

"She decided to retire early. So she retired a few months ago," Isabella says out of nowhere.

I glance back at her.

"How come?"

Isabella shrugs. "I think she just got tired of the hustle—especially with how crazy the housing market's been lately. She was stuck with three houses she couldn't sell for over a year, and that's when she realized it was more of a headache than it was worth. So, she bought a place on the lake a few towns over. Now she makes jewelry and runs her own Etsy shop," she says with a soft laugh as her fingers trace the edge of her cup.

"An Etsy shop? That sounds about right for her," I say with a smile, but as the words leave my mouth, a tight knot forms in my chest. It stings, hearing all this for the first time. Isabella's mom had always been like a second mother to me. Growing up, I spent almost every free moment at their house. Isabella's an only child, like me. Her parents always wanted more kids but I guess it wasn't in the cards for them, so they took me in with open arms and treated me like one of their own. I learned so much about Guatemalan culture because of them.

"Truly," Isabella says, a small, bittersweet smile tugging at her lips as she takes a slow sip of her coffee. "I don't think I've seen her this happy since... well, since before my dad passed."

I nod, trying to focus on her words, but hearing about it now stings in ways I can't quite explain. Her dad passed a few years after we stopped talking. I tried reaching out because I knew how close she was to her dad, but never got a response. Part of me wanted to keep trying, to be there for her, but I didn't want to intrude when there was clearly no space for me, so I stopped trying.

I did reach out to her mom, though, hoping to offer some small comfort. Marie and I chatted a bit, mostly about memories she had of her husband and Isabella. It wasn't the same as being there for Isabella herself, but it felt like a good way to remind her I was still there, holding space for her, waiting for the day she might be ready to reach back out.

I swallow before speaking "I'm sorry for your loss, Isa... He was such an amazing man."

She nods. "Yeah, he was."

We stay at the cafe for a while, sipping our drinks in silence.

Eventually, the reality of the day starts to creep in. I need to turn over my manuscript to my editor in a few days and I still don't have an ending. I look at my watch, then over at Isabella, who looks lost in thought.

"I should probably head out," I say gently. "Are you sure you don't want me to take you home? It looks like it's going to rain."

"You don't have to."

"I don't mind, I swear."

She nods, taking one last sip of her coffee. "Alright, yeah. That would be great."

I don't let it show, but my heart's so full I could burst.

We walk out of the cafe and head back down the street toward my place, the crisp morning air cooling our faces. Isabella walks close beside me, her steps matching mine. The streets are still relatively quiet, the town still waking up around us.

When we reach my house, I grab the hide-a-key and fumble with the key before finally getting the door open.

"Let me just grab my car keys."

"You don't have your keys?" Isabella says with a raised eyebrow.

"I locked myself out yesterday morning. I was going to go ask my mom to let me back in, but Clara insisted we were late and wouldn't let me, so I had my mom leave a spare out for me," I say, stepping inside. I spot them on the counter, right where I left them—which is a surprise, considering my cat usually knocks them off and plays with them until they end up under the couch or fridge.

Right as I grab them, I hear the sound of a door creaking. I turn around and see my mom step out into the backyard, a big smile on her face as her eyes land on Isabella.

"Isabella, sweetheart, it's been ages," she says, walking over to her with arms open for a hug.

Isabella smiles at my mom, but it doesn't quite reach her eyes, thankfully, my mom doesn't seem to notice. Mom wraps her in a hug, and Isabella awkwardly taps her back.

"It's good to see you too Lisa," Isabella says as she buries her hands in the pocket of her hoodie. I severely doubt it but points for trying.

As I watch them a pang of nostalgia tugs at my chest. Mom always adored Isabella so I know losing her was as painful for me as it was for her. Only maybe worse cause she never really knew why Isabella was there one day and gone the next.

Mom gestures toward the back porch, where two chairs sit under the shade of the old oak tree. "Come sit down, let's catch up. I want to hear all about your gallery. My friends say it's wonderful."

"Oh, Mom, we've got to go. Isabella has things to do," I say quickly, hoping to spare her from the pressure.

Isabella gives a small, awkward smile. "I do have some things to take care of, maybe another time," she says as she rubs the back of her neck. Something I know she only does when she's nervous. Or at least it used to be...

Mom studies her for a moment, her gaze softening. "Well, if you say so. I just wanted to hear more about it. You've always had such an eye for art. You know, I still have that painting you did for me all those years ago—it's hanging in the living room."

Isabella's face brightens in surprise. "You still have it?"

"Of course," Mom grins. "I wouldn't part with it for anything."

A tiny smile creeps up on Isabella's lips—the kind that's so subtle and quick, you almost wonder if you imagined it.

"It's one of my favorites," Mom adds with a wink. "Take care, sweetheart. We'll talk soon."

With a final wave, Isabella and I head back to the car, and we both slide inside.

She doesn't say much during the drive, only talking here and there to give me offhanded directions to her house.

As we pull up into her driveway. I realize we live less than five minutes away from each other, and that makes me very happy.

"Thanks for the ride," she says as she unbuckles her seatbelt.

"Of course," I reply.

I steal one last glance at her as she steps out of the car—messy hair, sleepy eyes, and all. She catches me looking and smiles softly. A smile that's making me question everything about how I left things between us all those years ago.

She closes my car door and I watch as she jogs up the stairs toward her front door but then pauses, her hand resting on the doorknob. She looks back at me and hesitates before yelling out. "Actually, can you wait here a minute? There's something I want to give you. I just need to grab it from inside."

"Uh, sure. Take your time," I yell back.

My mind instantly starts racing, wondering what she could possibly want to give me. I drum my fingers on the steering wheel, trying not to get lost in my thoughts—

because, let's be honest, overthinking is kind of my favorite pastime and I can't help but make up all sorts of stories in my head, just letting my imagination run wild.

A few minutes later, Isabella walks out of her house holding a small bag in her hand. I roll down the window, a bit more intrigued now.

"Here," she says, handing me the bag.

I carefully open the bag trying to keep my excitement contained but it's hard. I love gifts. Receiving gifts is easily my number two of all the love languages. Right after words of affirmation.

Inside, I find a neatly folded white blouse. I stare at it confused, until the memory clicks—the coffee shop. The shirt I wore that day, now discarded in the trash, stained with coffee. I pull the shirt out of the bag, and my breath catches in my throat.

"You bought me a shirt?" I ask, my voice barely above a whisper as I look up at her. My chest's so full I half expect it to burst.

"Yeah, I saw how bummed you were about messing up your shirt, so I found one that's pretty close to the one you were wearing," she says, leaning against the car with a smug grin on her face. "You're welcome, by the way," she adds.

The thoughtfulness behind the gesture catches me off guard. For the first time in a long time, I find myself tongue-tied, utterly speechless.

I swing the car door open. Isabella jumps back, startled, and as I step out I pull her into a tight hug. I feel her stiffen, but then she relaxes, and my pulse flutters wildly, as I hold her.

"Thank you," I say, still holding on to her, the shirt still in my hand.

"You're welcome," she replies, shrugging like it's no big deal.

But to me, it's everything. In this moment, it feels like the space between us shifts, just a little. And something clicks inside me—maybe, after all this time, there's still something between us that just fits. Like it always had. Maybe I'm not totally crazy for wanting to put our friendship back together. So, for a moment, I let myself believe our friendship can still be fixed, that someday it'll all go back to being what it used to be.

When I finally let her go, I lean in and kiss her cheek quickly before getting back in my car, my heart racing even faster now.

"Thanks again for the ride," she says, with a smile as she closes my car door.

She climbs up her front steps, pauses, and turns to wave goodbye, her smile brightening the morning even more. I wave back, feeling a warmth in my chest that lingers long after I drive away.

8

ISABELLA

"Could you please put those four pieces in storage?" I say, gesturing to the paintings on the wall. I'm at the gallery today, working with my assistant, Rachel, to help move things around for the upcoming installation, but I haven't done shit but argue with Myra all fucking day. I don't usually come in on Sundays, but I needed the distraction—even if my head's still pounding.

Clara makes the best drinks, but her pours are dangerous. You end up sipping one, then another, and before you know it, it's too late.

"Hey, what do you want to do with these?" I hear Rachel call from behind me. I turn to find her holding two paintings.

"Where'd you find them?" I ask.

"They were in the back. Sarah said to put them out but didn't say where."

Sarah is in charge of the layout for every show, so I know better than to make decisions about where these paintings should go without her.

"I don't know. Let's just wait for Sarah. I don't want to

have you put them somewhere just for her to move them later."

Rachel nods and walks toward the backroom, probably to track Sarah down.

I head to my office to try to pretend I'm doing something. I sit at my desk, log into my email, and, of course, my eyes go straight to the 126 unread messages. I swear, I'm trying to stay on top of it all, but no matter how fast I get through them, there's always more piling up. It's like this constant game of catch-up that I can never win.

I take a deep breath, roll my shoulders, and start sifting through a few. I'm already here, so I might as well do something. I get through about two, and then it hits me—I still don't have a collaborator for the exhibit. *Fuck.*

This next exhibit is deeply personal. It's meant to celebrate sapphic romance—ironic, I know, Clara lost her shit when I told her. The whole exhibit will feature abstract pieces and some of the more *risky* paintings I've kept to myself over the years. I usually feature a local artist at the show, but this time I want to spotlight a queer female artist to match the theme. The problem is that finding one in a small town like Stanwood isn't easy—but here I am—now finding two is near impossible.

So now, I need to go through my contact list, email a few friends from college, and see if any of them might be interested in a last-minute show. All while ignoring my desperate need to do a deep dive into why I can't seem to stop thinking about Lily.

I spend almost two hours scrolling through my contact list, doing some light research on the ones I'd like to feature. Making sure there's nothing problematic in their background. After a lot of back and forth, I narrow it down to three: Clark, Olivia, and Madison. I know them all from college—we practically lived in the studio together, and I've always loved their work. Plus, it helps to know we work well together.

I shoot off the emails, hoping one of them will reply within the week, and lean back in my chair, feeling a bit relieved. It's hard not to stress with the show just weeks away, but it's always worth it when opening night comes around. Still, I can't help but wish Myra would stop being such a drama queen so she can come over and help take the edge off some of the stress. But after the way she was acting yesterday, it's not even an option anymore. Seeing her get jealous and possessive during the hike made me rethink everything, and this morning, things only got worse.

Myra texted me about fifty times asking if anything happened between Lily and me last night, but no matter how many times I said no, she didn't believe me. Even if it had—not that I wanted to, but if it had—that should be the last thing on her mind. We're fuck buddies, and I can sleep with whoever I want, even if it's Lily—not that I want to sleep with Lily, but if I did want to sleep with Lily—it should be fine. That's what Myra agreed to a long time ago, as long as I was safe and got checked before fucking her, we were good.

But no matter how many times I explained that very point, she didn't get it, so I stopped replying. Which is when the calls started. I picked up once, letting Myra cry for at least an hour, telling me how she loves me and wants to be with me and how Lily doesn't deserve me and whatever the fuck else.

This isn't how it's supposed to go. We were just a place-holder until something better came along, and I thought I'd made it clear that I wasn't ever going to be that something better, but I guess I wasn't clear enough.

This is exactly why I don't date or let feelings be involved. First, they give you great sex; then, they give you mental health issues. It's all just too complicated and full of drama.

But honestly, this one is on me. I should've cut things off with Myra the second she told me she liked me a few weeks ago. Instead, I let her convince me it was just a passing feeling, something she'd get over.

Lesson learned, I guess. Next time someone tells me they like me, I'm running for the hills.

9

GROUP CHAT

Clara 7:30 p.m.: The fall festival is in a few days. do you guys want to go?

Alejandra 7:30 p.m.: I'm off Tuesday does that work for everyone? 👀

Clara 7:31 p.m.: Yeah, I work from home Tuesday. They won't even know I'm gone.

Lily 7:32 p.m.: Works for me!

Valeria 7:33 p.m.: Me 2!

Isabella 7:33 p.m.: if I must.

Clara 7:35 a.m.: Cool. let's meet there at noon. Also I can book the cabin for this weekend. Sorry for it being a last minute.

Alejandra 12:37 a.m.: Works for me!

Lily 12:37 a.m.: Me too.

Isabella 12:36 a.m.: 👍

Valeria 12:37 a.m.: Ditto!

Clara 12:39 a.m.: Booking now! night y'all

10

———

LILY

I've been holed up in my office for the past two hours, staring at my screen, desperately trying to figure out the ending to my book, but my brain refuses to cooperate.

My phone buzzes, and I reach for it. I freeze when I see a message from Isabella. I haven't heard from her since she gave me the shirt a couple of days ago.

> Isabella 10:00 a.m.: hey I know this is random, but do you think I could ride with you to the festival? I was supposed to go with clara and ale, but they both got stuck in meetings and I don't want to drive because parking is a nightmare

I stare at Isabella's text for a few seconds, feeling a flutter in my chest. I set my phone down and breathe in and out, trying to calm my pulse, when my phone buzzes again.

> Isabella 10:00 a.m.: please don't make me ride with valeria and brooke

I laugh, relieved that I'm not her absolute last option.

Lily 10:01 a.m.: Of course. Come over around 12.

The thought of her coming over has my heart doing somersaults, which is not helping my current state of distraction. I set my phone down and run my hands over my face, letting out a groan. *Focus. I need to focus.* But my thoughts keep drifting between the festival, the idea of spending the day with Isabella, and the giddiness I should absolutely not be feeling at the thought of seeing her.

I figure maybe some coffee will help me concentrate, so I push myself up from the desk and head to the kitchen. I put a pot on to brew, the familiar hum of the machine filling the silence and the smell of coffee fill the air, and I feel a brief sense of calm. There's nothing a little coffee can't fix.

I lean against the counter, waiting for it to finish, and drift into a daydream, thinking about how the day might turn out. I haven't been to one of these festivals since the last one Isabella and I went to. So going back and going with her after so many years feels... right.

The coffee machine beeps, breaking me out of my thoughts. I pour myself a mug and lean against the counter, sipping slowly, trying to ground myself.

I set my coffee down in the living room and head to my office to grab my laptop, hoping the change of scenery might help. But sitting on the couch doesn't make much of a difference. I spend the next thirty minutes staring at a blank page, watching the cursor blink, before moving on to some research, but I can't remember what I read because it left my mind the second I read something else.

I try doing some editing on the first few chapters, but every word I change ends up feeling clunky and forced, and I'm convinced I no longer know English. I guess it also doesn't help that my mind keeps drifting back to Isabella—her smile, the cute little dimple that appears on her left cheek when she talks. The thought of seeing her today and reliving some of my favorite memories of the festival with her is occupying the rest of my mind space. But I quickly press the stop button on that train of thought, because those thoughts are dangerous. Those same thoughts led me into the worst heartbreak I've ever experienced, and I can't... no, I won't, I refuse to go there again so eagerly and recklessly.

My goal is to fix our friendship, nothing else.

Before I know it, an hour has passed, and it's time to get ready. Isabella should be here soon. I toss the throw blanket off me, chug the rest of my—now cold—coffee, and head to the bathroom.

I hop onto the bathroom counter and lean in close to the mirror, carefully applying concealer trying to make myself look less like someone who's been staring at a blank screen for hours and more like someone who has their life together. Mascara, foundation, blush—check. Right eyeliner—done!

I glance at the clock—Isabella will be here any minute. Great. No pressure. Just as I'm about to start on the other eye, there's a knock at the door. Of course. Right on time. I set the eyeliner down and quickly head to the door, trying to calm the sudden rush of excitement that hits me. An excitement that quickly vanishes when I realize she might have brought Myra along. I mentally scan her text again trying to figure out if she said it in the plural but I can't remember.

Shoot... my stomach drops.

"Hey!" I say the moment I swing the door open. Quickly scanning outside to see if there's anyone else but it's just Isabella. Thank God...

"Hey," she replies.

"Come in! I'm almost ready." I say as I step to the side to let her in.

She gives me a slow once-over, smiling. "You look great already, but sure."

And I know I do because this is my favorite outfit and it never fails to make me feel cute. I'm wearing a sleek black long-sleeve top with a square neckline that shows just enough to keep it classy, and a fitted leather skirt with sheer black stockings and my favorite black Chelsea-style boots.

"Trust me, I need a few more minutes. You can follow me to the bathroom while I finish up."

She steps inside, kicking off her boots by the door before trailing after me. I lead her down the hallway and back into the bathroom, where my makeup is scattered all over the counter. I grab my eyeliner again, glancing at her through the mirror as she leans against the doorframe.

"So, parking's that bad, huh?" I ask while I try to focus on not stabbing myself in the eye with the liner.

She shrugs. "Yeah, you wouldn't believe how much bigger the festival is now. It's grown so much over the years. Kids come from all over for day trips with their schools—it's a big tourist attraction now."

"Wow, really?" I ask and Isabella nods.

I've been so focused on the eyeliner that I almost miss the way she's watching me—her gaze soft, almost thoughtful, like she's memorizing every little move I make. And suddenly I feel shy.

"There," I say, stepping back to check my reflection.

She shakes her head, still smiling. "You look perfect."

A flush of warmth creeps up my neck at her compliment, and I sprint past her, trying to slip into the hallway before she catches me turning red. "Alright, let's go!"

She pushes off the doorframe, and together we make our

way out of the house. As I lock the door behind us, a twinge of nerves flickers in my chest. We hop into my car, and as I start the engine, Isabella scans through radio stations before, settling on one playing some upbeat Indie music. The drive to the festival is short and neither of us says a thing. As we reach the town square, the roads get more and more congested. With people walking up and down the streets, and cars parked along every available curb.

Isabella wasn't exaggerating when she said it gets busy.

The excitement of getting here slowly turns into mild frustration as time ticks by and we can't find a parking spot. We spend about ten minutes slowly driving through side streets, both of us peering out our windows for any open spaces. Every now and then, Isabella points out a spot, only for it to be taken by another car.

Finally, I spot a small opening a couple of blocks away. "There! We're grabbing that one," I say, maneuvering into the spot as quickly as possible before the car in front of me gets any ideas. As we park, I can't help but feel a little victorious, a smile spreading across my face. Isabella laughs.

This might have been the most annoying part of the day, but there's something oddly satisfying about going through this ridiculous struggle with her.

"Alright, mission accomplished," I shout as Isabella unbuckles her seatbelt.

I step out of the car and stare out at the festival. It's mostly the same as I remember—booths lined up along the main street, familiar faces selling handmade crafts, and the same old carousel spinning lazily in the distance.

As we walk further into the festival, I spot Clara and Alejandra up ahead. They don't see us at first, but the moment I wave, Alejandras's eyes light up, and she calls out my name.

"Hey! You made it!" she says, pulling me into a quick hug.

"Yeah, sorry we're a bit late. Parking was a nightmare," I say as I reach for Clara.

"All good," Alejandra says as she grabs my hand and guides us further into the festival.

There are tents along both sides of the main streets. At the first stand, I see there's handcrafted jewelry, and next to that one, another overflows with stacks of homemade candles that smell like pumpkin spice and fresh pine. A few steps away from that one, Mrs. Buke—our old high school principal—is spinning wool into yarn, her hands moving with such practiced grace that I can't look away.

Alejandra and Clara must have walked ahead because the next time I look up Alejandra is laughing as she playfully shoves Clara toward the cornhole area. Clara rolls her eyes but follows her in any way. Isabella and I are just about to go in behind them when I notice a ring toss booth. I grab Isabella's hand and drag her towards it before she can protest.

"What are you doing?" she grumbles. But when I stop and she realizes where we're at she laughs.

Isabella and I used to spend all our summer allowance at the Fall Festival playing only one game: ring toss. I can still picture us trying—and failing miserably—at the ring toss year after year, laughing at how hopeless we were but determined to win something, no matter how small. We'd cheer each other on, even as the rings slipped off the bottles or clattered to the ground. We'd get so frustrated, but the whole time, we were having the best time. We never did win a thing.

The memory has always been sweet and comfy but

when I think about it now it stirs up something different. It's almost painful.

"You think we can win this time?" Isabella asks as I hand the guys at the stand a five-dollar bill. Which gets us five tosses.

I nod.

"Eight Summers of defeat and you still won't give up?" She says. Her smirk is lethal, and it's taking every ounce of restraint not to let her see just how much it's affecting me.

"I think I've got better luck now." I tease.

She raises an eyebrow, clearly thinking we're going to lose and I feel the need to defend myself. "I'm ready for a rematch. And this time, we're taking home a victory. Just you wait." I say.

"Alright, let's do it. But if we don't win, you owe me some mulled wine. For getting my hopes up."

"Deal!" I grin, watching her smile widen.

I throw the first ring and miss, Isabella throws the next two and also misses. I toss the last two and they both miss but the last one decided to tease me. It swirled around the neck of the bottle for a few agonizing seconds before finally flying off and landing in someone else's game earning them a ghost stuffy... We don't end up winning a thing—but with the way Isabella laughed as I fumbled through the game, I'd say victory doesn't matter at all.

"It's rigged!" Isabella shouts, loud enough for half the fair to hear. I scramble to cover her mouth, but I'm too late. The booth attendants already heard her, and now they're glaring at us.

Isabella laughs and wipes her mouth. "Alright, ready for mulled wine?" she says, already walking off with me trailing behind her.

The store is a cute little place, almost like something out

of a storybook—think cozy German style with wooden beams and warm lights glowing through the windows.

When we step inside we're immediately greeted by the smell of star anise and cloves. I hold the door for Isabella, and as she passes, she flashes me a smile that could melt even the chilliest October day.

This friendship thing is slipping out of my hands fast and edging towards something a little more dangerous every time she smiles at me.

We head up to the counter, and she orders for us both, that playful grin still on her face as she asks for two mulled wines. The barista pours our drinks and hands us two cups almost immediately. I was supposed to pay but Isabella ended up insisting she had this. And I wish it didn't but it leaves me feeling giddy. I take the cup and when my fingers brush against her, a silly little flutter runs through me.

We find a spot by the window, a perfect little corner to settle into. We both take a sip, letting the warmth of the wine chase away the chill from outside, as we watch Alejandra and Clara play cornhole. Clara is oddly really good at this game and sinks almost every bag, absolutely destroying Alejandra, who can't get a single one to go into the hole and is clearly getting more and more frustrated with each miss.

"Wow," Isabella chuckles, "Clara's got a hidden talent for cornhole. I didn't see that coming."

I laugh. "Yeah, Alejandra's gonna be mad about that for days."

"Lily!" I hear a voice call out. I turn to see Valeria and her girlfriend, Brooke, walking through the door hand in hand. Valeria's smile is as bright as ever.

"Well, look who finally made it!" I shout, waving them over.

"We got sidetracked at the caramel apple stand," Valeria says with a grin, holding up two sticky apples like trophies. Brooke stands next to her, offering nothing more than a tight-lipped smile and a small wave—she looks less than enthusiastic, but at least she's being polite enough to pretend.

"You better have brought enough for everyone," Isabella teases, leaning back in her chair with a smirk.

Valeria chuckles, shaking her head. "Sorry, these are ours. You'll have to fend for yourselves,"

Isabella pouts. "Fine, I guess we'll have to go get some ourselves."

"So, what have you guys been up to?" Valeria asks as she sits next to Isabella and takes a bite of her apple play-fully moaning into Isabella's face trying to make her jealous. Isabella grins and takes a big bite of Valeria's apple. Brooke immediately shakes her head and her face gets red like she's seconds away from spontaneously combusting.

Valeria laughs and pulls the apple away from Isabella. "Thief!" she says as she narrows her eyes. Gently placing a hand on Brookes and that seems to defuse the bomb.

"You were begging me to." Isabella jokes as she loudly chews on the big piece of caramel apple in her mouth.

Valeria rolls her eyes. "Anyways, what's the plan?"

Isabella and I shrug. We didn't come here with any plans.

"How do you guys feel about going to a haunted house?" Valeria asks.

I raise an eyebrow. "How haunted is this house?"

Isabella's eyes wide. "Yes! Let's go. I heard there's a really creepy one just outside of town. It's supposed to be one of the best. They say people don't even make it all the way through."

I shudder. "I'm terrible with haunted houses. I'll probably scream the whole time."

Valeria nudges me playfully. "That's half the fun! Besides, we'll be right there with you."

"We can go, but I probably won't go inside," I say.

"Oh, come on. We'll all go in together, it won't be that scary." Isabella says.

"Please," Valeria pouts.

Isabella sees Valeria pouting so she pouts too. Throwing in some puppy dog eyes for good measure.

I look between them and I hate the idea but seeing Isabella pout makes me fold.

"Fine," I finally agree.

Valeria claps her hands together. "It's settled then! We'll find Clara and Alejandra and then head straight over."

---- ♥ ♥ ♥ ----

I'm an idiot.

How'd I let myself get roped into this because a cute girl made a cute face at me...

The line to enter the haunted house snakes ahead of us and the sounds of screams and laughter echo from within. I shift from foot to foot, my heart racing. Isabella stands next to me, radiating calmness, and confidence, while I'm on the verge of passing out. Everyone promised I could be sandwiched in the middle once we go inside and that's the only thing keeping me sane right now.

"Can you believe this place?" I ask, wiping my sweaty palms on my skirt. "I mean, it's probably not even that scary right?" I laugh nervously.

Isabella shoots me a sideways glance and smiles. "You

don't look so sure." She says, and her teasing tone makes my heart race even faster making my anxiety worse. "You look a little pale."

"I'm just... preparing myself for the worst, you know, the creepy clowns, the jump scares... and those chainsaws!" I say pulling at the collar of my shirt.

"Chainsaws?" she laughs. "You're overthinking it. It's just a bunch of teenagers in costumes. And if there's chainsaws I can almost guarantee they're fake."

"Almost?"

"Definitely, she meant definitely." Alejandra cuts in. "Right, Isabella?"

Isabella rolls her eyes. "Sure," she says and Alejandra elbows Isabella in the ribs.

"Ow," Isabella says rubbing at her side.

"They're not real honey, I promise," Valeria says.

I breathe in deeply trying to believe what she's saying because of course it makes sense but to me... right now it doesn't.

The line moves forward, and before I know it, we're at the front of the line and our group is next. A sign hangs nearby, reminding everyone that no more than four can enter at a time.

"What is this?" I scream pointing at the sign. Feeling a panic attack brewing.

"Hey, it's ok. Isabella's got you, don't you Isa?"

"Oh, uh, sure."

Alejandra elbows her again.

"I mean, yes, of course, I do," Isabella says, correcting herself.

"You'll be ok," Alejandra says as she, Clara, Valeria, and Brooke step inside without us. Their excited laughter echo back as they disappear into the darkness. I watch as their figures vanish behind the heavy door, and my heart starts pounding even harder.

"Looks like it's just us, partner," Isabella says, stepping forward with unwavering confidence. "Are you ready?"

I take a deep breath, trying to shake off the nerves. "Mhmm."

I look back at the growing line behind us trying to figure out how many people I can let cut in front of us before Isabella drags me inside. When I look back at her she's staring down at me with an eyebrow raised. Like she knows exactly what I'm thinking.

"Guess we don't have much of a choice," I say, trying to sound brave, but my voice wavers slightly.

"Come on," she encourages, bumping her shoulder against mine. "It'll be fun."

"Easy for you to say," I shoot back, my heart pounding as we inch closer to the entrance. "You're not the one who's going to be scared out of their mind."

She laughs, and the sound settles my nerves just a bit, but not enough. Am I really about to let Isabella, of all people, guide me through one of the scariest moments in my life? Okay, sure, that's a bit of a reach, but at this moment, it feels true. And I don't think I can do this, but before I can back out or give Isabella a very elaborate excuse as to why I can't do this, we're being ushered in. Isabella walks forward, but I pull her back. She turns to look at me, and my eyes fill with tears.

Isabella steps closer and hugs me, something that quite frankly makes me want to cry even more.

"We don't have to go in Lily, not if you're this scared. We can get out of line."

I shake my head. "No, I want to do this, I just need you

to promise me that you won't run ahead and leave me behind."

"Lily, I promise I won't," she says, and I don't entirely believe her but I'm out of time. The door closes behind me and all we can do is walk through.

Isabella holds me at arm's length and stares into my eyes. She looks at me with such tenderness I almost feel... safe.

"If you change your mind, we can take one of the emergency exits," she says.

Having an escape plan eases some of the anxiety in my chest. But as we step into the darkened hallway, a chill runs down my spine, and I reach for Isabella's hand, the shadows swirling ominously around us

"You'll be fine," Isabella says.

We walk deeper into the haunted house, and I can feel adrenaline surge through me with every step. Every creak and distant howl sends my heart racing, and every time I squeeze Isabella's hand a little tighter. I know I must be hurting her, but you'd never be able to tell.

When we step into the first room, old circus posters are hanging on the walls, along with faded clown masks, and there's this weird off-key carnival music playing in the background that makes my skin crawl.

A pile of balloons in the corner moves slightly like something's hiding in it. Then, out of nowhere, a clown jumps out from behind a striped curtain, and I scream, instinctively pulling Isabella closer. Isabella laughs, but her grip on my hand is reassuring and steady. Her laughter rings out, and it somehow makes me feel a little less tense.

We step into the next chamber, and there are cobwebs everywhere, and dust particles dance in the air like tiny ghosts. I walk through, holding onto Isabella a little tighter, my eyes darting from one frame to the next, trying to figure out if the pictures are real or if someone's going to jump out of one of them. Suddenly, a loud crash echoes from the shadows, and a ghastly apparition springs to life, and air shoots into my face as its face twists in a sinister grin. I shriek, and without thinking, I hide behind Isabella, clutching at her waist, and bury my head in her shoulder blades.

I feel her laughter rumbling through her body, but instead of embarrassment, a wave of comfort washes over me. I tighten my grip around her, feeling the steady rhythm of her laugh against my cheek. Holding her like this feels so good, so... right.

"Scaredy-cat," she teases, and I can hear the grin in her voice.

"Whatever," I say, trying to sound annoyed.

We move through the haunted house, each jump scare becoming a little less daunting as I cling to Isabella. I almost look forward to something scaring me, so I have the perfect excuse to hold her tight.

Finally, we emerge into the cool night air, my heart still racing. The laughter of our friends echoes nearby.

"Look who survived!" Clara shouts, hands on her hips as she approaches me with a smirk.

Alejandra and Valeria each smack her, one on either side.

"Did you scream?" Clara teases, raising an eyebrow.

"Not even a little," I lie, still hiding behind Isabella, with my arms around her waist.

"Yeah, because she couldn't see much from behind me," Isabella jokes.

Valeria grins and nudges my shoulder. "I can't believe you hid behind Isabella the whole time!"

"Only a little," I say, my cheeks flushing as I finally release my hold on Isabella's waist.

"Just a bit, huh?" Alejandra laughs, crossing her arms. "We all heard you from outside. You sounded like you were fighting for your life in there!"

"I was," I yell.

Everyone laughs—well, everyone but Brooke. Brooke stands quietly to the side, unamused as she watches us.

"So, what's next?" Clara asks, looking around. "We can't let the night end here."

"How about we grab a drink?" Alejandra suggests. "There's a new bar nearby. I hear they have the best espresso martinis!"

"Yes, I need to calm my nerves after all that screaming," I say.

"Sounds perfect," Valeria agrees.

"Follow me!" Alejandra says.

Isabella places her hand on the small of my back and nudges me to follow. Her touch is warm and I can't help but smile.

"Thanks for what you did back there," I say.

"I couldn't let you ruin my night," she teases, bumping her shoulder against mine.

"I'm serious," I say, looping my arm in hers. "It means a lot more than you think."

She smiles but doesn't say anything.

When we finally make it to the bar, the adrenaline from the haunted house transforms into a wave of laughter and exaggerated retellings. Isabella and I keep sneaking glances at each other, the kind that feel electric, making the night feel like something out of a movie.

After a round of drinks, Isabella starts to lean into the fun a little too much. I watch as she knocks back cocktail after cocktail, her laughter bubbling up as she recounts her favorite scare from the haunted house.

"And then a clown jumped out of nowhere! Lily nearly took off running!" she exclaims, her hands animatedly illustrating the moment.

I chuckle.

After a few more drinks we decide it's time to head out.

"You're not driving, are you?" Valeria asks concern etched on her face as she stares at Isabella.

"No, Lily is," Isabella replies, her words a little slurred.

"Her car's at my house, but I'll make sure she stays with me tonight," I say firmly, giving Isabella a stern look.

She raises her eyebrows in surprise but doesn't argue. She just gives me a two-finger salute. I could just drive her home, but I've never been the type to drop off a drunk girl to an empty house, no matter how fine she claims to be.

Valeria glances at me, her brow furrowing slightly. "Text me when you guys get home?" she says, her voice softening.

I nod. "I will, I promise."

"Good," she replies, a smile breaking through.

As we step out of the bar, the cool night air hits us like a refreshing splash of water. We all quickly say goodbye and head to our cars. I catch Isabella's eye, and she flashes me a playful grin before looping her arm over my shoulder. Immediately an electric thrill runs up my arm.

"I can't believe we made it through that haunted house," she says, looking down at me with a playful smile. "Pretty sure you set a new record for the loudest scream," she teases.

My face starts to feel warm, but I laugh it off.

The walk back to the car is pretty uneventful aside from the fact that I can't keep my eyes off Isabella. There's something about the way she looks in the moonlight that's hypnotizing to me.

When we finally make it to my house, Isabella steps out of the car and sways slightly as she steps inside, her giggles bubbling up as she kicks off her shoes by the door.

"Make yourself at home" I chuckle softly as I guide her to my bedroom. I'm not planning on staying with her, but the thought of her in my bed sends a rush of nervousness through me and I'm glad I changed my sheets last night.

"Are you going to tuck me in?" she teases, her voice soft, playful, and slightly slurred. As she plops on my bed.

I playfully roll my eyes but lean down to tuck the blanket around her making sure it's nice and snug.

"There," I say, stepping back to admire my handiwork. "You're all set."

I head into my closet to change and when I step out Isabella looks like she's fast asleep. I watch her for a second and then I turn to leave.

"Where are you going?" she protests, scaring me.

"I'm sleeping on the couch," I say.

"Why?" she teases. "Are you afraid to share a bed with me?" She says as she bites her lip. Isabella must be plastered.

"No, I'm not afraid," I reply, trying to sound confident despite the flutter in my chest. "I just want to give you some space."

"No need," Isabella says, her smile widening as she holds the covers out, inviting me in.

"Are you sure?" I ask.

"Absolutely," she insists as she taps my side of the bed. I walk back towards her and settle in beside her.

This is innocent enough. Friends sleep in the same bed all the time.

But something not so friendly flutters in my chest as I watch her eyes grow heavy and the heat of her body envelops me. I want to freeze this moment and memorize every detail.

"Goodnight, Isabella," I whisper, brushing a strand of hair behind her ear.

She lets out a content sigh, her eyes finally closing as she drifts off to sleep. I snuggle into her allowing myself to bask in her warmth before surrendering to sleep.

11

ISABELLA

I wake up groggy, my head swimming in that fuzzy place between sleep and awareness, and I panic. This isn't my bed. I blink, trying to piece together where I am. The unfamiliar surroundings slowly come into focus. When I turn my head and see Lily, my breath evens out.

I haven't woken up in a stranger's bed in years, and I rather not start now.

Lily's face is turned toward the window, lips slightly parted, her hair a completely tangled up disaster, looking... kinda cute.

How did I end up here? Bits of last night flash through my mind—the festival, the haunted house, and the drinks. Ugh... those drinks. I groan, rubbing my eyes, a headache brewing.

Lily turns in her sleep, and somehow, her hand finds its way around my abdomen. I freeze, and I suck in a breath. Her fingers brush against my skin, and a nervous flutter sparks to life along the trail her fingers made. I think about shoving her hand off me, but instead, I let myself enjoy the warmth of her around me and try to relax, trying to memorize the weight of her arm draped across my waist, the soft rhythm of her breaths, the faint smell of her coconut shampoo on the pillowcase.

I wish it didn't, but it feels so fucking good to lie next to her.

My eyes start to feel heavy, and I almost fall back asleep. But reality crashes down like a bucket of ice water. I have to go.

I'm inching into dangerous territory with Lily, and I can't let myself fall into this again. This comfort is temporary. The butterflies will die. She's not staying at her mom's forever, and when she leaves, she'll take this with her, just like before.

I can't let feelings creep back in. If I do, I'll end up walking the same path of heartbreak I did ten years ago, and I barely made it out last time. I'm better off alone, no matter how good this feels. I can't let myself go there again.

I lift her arm and place it gently by her side. I slip out of bed slowly, doing my best not to shake the bed. When my feet hit the cool, creaky floor, I wince.

I look back, but Lily is still fast asleep. I grab my phone from the nightstand, stuff it into my pocket, and tiptoe out the door.

Once I'm out of her room, I let out a big sigh. I lean against it and try to steady myself before heading to my car, but my head is scrambled.

I've been fighting my feelings for Lily for years, building walls, burying them deep. And I hate that she's somehow destroying all the work I've put into forgetting her, but I need to figure out how to keep it all inside because it's better for both of us—ok, mainly me— if it's bottled up.

12

GROUP CHAT

Clara 6:26 a.m.: ok ladies are we ready to finally check off that night swim from our bucket list?

Alejandra 6:26 a.m.: YESSS, I'm so ready! I got this cute new bikini that needs to see the moonlight!

Isabella 6:27 a.m.: how cold is the water gonna be? I refuse to turn into an ice cube

Clara 6:27 a.m.: you'll survive.

Isabella 6:29 a.m.: rude

Alejandra 6:33 a.m.: I've got a better question: are we sneaking in or actually going somewhere legal for once?

Clara 6:33 a.m.: We're doing this right, people! Let's hit the cove near the cliffs. It's closed to the public during the fall, so we can wait there till we're ready to swim instead of trying to dodge beach security.

Valeria 6:33 a.m.: Sounds like a plan! Let's go Thursday night. It'll be a little warmer that day.

Clara 6:33 a.m.: As long as the snacks involve chocolate, I'm in.

Lily 6:36 a.m.: I'm in. What time are you thinking?

Clara 6:36 a.m.: Let's say 6? We can catch the sunset and then head into the water when it's fully dark.

Valeria 6:38 a.m.: 6 works. someone please remind me not to wear mascara unless we want me to look like a sea monster by the end of the night.

Clara 6:38 a.m.: LOL noted! No sea monster Val.

Isabella 6:38 a.m.: I'll pick everyone up.

Alejandra 6:38 a.m.: Finally! We're actually doing this. I can't wait!

13

LILY

When I woke up this morning I was expecting to find Isabella beside me, silly me. Sillier me to expect a message from her letting me know why she left, I guess. Instead, I woke up to fifteen messages from the group chat. She replied in there, but I didn't have a single one from her saying "goodbye". Not even a quick "GTG".

I grab my phone again, hoping there's something now, but there isn't. I stare at the screen as disappointment washes over me, sharp and heavy.

Waking up to an empty bed stung, and I still can't shake the hollow feeling. Somehow, I'm back in a familiar pattern of being left behind by her. The thought makes it hard to breathe.

I thought we made progress last night, but I guess not.

I just don't learn that I can't trust Isabella, do I?

I lean back in my chair and reach for my cup of coffee, but I'm out.

I've already asked the barista for six refills. If I ask for another, she might think I'm insane. So I set my cup down and groan.

I look back towards my computer and try to do some writing, but instead, I scroll through Target and buy a few candles.

About an hour passes, and I haven't written a thing, my editor is expecting this draft tomorrow and if I can't write out the last few paragraphs in my story in the next few hours, I'm going to have to turn this in late—again—and she might actually drop me this time, I can't even blame her. I sure would.

I close my eyes and rub at my temples. Trying to imagine the scene in my head. This is the second to last book in the series and I need to leave the ending on a cliffhanger, but every idea I have I hate, they all feel too cliche, too predictable.

When I finally open my eyes again, Isabella is standing right in front of me. I close my eyes and open them again, thinking I'm hallucinating, but sure enough, there she is with two coffee cups in her hands. My heart drops at the sight, and Myra's face flashes through my mind. I guess that explains why she left without saying goodbye.

"Sorry, I didn't mean to scare you," she says, as she bites down on her bottom lip.

"Oh, it's okay," I reply automatically.

She stares at me and just when I think she might say something. She doesn't and we're just awkwardly staring at each other, waiting for the other to say something.

"I should probably keep working," I finally say.

"Oh fuck, yeah, I'm sorry. I don't know why I came over here. You're busy."

I swallow, trying to steady my heartbeat. "Oh, it's fine. I'm almost done, anyway." I lie.

"Here. An I'm sorry for distracting you coffee," she says as she sets one of the coffee cups down in front of me.

My hero. Suddenly I don't care that she left without saying goodbye this morning. This coffee magically fixes everything. But then I think of Myra.

"Won't Myra care you gave me her coffee?"

Isabella knits her eyebrows together and laughs "What are you talking about?"

"Well, why else would you have two cups of coffee?"

"That wasn't for Myra. I just couldn't decide which coffee I wanted to try, so I got both," she says, narrowing her eyes.

And I'm sure my face does something ridiculous because she laughs. And my cheeks heat.

"We're not seeing each other anymore," Isabella mumbles. Her hand immediately rubbing the back of her neck.

"Oh, I'm sorry," I say, though I'm anything but. The sudden lightness in my chest makes that perfectly clear.

Isabella laughs.

"Don't be, it was just a fling. Anyways, I should head out."

"Oh, sure, thanks for the coffee, you saved me a very embarrassing seventh trip for a refill"

Isabella shakes her head. "You're a feen. I'll see you later," she says as she touches my arm lightly, her fingers brushing my skin before she quickly takes her hand away as if my skin burned her.

"See you," I mutter, feeling an ache in my bones at the absence of her touch.

She gives me one last smile, before walking away. And as the door closes behind her, I let out a breath I didn't know I was holding.

The room feels emptier without her, and the silence stretches on, too loud and too quiet all at once.

I try to refocus on writing, but my thoughts are tangled up in the memory of her, the scent of her cologne still faint in the air, obsessing over the exact spot where her finger brushed my arm, but most importantly the fact that she's not seeing Myra anymore. The thought makes me want to jump around.

I'm such an idiot for Isabella.

There's no way I'll be able to focus now so I head home practically skipping through the street.

Once inside, the world around me blurs into the background. I change into my comfiest pajamas and barely register the passing hours as I sink into the comfort of my couch, letting it swallow me whole obsessing over last night and how comfortable it felt to sleep next to Isabella. I sit with that feeling as I start writing again letting the fuzziness turn into inspiration. It takes a few hours but I finally write the perfect ending and as soon as I hit send on the email to my editor I cheer and run around the house jumping and screaming.

I haven't met my editor's deadlines in years, and it feels so freaking good! This whole move finally feels like the right choice.

Just as I start my fifth victory lap around the house my phone buzzes on the coffee table. I reach for it, and Isabella's name lights up the screen.

I do a double-take because that can't be right. Isabella never texts me.

> Isabella 9:20 p.m.: you up?

> Lily 9:21 p.m.: Did you seriously just 'you up' me? lol

Isabella 9:23 p.m.: what can I say? I like to keep it classic

Lily 9:24 p.m.: Haha, what's up?

Isabella 9:25 p.m.: i just wanted to apologize for not saying goodbye this morning. I've been thinking all day about how dickish that was of me. You took care of me and i didn't even say thank you.

Lily 9:25 p.m.: Oh, it's ok. I didn't give it much thought, I promise.

A lie of course. That's easily all I've thought about today, but she doesn't need to know that.

Isabella 9:26 p.m.: cool well, thanks anyway. it was nice of you to let me crash. I owe you one

Lily 9:26 p.m.: Can I collect tonight?

My heart races as my finger hits send.

I must be high on the excitement of having finished my manuscript and this overwhelming need I have to celebrate because I'm not usually so forward.

Nervousness takes hold of me as I watch the bubbles dip in and out of my screen. I've never been much of a nail-biter, but at this moment, I can't help it. My thumbnail finds its way to my mouth, and I bite down. Waiting for Isabella to reply.

Isabella 9:33 p.m.: what do you have in mind?

I sigh, sweet relief!

> Lily 9:33 p.m.: Movie? Or just hang out and talk? Your pick!

> Isabella 9:36 p.m.: already in PJs, so a movie sounds good

> Lily 9:37 p.m.: I'll be there in 10.

I quickly hop off the bed and head to my closet. Sure, I'm already in my comfy sweats, but if I'm going to see Isabella, I need to step up my pajama game. I pull out a sleek black silk pajama set I picked up from Target earlier in the week, and make a pit stop in the bathroom to check my face, making sure I look presentable. After a quick fix of my hair and a pinch of blush, I grab my keys and head out the door.

The drive feels longer than usual, and I wish I could teleport just to get there faster.

I really shouldn't be this giddy, but I can't help it.

When I finally pull up to her place, the warm glow of her porch light welcomes me. I hop out of the car, a nervous flutter in my stomach as I approach the door. I knock, and it swings open almost instantly, revealing Isabella with a playful smile on her face and I want to faint. She's in an oversized black sweatshirt and biker shorts. Her short hair is loosely tied back, a few strands framing her face, giving her a tousled, just-out-of-bed look that somehow makes her even more beautiful.

"Look at you," she teases, her eyes flicking up and down as she takes me in. "Those are some cute pajamas!"

I try not to blush under her gaze, but the way she says it makes it hard to keep my cool.

"Come in."

Her house looks exactly like I thought it would: very minimalistic, with art everywhere and not a plant in sight.

The sound of quick, excited paws on the hardwood floors grabs my attention. Before I can fully turn the corner, two dogs come barreling towards me. One is a black and white Border Collie with big, soulful eyes—he's the first to reach me, wagging his tail so hard that his whole body wobbles.

"Porter, calm down," Isabella laughs, but there's no stopping him as he eagerly sniffs at my hands.

Right on his heels is a sleek black Rottweiler. Her tail wagging just as hard, she quickly pushes Porter out of the way so she can get attention. She jumps up a little, excitedly sniffing my hands and licking my fingers as if we've been best friends forever.

"This is Shadow," Isabella says with a smile. Porter nuzzles his head into my leg, practically demanding to be petted.

"They don't know the meaning of personal space," Isabella teases as she rustles Porter's fur.

I laugh, crouching down to give both Porter and Shadow a good round of belly rubs and scratches. When I finally manage to peel myself away, I stand up and wipe my hands on my pajama pants with a smile. Isabella is watching, a smirk on her lips as she gestures for me to follow her.

"Come on, before they demand more of your attention," she jokes, stepping into the living room.

I follow her in, the living room is softly lit, with a few candles flickering on the coffee table, and I instantly relax. I sink into the plush couch, feeling the tension from the day melt away. Isabella plops down next to me, close enough that our shoulders are almost touching. Porter and Shadow trot in behind us, settling down by Isabella's feet but keeping an eye on me, just in case I'm up for more pets.

Isabella glances over at me, her eyes warm, and I can't help the flutter of excitement. Her eyes are different now. The iciness that's usually in them, melting.

"What do you want to watch?"

"I'm good with anything. What about you?"

She bites her lip, thinking, before grabbing the remote. "There's a scary movie I've been dying to watch. You down for that?"

"Sure! But you'll have to put up with me screaming."

Isabella laughs, the sound soft and easy, making me smile.

"It won't be the first time this week," she teases, scrolling through her endless list of streaming services. My cheeks heat up, and I look away, pretending to adjust the pillow behind me as my heart does a little flip.

Finally, she finds the movie she's been looking for and queues it. "Want some popcorn?"

I nod eagerly. "Yes, please."

She stands up, and heads toward the kitchen. Porter and Shadow lift their heads, watching her go before laying back down.

I shift around the couch, rearranging my limbs, trying to find a comfortable position. When I finally do, I reach for one of the throw blankets laid on the arm of the couch, and as I pull it over my lap, the smell of her cologne hits me. It lingers in the fabric, warm and familiar, and I have this ridiculous urge to bury my face in it and just breathe it in. I don't, of course, because if she sees me, she'll think I'm a freak. But I do bring it up to my neck and lay it around me so her smell is near me. Which I think is a perfectly acceptable middle ground.

After a few minutes, Isabella returns with a big bowl of freshly popped popcorn, the buttery smell filling the room. She hands it to me and then settles back into the couch, close enough that one of my crossed legs ends up slightly on top of her. I freeze at the proximity of her body next to mine. My attention immediately consumed by the tingle on my knee, right where her thigh is.

"Okay," she says with a triumphant smile, "Ready?"

I gulp, trying to ignore the heat growing between my thighs. All I can do is nod.

She presses play and the movie flickers to life on the screen. I try to focus, but the warmth of her thigh brushing against my knee keeps pulling my attention away.

Every time something jumps on screen, I flinch, and she nudges me, smirking as if she's waiting for me to lose it entirely.

A brutal jumpscare catches me off guard and I reach for her, curling into the side of her neck as I clutch her arm. I feel her tense up, but then she laughs, a soft, melodic sound that makes my pulse race even more and I can't help but laugh, too.

The smell of her cologne hits me again. It's stronger now mixed with the smell of her skin and it's intoxicating. I want to rub my face against her neck and bathe in it.

The movie plays on but I don't let go. Enjoying a little too much being so close to her.

By the time the credits roll, I realize I've barely paid attention to the movie. Instead, I've been wrapped up in her. I look over at Isabella, and she catches my eye, holding my gaze. It feels as if the world around us has faded, and all that I can focus on is the space between us.

And I can't wish any harder that the space would just disappear—that I could close this gap between us, and feel the heat of her fully, without any of the hesitation that's holding me back.

14

ISABELLA

Lily's had a death grip on my arm all night, and as much as I enjoy her hands on me, she's squeezing so hard I think I'll have a bruise tomorrow. But oddly, I don't mind. There's something about the way she holds on to me, something that makes me feel needed, and it's hard not to let that drive me wild.

I've always had this dom/femme energy going for me, and I love the feeling of being in control, of being the protector. But right now, being her protector is probably my favorite role yet. Which is kind of weird, considering this whole identity of mine was meant to protect me from her. But the way she's looking at me right now makes it hard for me to think about anything else but how her lips would feel on mine.

This whole damsel in distress thing is doing it for me, and I want so fucking desperately to kiss her, but I know I shouldn't—or maybe I should just go for it. You know how they say sometimes you have to just get things out of your system? Holding back only makes it more intense. But even as I try to rationalize that thought, it sounds ridiculous.

Lily finally lets go of my arm and lets out a long, shaky breath. "Never again," she declares, looking at everything in the room but me. "Next time, we're watching a rom-com."

"Next time?" I say, raising my eyebrows high into my forehead. I kind of like the sound of that. Or, I would if it were someone else.

Lily rolls her eyes, but I can see the hint of a smile on her lips.

"Anyway, what now?" she asks, and the question throws me off. I was sure she'd want to go home. And for the first time all night, a nervous energy creeps in. Lily is in my house... We haven't hung out like this since we were dating, and it should feel wrong and weird and awkward, but it doesn't and I kind of hate that. I hate that things feel so natural with her. I hate that I can't hold on to my anger when she's around.

"Mmm... I'm not sure," I say as I look around my living room. "We can do a puzzle or we can just talk."

"Let's talk. We have about ten years of catching up to do," Lily says as she turns to face me.

"Do we, though? 'Cause I'm sure the girls kept you just as up-to-date on my life as they did me with yours."

Lily laughs, "Yeah, I guess that's true. My updates even came with pictures sometimes," she jokes.

"God, I hate them. I'm sure if I had let them, yours would have too."

We both laugh.

The girls are too nosy, but I don't know what I'd do without them.

Lily looks around the room and I follow her eyes.

"Isabella?"

"Yeah?"

"Do you think we could ever go back to being friends? Like we used to be?"

I think the question over and over, could we? I don't know. There's too much baggage attached to our friendship now, but we were friends longer than we were anything else so it's not impossible. But that's a whole lot of hurt we'd both have to get over and I'm not sure if we ever could.

"I don't know Lily, but I'm trying," I say honestly.

"I know, but is it because you want to or because you're being forced by the girls?"

"A little of both, I guess."

She lets out a small laugh.

"I really hate that I left the way I did," she says.

And the air gets sucked out of my lungs. I never thought I'd hear that. It doesn't fix anything, but it does mend something deep in my soul. Something that makes breathing a little easier.

I give her a tight-lipped smile and nod. Lily doesn't say anything else. Both us us just sit in silence for a few minutes, the easy air is now a little heavier and I kind of want her to go home before this gets any more tense, but I can't exactly kick her out.

"I should probably head home." She finally says and I nod. *Bless.*

We both stand without another word and walk out the door.

"Thanks for tonight," Lily says standing at the threshold of my front door.

"Of course."

She steps closer and leans in to hug me and to my surprise I let her. I wrap my arms around her and a flood of warmth washes over me. I hold her even tighter afraid that if I let go this feeling will disappear, Lily holds me tighter and the warmth of her body against mine sends a jolt of electricity through me.

When I ease my grip on her she looks up at me and whispers "I missed you."

Her eyes start to shimmer and I hate the sadness in them. Because no matter how things ended with Lily. She was my best friend too and I missed her. Even when I hated her I missed her.

"Did you mean it when you said we had been a mistake?" Lily asks, and everything in me drains. I want to lie and tell her I did, but I can't.

I pinch her chin between my index finger and thumb. "No," I whisper as I lean in and kiss her. It's almost instinctive. I couldn't have stopped myself if I tried.

Lily freezes, and I know I just made a big mistake, but when she kisses me back, I don't care. Her lips are warm and familiar, and it feels so fucking good to kiss her. It's not hurried or desperate—it's something softer, safer. The world outside Lily and me disappears, leaving behind this intense, magnetic kiss that ignites a fire within me, and I hate that it makes my heart feel full and my brain feel fuzzy. As I pull away, the air crackles and I can hardly breathe. The pressure of her lips lingers on mine like a sweet, intoxicating memory.

"I'm sorry," I say almost immediately.

"Don't," Lily says her thumb caressing my cheek. "Let that be the goodbye we should have had."

I nod, but my heart tightens, and pressure starts to build behind my eyes. I bite hard on my bottom lip, trying to distract my brain from the ache in my chest, but it's not working.

"Goodnight."

"Goodnight, Lily," I manage to choke out before she turns to walk toward her car.

When I make it back to my house. The quiet is almost too loud. I move past the living room, my feet carrying me automatically toward my bedroom. I try to push thoughts of our kiss from my mind, but they linger like the scent of her perfume on my chest. *God, even my thoughts sound mushy and gross.*

Every step I take feels heavier, weighed down by a truth I don't want to admit—I never let her go.

Nights like tonight make me want to give in, to let every moment stretch out forever, even when I know they can't, not after everything that has happened.

I try to tell myself that she won't disappear this time. She just moved back, and we're talking again. But that doesn't stop the fear from creeping in—the thought that she could decide, *again,* that she wants nothing to do with me is enough to never let me want to try. I don't think I could go through that again. Not with the way things have been lately, not when it feels like the parts of me she broke are only just beginning to heal with her around.

I want to keep her close, but I also know the danger of holding on too tight. One wrong move and it could all unravel. And then what?

It's not worth it.

I stand at the edge of my bed, staring at the rumpled sheets, unable to move. My mind won't stop spinning, replaying the night over and over. I sit on the edge of the mattress, dragging my hands through my hair, trying to shake off the emotions that cling to me like shadows.

My plan was solid. Keep her close, but not too close. It's supposed to be about control. But I'm losing that control fast because being with her feels right. And that's scary and a little unhinged, Lily is the worst thing that ever happened to me. Wanting her is like standing on the edge of a cliff, and every second I spend with her I'm one step closer to falling into something that will ruin me.

I pull the covers over me as if that will smother the thoughts, but they come flooding back.

Maybe this time will be different. Maybe she won't leave again. Even as I tell myself that I know better. But, there's a part of me that doesn't care. A reckless part that just wants to be with her, even if it means risking everything.

What am I even doing? If I were smart, I'd cut things off now before it goes too far. Before I find myself standing in the ruins of my own heart again, wondering how I got there. But I'm not smart. Not when it comes to Lily.

15

LILY

I stare at the eggs and bacon on my plate, pushing the eggs around with a fork. I couldn't sleep last night. I lay in bed for hours, tossing and turning. Now, here I am, sitting in my mom's kitchen, poking at my breakfast, barely able to keep my eyes open.

"Are you ok, honey?" Mom asks, concerned, as she watches me push around my food.

I nod. "Yeah, just a little tired."

She narrows her eyes at me but doesn't push it.

I adore my mom but I don't exactly want to talk to her about what happened last night or about everything that kissing Isabella made me feel or how that kiss has—despite everything—given me a small surge of something that could maybe be hope. But hope for what? For a chance? For something I'm not sure I should want?

It was a goodbye kiss, a goodbye to our past, not a hello to our future. God, why can't I ever get my emotions to cooperate?

My mind feels saturated. Ten years' worth of anger and

hurt and yearning, all wanting to be processed at the same time.

Since she came back into my life, every little thing she does sparks old feelings and brings them crawling back to life, but that kiss really broke the last shred of control I had, and now I feel lost and confused, and I want more. More nights like last night. More kisses from her, even if she never wants anything else, and I'm terrified. Because I've been here before. I've felt this pull, and I've watched it turn into something that ended up breaking me. And I'm scared. I'm scared of getting too close, of letting her in, and then losing her again.

I glance over at my phone and grab it, silently debating whether to text Isabella so she can clear things up, and I can let go of the idea that our kiss meant more than it did.

My fingers hover over the screen, but I hesitate. I don't know what to say, because what if it meant nothing and she realizes I thought it did and I ruin my chance at a friendship because I can't let her go? Why does this have to be so complicated?

"Do it," Mom says, her eyes fixed on my phone. Isabella's name flashing on the screen.

"But you don't even know what's going on."

"I don't need to. If your gut is telling you to text her, trust your instincts."

I close my eyes and try to make sense of what my gut's telling me. But honestly, all I can think about is our kiss, how amazing and sweet and perfect it felt, and how I probably messed up any chance I had at doing it again by telling Isabella that kiss meant goodbye.

She doesn't need to clear anything up for me... I made the decision last night.

16

ISABELLA

From the moment I woke up today, there's been this restless energy buzzing under my skin, and an unwelcome carousel of Lily has taken permanent residence in my brain.

I wander through my house trying to ignore it by pulling out every art supply I own, trying every medium I can think of on canvas, I even try painting with condiments —Don't judge me, I saw someone do it on TikTok. But when none of it works, I wander into my office and walk over to my easel, my eyes scanning the half-finished paintings I've been working on.

Maybe something more detailed will take up enough space in my brain, so I can't think about anything else. I grab a brush and try to lose myself in my work. With each brushstroke, I feel a sense of calm, a quiet focus that lets me forget about everything except the canvas in front of me. For hours, the rhythm of my strokes grounds me, and everything else fades away—the Lily carousel finally stops, along with the restlessness in my chest. And for the first time today, I feel like I can breathe.

But the peace doesn't last very long.

It's Thursday today, and the girls and I are supposed to go on our night swim. And this whole thing with Lily is so fucking confusing I don't even know if I should go. I need to stay away from her until I can figure out how to get a hold of my fucking feelings. I hate that this is happening with her, of all people. I hate that one kiss has got me feeling this fucking confused. I hate feeling like an idiot. This girl wrecked me. Why can't I seem to remember that when she's around?

No matter how much I paint, I can't fully escape my thoughts. No matter what I do, there's one person in my head, and being at home is starting to feel suffocating. I need to get out of here.

I grab Porter's and Shadow's harnesses, and the moment they hear the jingle, they come running. Their excited barks ring in my ears.

We pile into the car and head to the dog park.

The second I open the liftgate, Porter and Shadow run off, tails wagging like little flags in the wind as they race toward their favorite spot.

I sit on a bench at the end of the dog park, making sure I have a full view of my babies, and smile as I watch Porter and Shadow run around, chasing each other in circles. The sun is shining, and the air is filled with the sounds of dogs barking and their owners chatting. The fresh air is like a balm on my frazzled nerves, and my brain feels a little lighter.

I lean back on the bench and pull out my pocket-sized

sketchbook. I always bring it to the dog park—it's the perfect place to sketch while I people-watch.

There's an old man sitting in front of me, slowly dozing off... he's perfect, but right as I press pen to paper, something catches my attention out of the corner of my eye. I turn towards it and see Lily walking by, her black cat on a leash.

Fucking hell. I can't escape her today, no matter what I do.

But seeing her with her black cat on a walk is so cute it brings a smile to my face, and it's hard to be mad at that.

Lily starts to cross the street, her laughter echoing faintly as she calls to her cat, who has gotten distracted by a fluttering butterfly. As she disappears from view, I turn my focus back to Porter and Shadow, who are happily chasing after a falling leaf.

I try to push Lily aside, but I can't help the need I have to talk to her, so I ignore the tiny voice in my head telling me not to and pull out my phone and text her. Because apparently, I'm a masochist.

> Isabella 12:30 p.m.: you look cute today

I hit send before the voice from before gets louder, feeling a rush of nervousness. I haven't felt nervous about texting someone in ages. My heart races as I watch the bubbles appear on my screen. I look at the spot where I last saw her, half hoping she might come back my way.

A few seconds pass, and my phone vibrates in my hand.

> Lily 12:31 p.m.: Did you mean to send that to me?

Isabella 12:31 p.m.: yes I just saw you walk past the dog park with your cat

Lily 12:35 p.m.: Oh no, I didn't see you!

Isabella 12:36 p.m.: i'm on the bench at the end of the park. Kinda hard to see from up the hill

Lily 12:37 p.m.: I'll be right there!

Isabella 12:37 p.m.: i'll meet you at the top of the hill

I turn to look for my dogs, and they're both running around chasing after another a gray Pitbull. I get up and make my way towards the top of the hill, and that's when I see her. She looks even better up close. She's wearing a long black dress with a black jean jacket. Her Dr. Marten boots make her look almost as tall as me.

"Hey," Lily calls out and my heart thumps a little faster.

"Hey yourself," I say, hoping I didn't leave the house looking a mess, but then again, why should I care, it's just Lily.

"Did you see her chasing after the butterflies earlier?" Lily asks almost breathless.

"Yeah, I saw. It was pretty cute," I say, as I crouch.

I stick my index finger through the fence and try to give her cat some pets. But she's too far.

Porter and Shadow come barreling toward me, tails wagging and tongues lolling. I brace myself for the chaos that's about to go down, but nothing happens. They see the cat and almost immediately start sniffing through the fence. She even gets closer and rubs the side of her mouth against the fence where the dog's noses are.

"Wow, Pickles doesn't usually like dogs," Lily says surprised.

"Yeah, they don't usually like cats either," I say, looking at them. Pickles is on her back, belly up, and both Porter and Shadow are whining, trying to get closer. They met Myra's cat once, and they absolutely hated it, so this is a nice surprise.

"Are you ready for tonight?" Lily asks.

"Yeah, I found my bathing suits this morning, so I'm good to go."

"Nice! I'm excited to see it."

I look up at her and raise an eyebrow. I don't know if this is a Freudian slip or if she's trying to flirt with me, but the butterflies in my stomach decide it's the latter.

Lily's eyes widen. "What I meant was that I can't wait to see you later... Not in the bathing suit, just you."

I stand and cross my arms in front of my chest, tilting my head. I don't say a thing, I just stare at her and smile.

"What I mean is I'm sure you'll look great in the bathing suit, but it's not *why* I'm excited"

I nod, and a big ol' smirk spreads across my face. Lily wipes her forehead, blows out a raspberry, and giggles. I think watching her squirm is my new favorite thing.

"I'm just excited to hang out with you later." She says, her voice breaking. "And with the girls, obviously," Lily adds before dropping her head.

Her cheeks are crimson red, and she's got the cutest smile on her lips.

"Yes, of course, the girls." I tease.

I bite my bottom lip, trying to hold back a laugh, but I can't. This is insanely cute—Lily is flustered by the thought of me in a bathing suit, and it's giving me all kinds of ideas.

The bathing suit I found this morning is simply not going to cut it. I need to go shopping.

I watch her play with her cat's leash, twirling it around her fingers. For God knows how long. Letting myself enjoy the fact that maybe I still make Lily nervous.

"I should get going," she finally says. "I promised my mom I'd have lunch with her downtown, and I still have to take Pickles home. I'll see you later, though."

I nod, doing my fucking best to try and hide my disappointment. We both say bye, and she turns around, wrestling her cat away from my dogs.

I shouldn't feel sad about her leaving for one because I will see her in like six hours but also because Lily shouldn't be missable. At least not to me.

A loud bark pulls me from my thoughts, and I turn to find Shadow barking at another dog who keeps trying to play aggressively with Porter so I decide it's time to take them home. Last time this happened, Porter got bit in the forehead and spent about a month milking it for attention.

I call for them and wrestle them back to the car, head home, drop them off, and beeline to this cute boutique downtown.

As I browse through their summer collection, something catches my eye: a black two-piece with an intricate lace top I grab it and make my way to the fitting room.

I slip out of my clothes and into the swimsuit, feeling the fabric hug my curves. It's a perfect fit, and I love the way it makes my boobs look, I can already picture Lily's face when she sees it tonight. But as I think that, I realize I'm so fucking stupid. Why am I doing this for her? What am I hoping to get out of this? This is dumb. I'm dumb.

I slip back into my clothes and step out of the fitting room.

"Would you like to try another size or is this fine?" A sales associate asks.

"I'm not taking it, thanks," I say as I hand her the bathing suit.

Next time the butterflies in my stomach flutter, I'm chugging down whatever is near me and drowning them, they make me do dumb shit.

———— ♥ ♥ ♥ ————

The day passes by in a blur of chores and supply orders for the gallery. When I glance back at the clock, it's 5:30 p.m., and I need to start getting ready. I promised to pick everyone up, and if I'm not out of the house in 15 minutes, Clara will kill me for being late.

I close up my laptop and head into my room to change into a random bathing suit and throw on a hoodie and some sweats. I grab a couple of beach towels from my closet and head to my car.

Just as I'm pulling onto Clara and Alejandra's street, my phone pings in the cup holder, I quickly tap the voice command to read it out loud.

Clara 5:42 p.m.: You better not be late.

I roll my eyes. She's so fucking impatient.

Isabella 5:43 p.m.: relax i'm a minute away

I pull up to Clara and Alejandra's driveway, and they're already waiting outside, leaning against their front door with giant bags at their feet. Clara spots my car, and they make their way toward it. Clara slips into the passenger seat while Alejandra climbs into the backseat.

"Took you long enough," Clara says as she fastens her seatbelt.

I roll my eyes. "You're impossible."

Clara shrugs and laughs.

"Thanks for picking us up," Alejandra says, hitting Clara on the shoulder.

Next stop: Lily's.

I pull up Lily's driveway, shoot her a quick text, and a few minutes later, the front door swings open. Lily walks out barefoot, carrying an obnoxiously oversized beach towel in one hand and her shoes in the other.

"You okay? Alejandra asks. After Lily lets out a long sigh.

"Yeah, I just woke up. My alarm didn't go off. So Isabella's text woke me up."

I look at her through the rearview mirror, and now that I can see her clearer, her eyes are still full of sleep, and there's a faint line imprinted on her cheek, probably from the pillowcase. It's unfair how pretty she looks, frazzled hair and all. Lily catches my eye and I quickly look away. Good thing I'm wearing sunglasses. She'll never know.

With three down, it's time to grab Valeria.

I pull up to her house, and she's already waiting for us on the porch. The second she spots us, she runs to the car.

"Hey," we all say as she slips into the seat next to Alejandra. With everyone in the car, I turn the wheel toward the coast.

The cove is just five minutes away, so we get there quickly. After parking the car, we walk for a few minutes until we find a spot we like. We spread our blankets and towels on the sand and wait for the sun to dip below the horizon, which, by the look of it, won't be for another hour.

"Anyone up for a game?" Alejandra asks as she pulls out a box of UNO cards. I hate how much she loves this game... We play it every single time we hang out.

"I'm in!" Valeria exclaims.

The rest of us groan but sit in a circle, anyway.

Luckily, Valeria brought a portable bonfire, so we huddle around it while Alejandra shuffles the cards and deals them out. We play for about an hour but miss the sunset. In true PNW fashion, the sky gets covered in a dark gray cloud.

"Absolutely not," Alejandra screams as Clara throws a draw four on my draw four.

"What, why not?" Clara shouts.

I tune them out. They have this very same fight every single time we play. I think Clara does it on purpose.

"How was the rest of your day?" Lily asks as we wait for Clara and Alejandra to finish arguing over the right way to use a draw-four card.

"Fine, didn't do much," I say as I lean back on my elbows and throw my cards to the side. This argument is going to go on for a while.

"Well, that's good, I'm sure you've been swamped trying to get the show ready"

"Yeah, everyone's hyped about the show, so people keep popping in, hoping to get a sneak peek at the new collection."

Pride starts bubbling in my chest as I speak because my art is finally getting the recognition it deserves. It's taken years of pouring my soul onto canvases to get here. Years of rejection and self-doubt. But in the last couple of years, everything's changed. I somehow got my paintings in a big gallery, and suddenly, people started whispering my name. That whisper turned into a buzz, and eventually, it was loud enough for me to open my own gallery.

Lily smiles. "That's amazing," she says, her voice softer now. "I remember when you used to sketch on the corner of every piece of paper you got your hands on, and now look at you. You're—" she pauses, and her voice gets lower. "You're really doing it. I know this might not mean much, but I'm so proud of you."

But she's wrong. It means everything. I've always been so fucking proud of myself. But something about hearing Lily say it, feels different. It's like her words mend something inside me I never knew was broken. My whole body feels warmer and lighter and a piece of me just clicks into place.

Lily tucks a strand of hair behind her ear, her gaze dropping to the crackling flames of the bonfire. "You deserve it, you know. All of it."

My heart does a little twirl, and I smile. The happiness bubbling up inside me feels like it's about to burst out, so I focus on something small—picking out single grains of sand and counting them until I can ground myself.

"Thanks," is all I manage to say. It's the only thing that comes to mind, the only thing my brain can process while I'm trying not to throw myself into Lily's arms. But as soon as I say it, I wish it was more, that I'd said something... I don't know, meaningful. But before I can add more, Clara yells out something ridiculous about being able to stack draw fours on draw twos. And the moment is gone. Lily looks over and laughs.

Valeria finally steps in, and once Alejandra and Clara agree on the rules, we play a few more rounds until the sky has gone completely dark.

"I think it's time!" Alejandra sings.

"What if... hear me out," Clara says with a big ol' grin.

We all stare at her, waiting to hear what she's going to say, but she drags the silence on so long I think she froze.

"Say something!" Alejandra screams.

"I knew you'd break first" Clara laughs.

Alejandra rolls her eyes.

"Well?" I finally say, getting a little annoyed.

"How about we go skinny dipping?" Clara says.

"Are you serious?" Alejandra yells, and I can't tell if she's excited or if she thinks Clara has lost it. I however think Clara has lost it.

"Absolutely!" Clara says eagerly.

"I'm in if you all are," Alejandra says, looking around. "But you're on your own if the water's freezing!" she adds.

Valeria sighs. "You guys go ahead, I don't think I could explain that one to Brooke."

Lily turns to me. "I'm kind of down. What do you think?"

I think Clara is insane. I think the water is probably freezing, and I think hypothermia doesn't sound like fun. But none of that makes it out of my mouth. What does come out is a nervous laugh followed by "Fuck it."

Common sense has left the building...

And with that, laughter erupts as we scramble to strip down, clothes flying off and landing haphazardly all across the sand. Clara and I run in and submerge ourselves entirely, knowing if we do it slowly, we'll just back out. Alejandra lowers herself in inch by inch, and Lily is still lingering by the shore, fighting with her skinny jeans. Watching her hop around, trying to free her foot, is insanely cute.

"Need some help?" Clara calls out laughing.

"I've got it!" Lily laughs.

"That's exactly why I don't wear skinny jeans anymore," Alejandra jokes.

When I turn back to check on Lily, she's freed her foot and has taken the rest of her clothes off. My heart stops, and my mouth goes dry. I look away, but my mind has already xeroxed the curve of her body, the way the moonlight draped over her like some kind of spotlight from the Universe pressing every inch of her to memory and tucking it away for safekeeping.

I hear her run toward the water, squealing as the cold hits her skin.

"It's freezing!" she laughs.

The second I turn towards her, I can't look away. There's something magnetic about her, and the closer she gets, the faster my heart beats.

"Let's go in deeper," I hear Alejandra say when Lily finally makes her way to us.

Lily nods and without a second thought, I follow her.

Swimming next to Lily heightens all my senses, and a glimpse at her hardened nipple sends a surge of desire running through my body in a way I haven't felt in years. Not since I was with her. My palms tingle, and my fingertips feel like they're on fire, aching with the crazy need to feel her skin against mine.

I am so fucked, this was a terrible idea.

My hand accidentally brushes against Lily's, and what I felt earlier pales in comparison to the jolt that I feel now. And I wonder if Lily feels it, too, because our eyes lock, and the world outside the water dematerializes—who knew I had such a flare for the dramatic? I feel breathless and overwhelmed by the intensity of it all.

Lily's chest starts rising and falling a little faster as I

reach for her hand. She intertwines her fingers in mine, and I want to pull her close to press her body against mine, but I can't, not with the girls around. To be fair, I shouldn't, period, but I can't be convinced of reasoning right now because Lily is naked and staring at me with intense lust in her eyes and I feel like I'm going to explode.

I pull her closer, and thunder crashes nearby. The first droplets of rain start to fall, splattering against the surface of the lake. I don't have a single second to process it all before chaos erupts. We all swim to shore, limbs flailing in a frantic scramble to grab our belongings before the rain snuffs out our fire and plunges us into darkness.

"Quick! Grab everything!" someone shouts, and we move like a whirlwind, hurriedly dressing and packing.

Once we have everything, we sprint toward the shelter of my car, laughter echoing through the rain-soaked air.

"Whose idea was it to come today?" Clara yells through her laughter, her voice rising above the downpour.

"I think it was mine," Valeria yells out.

I fumble with my car keys, my hands slick from the rain, while the others huddle close, shivering and giggling. The sound of the rain pounding on the metal roof as another loud crash of thunder rings nearby.

Finally, I unlock the car and we tumble inside, dripping wet.

"What a night!" I say, catching Lily's eye.

Her smile is big, and that spark comes roaring back in. I worry it's my new favorite thing because I only want more.

"Next time, we'll check the forecast!" Valeria jokes, wiping her hair out of her face.

"Deal," I say as I turn the key in the ignition.

"We barely swam! Does that still count as the night-time swim, or do we need to do it again?" Alejandra whines.

"I think it counts," Lily says. "I'll cross it off once I'm home."

"Ok good, I don't think I'd be able to do it again. The water was too cold."

We all nod in agreement.

"Alright, let's get you all home," I say once my fingers warm up a bit.

Clara is still laughing, her hair a tangled mess as pink dye streaks down her face. Alejandra complains about rainwater sloshing around in her clothes. But I don't feel a thing aside from the tingle at my fingertips from holding Lily's hand.

I drop Alejandra and Clara off first, then Valeria. It's not the most practical way to drop everyone off, but I want some more time with Lily.

But it's not enough because before I know it, I'm pulling into the front of her house.

Her hand hovers over the seatbelt release button lost in thought. She turns to me, and before she can say anything, I kiss her.

The second my lips touch hers, I decide this is the best idea I've ever had. Her breath mixed with mine is intoxicating, and with every second of this kiss, I think about taking her back to my place.

Lily's hands find their way into my shirt and she digs her nails into my back, driving me even wilder. I want to undress her and taste her and fuck her in the car.

"Should we be doing this?" Lily asks as she kisses me.

"No, probably not," I say as I pull her closer to me. And we shouldn't, but I don't care. Not right now.

I push my seat back, and I pull her towards me. And I love that she knows what to do without direction. Lily climbs over the center console and straddles my hips. I unbutton her jeans, but we both freeze when we hear a door slam. Lily jumps off of me and into the passenger seat, buttoning up her jeans, But when we look around, we don't see anyone.

We both laugh, but my heart is beating a thousand beats per minute, and I can't seem to catch my breath.

"Come inside," she whispers, her voice a bit unsteady.

I stare at her, trying to figure out if this is a good idea, but my brain is offline right now, and my body is screaming at me to follow her in, I close my eyes, not knowing what to do, but what's the worst thing that'll happen if I do?

—————— ♥ ♥ ♥ ——————

We kiss from her front door to her bathroom, undressing each other feverishly as we step into the shower, letting the cold water pour over us, not waiting for it to warm up. Our lips never leaving the others.

I turn Lily around and press her ass against me. *Fuck.* Her body pressed against mine feels so good I nearly cum at the contact. I wrap my hand in her hair and bend her forward, tracing her spine with my other hand watching the water glide off her body until my fingers find their way down her pubic hair and reach her clit. Lily sucks in a breath and I smile. I rub slow circles against her and she moans. I feel a little smug knowing I'm the one making that happen. That after ten years I still know how to get that noise out of her and it only makes me press harder. Lily's arms shoot forward, trying to hold herself up. Her breaths get ragged, and her moans get louder, making my clit swell at the sound. I need to taste her, now.

"Let's go to your bed," I say, and Lily nods.

She turns the water off and guides us to her room. She hands me a towel and we both quickly dry off.

I lay in bed before her, and for the first time since tonight, I take a moment to drink her in. I trace the curve of her breast and memorize the softness of her belly as she climbs in after me. Her lips swollen and red from kissing.

She tries to lay next to me but I shake my head.

"Sit on my face," I say as I lay on my back.

Lily climbs on top of me without protest and I've always loved that she's such a good listener.

She moves her way up my body until her legs are straddling my face.

"You have the prettiest pussy I've ever seen," I say before flicking my tongue against her clit.

Lily sucks in a breath and I smile.

I lock eyes with her as I run my tongue down her slit. And I moan, fuck she tastes so fucking good. I could spend an eternity between her thighs and never need another thing.

I stick my tongue in her craving more of her on my tongue and Lily moans as she buries her hand in my hair.

"Isabella," she moans and my name sounds so sweet on her lips I never want to stop hearing it.

I suck on her clit and her hips start to ride my face, Lily's eyes roll back and she lets her head fall. Pushing herself into my mouth harder.

"Look at me," I say, wanting to see the moment she cums.

Lily does, and I suck harder. Her fingers tread into my hair, making the tension in my clit build as she pushes into me until she...

"Isabella? You there?" Lily asks, snapping me out of my day dream.

I blink against the dark and take in my surroundings. We're still in my car. Fuck, it all felt so real.

"Huh?"

"Where'd you go?" Lily asks sweetly.

"I should head home," I say, ignoring her question.

"Are you coming inside?"

"No, I don't think that's a good idea."

"Oh, ok," Lily says looking down at her hands. "Thanks for the ride," she whispers, her voice a bit unsteady, before stepping out of the car and leaving me sitting there, breathless.

I watch her walk up to her door, pausing under the porch light to look back at me before she slips inside.

I sit in my car for a while, trying to regain control of my thoughts as I try to block out everything I just pictured us doing because it can't happen. That's a line I absolutely can't cross.

Once I'm home, I stare out the window, watching the rain streak down the glass as if it could wash away my confusion. The past couple of days have brought me so much closer to Lily, and with each passing day, the barriers I very purposefully erected around my heart weaken.

It isn't that I don't want to let her in. I do—probably more than I'd admit out loud. But that's the problem.

All night I'm in this tug-of-war—torn between wanting to dive deeper into whatever this is with Lily and the nagging instinct to keep her at arm's length. I told myself I'd never do this again, but here I am.

Our weekend getaway is just a couple of days away, and the thought of being stuck in a cabin for three days with Lily has me spiraling. Three days. In a tiny cabin. With the girl who makes me question every emotional defense mechanism I've perfected.

What could go wrong?

17

LILY

I've been sitting in my office for hours, staring at the blank page on my screen, the blinking cursor mocking me. I should be writing my query letter, but it's impossible to focus on anything else but the throbbing between my thighs. Isolating myself in my office seemed like a good idea this morning. I thought it would help keep my mind off Isabella. Instead, I've been sitting here doing the exact opposite.

Last night, playing on a loop. I can still feel Isabella's lips on mine, her body pressed tightly against me, along with the desperate need I had for her to come inside and lose ourselves in each other.

When she drove off, every part of me ached, and I spent the rest of the night beating myself up for asking her to come inside. Of course, she wasn't going to. The kiss was a fluke, just a wild, crazy moment.

Frustrated, I close my laptop and let out a long sigh. There's no way I'll be able to concentrate right now, so I'm calling it. I grab the dark academia book I've been reading from my desk and head towards my newly finished reading nook. Hoping some reading will distract me.

Mom helped me finish building all my shelves this morning, and I absolutely love how cute it turned out. I bought a teal armchair and ottoman and placed them near the largest window in the living room, added a small side table, and hung a beautiful vintage lamp just above it. Then, I unpacked every book I own and filled the shelves to the brim, organizing them by color—because that's the only right way to do it.

Just as I get comfortable, Pickles leaps up beside me, curling into a warm ball of fur purring softly in my lap. I reach over and scratch her head. Just as I open my book, my phone buzzes. It's Clara. She is either about to make a suggestion that pulls me out of my cozy reading bubble, or she's sharing a meme. I swipe to unlock the screen and read her message.

> Clara 3:00 p.m.: Hey! What are you up to tonight? The girls are coming over today for our Tuesday night game night. Wanna come? It's pretty low-key. Just some board games and dinner.

My first instinct is to say no. My introverted side craves quiet and comfort and I really want to stay put, eat cookies, and snuggle into the couch with my book. But then, a tiny voice—that sounds a lot like Isabella's—tells me to go, that I can read and be anti-social another day.

> Lily 3:01 p.m.: What time?

> Clara 3:01 p.m.: Around 7.

It's only 3:00 p.m. I still have some time to relax and read before heading over. Best of both worlds.

Lily 3:03 p.m.: Okay! I'll see you then.

I set an alarm for 6:30 p.m., giving myself a solid three and a half hours of reading before I need to get up and get ready.

I snuggle deeper into the couch, pull a weighted blanket over me, and get lost in my book.

My phone's alarm suddenly jolts me from my book.

"No!" I yell, frustrated.

Not when I was getting to the juicy stuff... I hit the book against my forehead a few times, trying to think of a solid excuse as to why I can no longer make it to Clara and Alejandras, but my mind draws blanks.

Knowing them, they'd probably just move the party here—and then I'd be stuck cleaning up. That thought alone is enough to make me set my book down and shuffle toward my closet. I throw on some jeans and reach for the shirt Isabella gave me and throw it on, the soft fabric feeling like a warm hug against my skin. I look in the mirror, and I can't help but smile, it fits just like the other one did but this one smells faintly of Isabella making it my new favorite shirt.

I head back into the kitchen, and I pack up most of the cookies my mom dropped off yesterday. With the cookies securely packed. I grab my jacket and head out the door.

When I pull up to Alejandra and Clara's house, I take a deep breath, feeling nervousness build as I hop out of my car. I haven't joined the girls for a game night in years. I knock on the door, and it swings open almost immediately. Clara stands there with a big grin, her pink hair pulled up in a messy bun.

"Perfect timing!" she exclaims, stepping aside to let me in.

The sound of laughter and chatter drifts from the living room, and I can see Valeria and Alejandra sitting on the couch, a game spread out in front of them.

"Hey, you made it!" Alejandra says, looking up and waving enthusiastically. Her long hair is in French braids that swing as she moves. "We thought you might bail on us!"

"I was reading, so I almost did!" I joke.

"Mean," Valeria teases.

"But I come bearing treats!" I say as I hold up the cookie container triumphantly.

"Yes!" Alejandra says. "You know that's the real reason we invited you!"

I laugh and step further inside. Clara leads me to the kitchen, where she sets out a plate for the cookies.

"Do you want some wine?" Clara asks

"Yeah, that sounds great," I reply.

As she pours the wine, I glance around the kitchen and realize Isabella is missing. And a pang of sadness hits. I really wanted her to see me in this shirt.

"Is Isabella coming?" I ask, trying to mask my disappointment.

"Yeah, she is," Clara says. "She had a couple of interviews today about the exhibit. She should be here soon, though."

Relief washes over me, but it also makes me a little nervous because I can't let myself get sad over not seeing her. But friends can miss each other, so I tell myself it's friendly because it is! What else would it be?

Once the cookies are on the table, we all gather in the living room. Clara plops down next to Alejandra while

Valeria grabs a cookie and dives into the game instructions.

"We're playing a murder mystery, and each of us has a role—one of us will be the murderer. All the clues we need are in these envelopes. We have to figure out who the murderer is by piecing everything together. When we think we've cracked a clue, we can open the next set of envelopes to move forward. Does that make sense?"

"I think so," I say, grabbing a cookie. Just then, the door swings open, and Clara looks around with a smile. "That must be Isabella!"

Without thinking, I shove the cookie in my mouth, smooth my hair over, and sit a little straighter.

Isabella steps in with a smile, her hair slightly windswept. She looks a bit flustered, and my heart does a little flip.

"Sorry, I'm late!" Isabella exclaims, shaking off her jacket and letting her eyes wander over the room before landing on me. She throws me a smile and a wink and my cheeks redden. I look away almost on instinct.

"No worries! We haven't started," Clara reassures her.

Isabella walks over and joins us on the couch, sitting right next to me. Our thighs are so close they're almost touching, and I can feel the warmth radiating from her.

"What did I miss?" she asks, glancing at the game board.

"Not much, I was just explaining the game to Lily," Alejandra says.

"Perfect!" Isabella replies. She leans forward slightly. "So, how do we play?"

Alejandra takes a deep breath and gestures dramatically.

"Okay, everyone, gather around! Here's the deal. The game takes place at an extravagant masquerade ball hosted in an opulent mansion. Guests wear elegant costumes and mysterious masks. They mingle while enjoying champagne and hors d'oeuvres. Just as the evening reaches its peak, a blood-curdling scream echoes through the halls, and the lights flicker ominously. The host of the ball, the wealthy and enigmatic socialite Margaret Sinclair, is found dead in her private study. With all the doors locked and windows sealed, it's clear that the murderer is among the guests. So, each character must unravel the mystery of who killed Margaret and why. But remember, the killer will be one of us!"

Isabella's eyes widen, and she leans in closer. "Finally, something other than UNO. I'm into it."

Alejandra sticks her tongue out at her.

"Who do I get to be?" Isabella asks.

Clara grins, flipping through the character cards. "Let's find out!"

We all dive into the game, shouting out our theories about who might be the murderer. Clara teases Alejandra about her questionable strategy, while Valeria is too focused on winning to even notice, and Isabella quietly watches us all.

As laughter erupts alongside the banter, I realize how much I've missed these moments. It feels so good to be back here, surrounded by my best friends.

I take a sip of my wine, feeling the warmth of the room wrap around me like a cozy blanket.

My phone buzzes, startling me, and when I fish it out of my pocket, I have a message from Isabella.

> Isabella 8:00 p.m.: I like the shirt 😊

I look up at her, and she's watching me from the

kitchen, with an annoyingly cute smirk plastered on her face. My heart skips a beat, and a massive smile spreads across my lips. Then there's another buzz.

Isabella 8:05 p.m.: You look cute

All I can do is smile and shake my head at her playfully. My face feels hot and I press my icy fingers against my cheek. I don't reply, partly because I don't know what to say, but mostly because I'm flustered.

"I mean it," Isabella says as she sits next to me again. The way she holds my gaze is overwhelming, like she's looking straight into my soul, and it makes me want to lay myself bare and show her all the parts I hide.

My eyes land on her lips, and our kiss in the car replays in my head so vividly I swear it's happening, and I can feel the warmth of her lips on mine.

"Uh, what's going on between you?" Clara says as she glances between Isabella and me.

The sudden attention makes my stomach flip. I open my mouth to respond, but nothing comes out. Isabella shifts slightly, and I can see a hint of a smile on her lips, as if she's amused by the situation.

Before I can gather my thoughts, Isabella smirks at me and leans in closer. "Well, Lily, it's not like they don't have their suspicions," she says playfully, and I nearly choke.

I look around, and Clara, Valeria, and Alejandra's eyes are boring into me.

Isabella's smirk widens, and I can tell she's loving every second of this.

"Well?" Alejandra presses.

But I don't know what to say, because I have no clue what's going on between us. Do I tell them about our kiss last night? Or do I tell them about Isabella flirting with me a few minutes ago? Or about how I desperately want to kiss her again?

"Lily…" Isabella pauses, and everyone turns to look at her, their eyes wide and expectant, waiting to hear what she's going to say. My heart hammers in my chest, and I think I'm going to pass out. I have no idea what Isabella is going to say.

"Lily is the murderer," Isabella announces and I let out a breath. I was definitely not expecting that. Damn… that almost went a completely different way.

Clara bursts out laughing. "What? Why?" she asks, completely caught off guard.

I couldn't tell you what Isabella said. My head is reeling and my heart is thumping in my ears.

I pull out my phone and text her.

> Lily 8:22 p.m.: Asshole

I don't usually swear, but she deserves it.
Isabella looks at her phone and laughs.

> 😘😘😘

If she weren't so infuriatingly cute, I'd seriously consider plotting her demise. How can someone be so adorable and so maddening at the same time? It's completely unfair.

When we finish the game, everyone realizes that I am, in fact, the murderer. I'm not sure how Isabella figured it out or if her accusing me earlier was plain dumb luck, but she's the only one who guessed it right.

I shoot her a playful glare, half impressed, half annoyed,

as she flashes me a triumphant smile. It's almost as if she's reveling in my downfall, and I can't help but admire her for it.

Isabella stretches, and she yawns. "Well, I should head out," she says, looking around the room.

"Yeah, I should, too," I say. But inside, I feel a twinge of disappointment because I don't want the night to end.

"So soon?" Alejandra pouts.

"Yes, I'm exhausted," Isabella replies.

"Fine." Alejandra says.

After a few more goodbyes and promises to do this again soon, it's just Isabella and me standing at the door.

"How'd you know I was the murderer," I say just as Isabella turns to leave. Caught off guard by how much I want her to stay.

She laughs, "Lily, you were my best friend for like twelve years. I can still tell when you're lying,"

I roll my eyes, but smile because I kind of love that she still knows me even if it's something dumb like knowing when I'm lying.

"Great, so I can never hide anything from you?"

"Exactly," she replies with a wink. "You should know better than to think you could get away with it."

"Whatever," I say, looking down at my boots as I kick at a pebble around, trying to distract myself from the flutter in my chest.

"Goodnight, Lily," Isabella says softly, brushing her hand lightly against mine before turning to leave.

"Goodnight," I reply, watching her walk away, already counting the hours until I see her again.

18

ISABELLA

The girls and I are going to the cabin today, and I haven't packed a thing.

I yank open my suitcase and toss it onto the bed, my hands quickly rifling through drawers, grabbing whatever clothes are within reach.

I'm supposed to pick Lily up today, which only makes this entire morning even crazier.

It wasn't my idea, but with everyone else heading out around 6 a.m. to make it there around check-in, I knew I'd be driving in later, and I guess Lily had the same idea. Alejandra somehow volunteered me and let me know last night that I was supposed to pick Lily up at 8:30 a.m. She didn't give me much of a choice, and honestly, arguing with Alejandra is pointless. So I just agreed.

I find my phone buried under some jeans and send Lily a quick text.

> Isabella 7:22 a.m.: I'll pick you up in an hour ok?

Hopefully, she set an alarm this time.

I mentally run through what I might need for the weekend and I can't shake the feeling that I'm forgetting something, but my headspace is currently taken up by what the fuck Lily and I are going to talk about for three whole hours.

My 'you need to leave now' alarm goes off, but I still need to shower, and get my dogs in the car so I can drop them off at the sitter before, check in on the gallery. *I should've woken up earlier.*

I zip the suitcase shut and collapse onto my bed for a second, trying to catch my breath. What's another minute? I'm already running behind.

My phone pings, and when I reach for it, I realize I've been in bed for five minutes. How did I lose track of so much time?

"Fuck, fuck, fuck," I yell as I run to the shower and take the quickest shower known to man. Barely dry myself before throwing on a T-shirt and jeans. Then comes the mad dash to grab my things: phone, keys, wallet, bag, and dogs. One last quick scan of the room, a deep breath, and I head out.

I drop my dogs off at the sitter and then speed towards the gallery. Once I park, I hurry inside, looking over the space to make sure everything is in order. I type out a few emails, barely paying attention as I do. And after what feels like an eternity, I head back to my car.

> Isabella 8:20 a.m.: I'm on my way. Are you ready?

As I pull up to Lily's house, I text her again to let her know I'm outside. While I wait, I map out the best route to the cabin and read a few emails on my phone. Five minutes pass and Lily's still not out, and now I'm worried she overslept. I pull my phone out to call her, but just as I'm about to, Lily finally steps out of her house.

She's wearing a long, black cardigan layered over a fitted turtleneck with high-waisted jeans. Looking devastatingly good.

I pop the liftgate open for her and watch as she struggles with her luggage. Her determination is both adorable and a little worrying. I almost jump out to help her, but before I can make a move, she's got everything stowed away and slides into the passenger seat.

"Thanks for picking me up, sorry I took so long, my mom is taking care of Pickles, and she insisted I run through everything again," she says.

"No problem," I say as I give her a quick once over before turning my attention to the road, but it's hard when she looks and smells so fucking good.

Her arm is resting on the center console, brushing against mine now and then. I keep moving my arm, trying my hardest not to accidentally bump into her because her touch is electric, and it makes it hard to stay focused on the road.

"So," Lily says. "Have you been up to anything exciting lately?"

Damn, I knew the conversation up to the cabin was going to be awkward, but did she just pull out the number one question in the awkward conversations handbook?

I try not to laugh and instead focus on trying to answer her question without bursting out in an uncontrollable cackle.

"Yeah, I started designing the installation for the upcoming show at the gallery."

"Really? That's amazing! I'm sure it's going to be great."

And that same annoying warmth I felt during our

conversation around the bonfire takes over me again. It's nice to know she's in my corner, cheering me on.

"I recently found some of our high school notebooks, and it brought back so many memories of you turning our notebooks into your canvas," Lily says.

Immediately, I'm transported to the biology class I had with her during our senior year. We had come up with this great idea to pass around a notebook full of our notes back and forth, hoping our teacher would just assume it was our class notebook, and honestly, it worked. We never got caught. I'd draw all sorts of things in the margins. Sometimes, Lily would join in and add to my drawings, and eventually, they'd take over the entire page.

I'd completely forgotten about those. Teenage Isabella pops into my mind, reminding me of all the fun Lily and I had passing around that notebook. A wave of nostalgia hits me, and all I can do is smile at the memory back when things were so much simpler.

"Yeah, I think I still have one of them stashed away somewhere," I reply, trying to remember the last time I laid eyes on it and then I do, I threw it away a couple of years ago... *oops*.

Lily smiles at me and adjusts herself in the seat.

The rest of the car ride is pretty chill. Lily puts on a true crime podcast I haven't heard before, and we listen for a good two hours. We get so wrapped up in the details that we keep pausing to swap theories and gasp over the latest twist like we're co-detectives on a case.

For the last hour of the drive, Lily decides to switch gears and takes out a trivia book and asks me all sorts of questions I don't know the answer to, like she's hosting a game show and I'm the star contestant. "What's the capital of Mongolia?" "Which movie won the Oscar for Best

Picture in 1994?" I stumble through the questions most of my answers guesses and wild speculations. Every wrong answer gets a laugh from Lily, who's having the time of her life. We laugh, she teases, and despite my less-than-stellar performance, I have a great time. And it's like those ten years apart never happened. It's a little scary, though, because I know that's not true. I know all the hurt that came with those years, but at this moment, I can't seem to conjure up any of that negativity and I decide that for the rest of this trip, I will try not to.

————— ♥ ♥ ♥ —————

The gravel crunches under my tires as I turn into the driveway of the cabin. It's nestled among tall pines and evergreens, their dark silhouettes standing out against the afternoon sky. The cabin is perfect, almost too perfect, like something out of a postcard.

I put the car in park and roll my window down, taking a moment to enjoy the gentle rustling of leaves and the distant calls of a bird. I take in a deep breath of the crisp, pine-scented air, and then I turn to Lily.

"Well, here we are!"

Lily leans in and gives my cheek a light, tender kiss. My body tenses up, and my mind goes blank. The scent of her perfume—a blend of something sweet and floral—is intoxicating, and the outline of her lips burns on my cheek. I press my fingers against it, trying to savor the tingle she left behind, doing my fucking best to rein my thoughts in, not allowing myself to overthink what it means or what I want it to mean. *It was just a thank you for driving three hours, so I didn't have to kiss. Nothing more.* I tell myself.

"Thank you for driving," she says before she steps out of the car. *See? I was right.*

Lily and I fish our bags from the trunk and head up the stairs of the cabin. I can hear the chatter of our friends from outside, but the second we open the door, they go silent. *That's never good.*

"Lily? Isabella? Is that you?" Alejandra calls out.

"Yeah," I yell back and hear their chairs push back.

We haven't made it two steps inside when Alejandra comes marching straight at us and says, "We have a problem."

"Not even a hello?" I reply, letting my bag drop to the floor.

Clara smiles and rolls her eyes, but before she can say anything, Valeria comes down the stairs, followed by her girlfriend, Brooke. *What the fuck is Brooke doing here?*

"Okay, a couple of problems," Alejandra whispers as she leans in.

Valeria walks past me with a tight smile. Followed by Brooke, who mean-mugs us all. They go out the front door, and we all awkwardly watch after them. Once the door closes behind them, Lily asks, "What's Brooke doing here?"

Something I'd also like to know...

"Brooke invited herself here, and now Valeria is pissed," Clara says.

"Well, she shouldn't be here so who can blame her," I say. Everyone nods. "What's the other problem?"

"The second one is that I accidentally booked the wrong cabin," Clara says as she rubs her forehead. "There are two on this property, and I meant to book the one with five rooms. This one only has three, so we're all going to have to share. Since you two drove up together, we were hoping you wouldn't mind rooming together."

Lily turns to me wide-eyed. My own feel like they're about to pop out of their socket.

"There's a room with bunk beds you can use if that helps. Ale and I can share the queen bed in the other room," Clara adds.

That makes me feel the tiniest bit better.

"Absolutely not," Alejandra chimes in, shaking her head. "I've shared a bed with you before, and It's like being trapped in a whirlwind of never-ending limbs. No way," she says, crossing her arms.

Fuck.

"Then why don't you stay with Lily?" I ask, getting more and more annoyed.

"Because I don't want to share a bed," Alejandra says.

"Well, neither do I." I push back.

Sharing a bed with Lily sounds like an awful idea. I cannot let this happen.

"Then you should have been here early to claim a bed," Alejandra says, narrowing her eyes at me.

God damn it. Why is she so fucking impossible?

"Clara?" I say, almost whining.

"Sorry friend, I do move around a lot. I don't wanna do that to either one of you."

I roll my eyes so far back I think I see my skull.

"I guess we don't have much of a choice. Looks like it's you and me," I say to Lily, who looks like she's about to throw up and she's not alone.

"Looks like it's you and me," she repeats her voice shaky.

"You sure you're okay with this?" I ask. "We can just throw their shit out of the room with the bunkbeds."

Her lips quirk into a half-smile and she takes in a deep breath. "Yeah, it's ok," she finally says adjusting the strap of her bag. "Lead the way."

"Thank you," Alejandra says, reaching for both our hands and squeezing before guiding us up the stairs.

Why did I come?

"Alright, you two, this is it," Alejandra says as she guides us to the door of our room.

Our room... mine and Lily's room... fuck.

"Get settled, and then come down. We're having lunch soon," Alejandra adds.

Lily nods, and I try to swallow past the knot at the base of my throat as I watch Alejandra skip down the stairs.

Lily and I turn to face each other, then at the closed door. She pushes it open, revealing a small room. It's exactly what you'd expect from a cabin—It's got this cozy, rustic vibe and wooden walls, massive windows that take up half the room, and in the center, a single *full-size* bed. If I wasn't sharing this tiny room with Lily, I'd love this room.

"Guess this is it," Lily says, her voice light, but I can hear the strain behind it.

"I thought Clara said this was a queen," I say feeling a little lightheaded.

"Yeah... me too."

We both stand in the doorway, staring at the bed.

When I finally get my legs moving, I step inside, drop my bag at the foot of the bed, and let out a gigantic sigh. The bed looks impossibly tiny, and I don't know how we're both supposed to fit on it. The room starts to close in on me, and I feel claustrophobic. I need to get out of here and not think about this, or I'm going to give myself a panic attack.

"I'm going to go see what they're making," I say, practically running out the door. Not waiting for Lily to reply.

I close the door behind me, and as soon as I hear the door click shut, I let out a sigh. These next few days are going to be miserable.

I bounce down the stairs, heading straight for the front door to get some air, but Valeria stops me.

"There you are!" she says, looping her arm in mine and guiding me towards the kitchen. We walk in to find Clara and Alejandra in full chef mode, pots bubbling on the stove, and the entire kitchen smells like heaven—way better than anything I'd expect them to make.

Valeria walks around the counter and starts pouring herself a glass of white wine. "Would you like some?"

"Ew... No. Is there red wine?" I say as I slip onto the stool in front of her. Valeria crouches under the kitchen island and pulls out a red bottle of wine and uncorks it.

"What are you guys making? It smells amazing," I say, taking the glass of wine from Valeria with a quick, mouthed "thanks"

"Oh, we're not cooking. Brooke is. She just stepped out to take a call, so we're keeping an eye on it for her. You know Clara and I live off takeout," Alejandra jokes.

Clara looks over her shoulder from the stove. "Hey, I'm making garlic bread," she pouts.

"It's pre-made! You're just sticking it in the oven," Alejandra shoots back, shaking her head. "I, however, am crafting a gourmet salad."

"More like a—uh—a very questionable salad," Clara teases.

"Questionable salad?" I ask, raising an eyebrow.

"She added pickles to it," Clara says, dramatically pretending to gag.

"Yeah, that's gross Ale."

Lily walks into the kitchen and I watch as she moves through the room, commanding my attention. It's like she has this gravitational pull, and without even trying, my focus locks onto her.

"Who in their right mind puts pickles in a salad?" Lily says, scrunching up her face as she slides onto the stool next to me, stealing my wine.

"They're not chopped into the salad weirdos. It's in the dressing!" Alejandra clarifies. "It's called creativity, people."

"It's called being gross," Clara mutters. "But hey, you do you."

I laugh, shaking my head at them. "Alright, enough about the salad. What's the plan?" I say stealing my wine glass back from Lily who gives me a tiny pout. I roll my eyes and set it back in front of her.

Alejandra wipes her hands on a towel and then whips out a deck of cards from the drawer with a wicked grin. "We're playing Dare or Drink. You know the drill."

We all stare at her in shock as we recognize the deck.

"Wait, is that the one we made in high school?" Valeria asks.

Alejandra nods and wags her eyebrow.

I can't believe she still has it. We made that deck back in our sophomore year of high school. We were all in charge of making up ten dares, and we all filled the cards with dares we thought were hilarious at the time. Like, call a random contact on your phone and sing them 'Baby Shark' and other stupid things like that.

"I thought it would be perfect for our little getaway," Alejandra says, shuffling the cards.

"Oh, this is going to be a disaster," Clara says, laughing.

"Don't act like you don't love it," Alejandra replies with a wink.

I swear, sometimes I think these two are in love.

Clara slides into the stool next to Lily, abandoning her garlic bread duties without a second thought. "Just remember, I'm in charge of our lunch. Dare wisely."

Alejandra grins at her. "No promises."

The first few rounds are harmless—Valeria has to wear a dish towel as a cape and proclaim herself the "Queen of Garlic Bread" while Lily has to sing Twinkle, Twinkle, Little Star in the world's worst opera voice, which—annoyingly, was way cuter than I thought possible. Clara gives a dramatic monologue to... a fork. She grabs it like it's a Shakespearean prop and begins, "Oh, loyal fork! Stabber of pasta, defender of meals..." It was so over-the-top that we were doubled over, laughing until our cheeks ached.

Then it's my turn.

I draw a card, holding it up like it's a life sentence. And of course... it's a blank dare card. This means the person to my right gets to come up with a dare for me, and to just my luck... It's Lily. The tension in the room shifts as all eyes turn to Lily, who's grinning like the Cheshire cat.

"Alright, I dare you to serenade us with a dramatic love song," she says.

"Easy enough," I reply.

But it isn't. Because my mind is now hung up on why Lily wants *me* to serenade a love song. My mouth goes dry, my throat tightens, and just like that, I forget every love song I've ever known.

Lily stares at me, her cheeks flushing red. "Oh, but there's a twist. You need to use a kitchen utensil as your mic!" she blurts out, the words tumbling from her mouth a bit too quickly.

Everyone laughs, and I just roll my eyes.

Whatever nervousness took over me earlier is now gone at the thought of making a fool of myself.

"Go on, rock star," Clara says, passing me a spatula.

I laugh, grabbing the spatula and pretend it's a microphone. With all the grace of a professional singer—okay, more like none at all—I launch into the most over-the-top rendition of Whitney Houston's I Will Always Love You imaginable. I belt the chorus like I'm on stage at the Grammys, falling to my knees in front of the stove. The girls laugh so hard they can barely breathe.

"Okay, okay!" Alejandra cries, wiping fake tears from her eyes. "You win this round!"

I take a mock bow, still clutching the spatula.

Brooke turns to us, pulling the garlic bread from the oven. "Lunch is ready," she announces.

We all eagerly stand and make ourselves a plate. We dive into the spaghetti like we haven't eaten in days. The garlic bread disappears in seconds, and even Alejandra's pickle salad isn't as bad as it sounds—though none of us are ready to admit that to her. And annoyingly lunch is delicious. If Brooke wasn't such a cunt I'd spend every day at her house eating everything she made.

After lunch, the cards come back out, and things only get crazier. Clara struts around the kitchen like it's Fashion Week, wearing a pot on her head as a makeshift hat, striking poses between the fridge and the stove. Brooke writes and performs a passionate poem about Bigfoot, complete with dramatic sighs and longing stares out the window, swooning over his "hairy magnificence." Valeria prank calls her brother, frantically claiming aliens have abducted her and desperately needs him to go to the moon to rescue her. Then it's Lily's turn, and of course, she pulls a blank card. What are the odds?

Clara taps at her chin as she thinks about what to dare Lily with. We all look around at each other, worried for Lily. Clara always makes up the worst dares. One time, she dared Alejandra to drink a whole glass of pickle juice mixed with mayonnaise and the juice of a tuna can. Alejandra barely made it through before gagging and running for the sink, coughing and crying. But the rest of us couldn't stop laughing.

"Isabella you have to let Lily blindfold you and feed you two random ingredients," Clara announces.

Lily freezes, and so do I. I'm such an idiot, of course, Lily and I are the only two to pull a blank card. This has Alejandra and Clara written all over it. I can't stand them.

"What? No, this is Lily's dare, not mine," I protest.

"So?"

"So, give her something to do not me."

"She *is* doing something; she's feeding you two random ingredients," Clara says with a shrug.

I roll my eyes. I fucking hate this.

"Have her pull another card then because I think it's pretty fucking weird that she and I are the only two to pull a blank, and now you're giving up your dare? Something isn't right."

"She pulled a blank, do the dare or drink. Don't be a baby, come on, we don't have all night. Chop chop!" Clara says as she hands me a scarf to cover my eyes.

"I hate you," I say, snatching the scarf from her hands. But Clara just blows me a kiss.

If it were any other dare or if Clara was doing it herself, I'd drink, but this one seems pretty harmless, how many gross things could they even find?

Lily stands slowly and makes her way to the kitchen.

I put the blindfolds on, and everything goes black.

I hear footsteps but can't figure out if they're coming towards me or away, but then I hear Clara and Alejandra talking to Lily in what I'm assuming is the kitchen. *Great.*

I try to focus on whatever is happening in there, trying to hear what they're doing. A bag crunches, and a lid pops, but that could be anything. I try to remember everything I saw in the kitchen earlier, but all I can think about is the pickle jar.

"We're back," Alejandra sings.

"Good luck," Clara says as she massages my shoulders.

I feel a draft on my face followed by a floral smell, and I immediately know Lily's in front of me. My body tenses up, and I grip the seat of my chair. *I should have drank.*

"Will you come closer," Lily says.

Inch by inch, I scoot forward, not sure when to stop, continuing until my knees hit something. I don't know if it's Lily's knees or her chair, but knowing we're this close makes my heart race.

A few things clink, and then Lily gently grabs my chin and tilts my head up. The moment her fingers touch my skin, I gasp, and butterflies flutter to life in my stomach.

I wait for something to drop into my mouth, but nothing does.

"Ahem," I hear Clara say, followed by a giggle that sounds a lot like Valerias.

Lily clears her throat and pulls me in closer.

Something that sounds a lot like a fart rings in my ears, followed by something cold and wet landing on my tongue.

I don't close my mouth, too afraid to figure out what it is. I pull on my sleeve and wipe my tongue. A bitterness taking over my taste buds.

"Ugh, that's disgusting. What is that?" I protest.

"Mustard," Clara laughs.

Ugh...Of course, they picked that... I hate mustard.

"Why did it fart?"

Lily giggles. "It's just trapped air."

Someone places a cup of water in my wand, and I swish it around, trying to get the taste of mustard out of my mouth. Just one more, and we're done. Which shouldn't be too bad because there's nothing I hate more than mustard.

"Okay, open wide," Lily says, and I hesitantly open my mouth. But not wide enough because, again, Lily has to grab my chin. And the same butterflies from before flutter awake.

"I'm sorry," Lily says, and my anxiety level spikes. Before I can say or do anything, something sour and slimy lands on my tongue. I wince and immediately spit it out.

The girls go into a fit of laughter and I rip the scarf off my face. "What is wrong with you?" I yell as I take a big gulp of my wine. "What was that?"

Lily holds up a can of pickled mushrooms. I was wrong... there is one thing I hate more than mustard, and it's this. Why is it even here?

"You could have just drank, you know," Clara says through her laughter.

"Whatever," I say as I take another big gulp of my wine, and we all keep playing.

After a while of torturing each other with dare or drink, we start to wind down, and everyone retreats to their room one by one. It's not even ten o'clock, but we're all exhausted and a little too drunk to keep going, so we decide to go to bed early.

Lily and I head upstairs, and when we reach our room, I nervously slip inside and sit on the edge of the bed. Lily quietly closes the door behind us, her movements slow.

The room looks smaller than it did earlier—especially the bed, which suddenly looks impossibly small.

Thankfully, this room has an ensuite bathroom, so I lock myself in there trying to ease the tension settling in my shoulders. I change into my pajamas, wash my face, do my best to tame my frizzy hair, brush my teeth, and stare at myself in the mirror. I look exhausted; I'm so ready to get in bed and rest, but I know I won't get much sleep tonight, not with Lily inches from me.

When I open the door, Lily's not in the room.

Maybe she decided to sleep elsewhere after all. The thought helps me feel a little more relaxed, but I know there's no way. Where else would she stay? Lily's never been a fan of sleeping in the living room, courtesy of one too many true crime podcasts. But I guess things change. It's been ten years.

I cross the room and flop down on my side of the bed. I shift around, trying to find the perfect spot, but when I can't, I just give up and lie on my back. I grab my phone and start scrolling through some emails—mostly just confirmation stuff for Clark's hotel and flight. She signed the contract my lawyer sent her earlier, so now it's official she's the featured artist at the exhibit. She'll be down at the gallery in a few days to start on her installation.

I throw my phone on the nightstand and look up at the ceiling. There are glow-in-the-dark stars plastered everywhere. I haven't seen these in years, and now I kind of want to put some in my room.

The creaking of the door scares me, but it's just Lily walking in with two glasses of water in hand. She hands me one and sets the other on her nightstand.

She stands by the foot of the bed for a second, like she isn't sure what to do, and then she starts to play with a strand of her hair, looking around the room like it's her first time seeing it.

I almost want to tease her about how nervous she is, but I don't. Instead, I lift the blanket and pat the side of her bed. She smiles and shuffles awkwardly into bed. We both move around, trying to find the comfiest position. I hadn't noticed, but there's a second blanket under the duvet, and as Lily tries to pull it over her, she yanks so hard that she loses her grip and smacks me right in the nose.

"Fucking shit," I yell, immediately grabbing my nose.

My eyes water, and my sinuses sting so bad I honestly think Lily might've broken it.

"Oh my god, I'm so sorry!" Lily yells, her voice full of panic. She quickly reaches out, trying to help, but I pull away, still holding my nose.

"I think you broke it," I mutter.

Lily's face turns pale. "No, no, no!" she yells, looking frantic.

"Everything okay in there?" Valeria calls out from the other side of the door.

"Come in," Lily says.

Valeria peeks in, her brow furrowed. "What's going on? I heard someone yell."

"Will you take a look at Isabella's nose?" Lily screams.

Valeria's a vet, so I have no idea what Lily thinks she can do for me, but I guess we're out of options at this point.

"I accidentally hit her," Lily adds as she gets up from bed, letting Valeria take a seat next to me.

"You what?" I hear Clara and Alejandra say from behind Lily.

"Guys, it was an accident," I say, still holding my nose, the faint taste of blood lingering in the back of my throat.

Valeria scoots closer, inspecting my face carefully as she gently touches my nose.

"It's swollen, but I think you're fine. It will probably bruise, though."

"So, no broken nose?"

Valeria shakes her head. "Nah, I think you're in the clear. You should ice it though."

I nod.

"Thank God," Lily says letting out a big sigh.

"I'll go grab you something from the freezer," Clara says.

"How did this happen?" Alejandra asks.

"I was trying to get under the covers, and I lost my grip on the sheets," Lily says, rubbing her forehead. "I didn't mean to hurt you. I'm so sorry," She says, looking back at me with such guilt I almost feel bad that my face was in her fist's way.

"I know," I say. "It's fine."

Clara runs in and hands me a bag of frozen meatballs.

"Meatballs? Really?" I say, annoyed as I press the bag against my nose. The smell of the meat leaking through.

"It's all we have!" Clara says.

"Are you sure she's ok?" Lily asks Valeria.

"Yeah, she just needs to ice it."

"Well, we'll let you both rest then," Alejandra says.

Alejandra leans in and gives Lily a quick kiss on the cheek. "Goodnight, please don't hit her again," she teases, and Lily buries her face in her hands.

"Goodnight, guys," I say, leaning my head back to keep snot from dripping down my face.

Lily gets back in bed and pulls my head into her chest, smashing my nose on her shoulder, and it hurts like a bitch. My eyes water and I bite the inside of my cheek, trying not to make a sound because I know if I do, Lily and I will end up on a never-ending loop of "I'm sorry" and "It's okay."

"I'm so sorry," she whispers.

"Lily, it's fine." I laugh freeing my head from her.

"You sure you're okay?"

"Okay... well goodnight," Lily says quietly.

"Goodnight, Lily," I whisper back.

I throw a few pillows in the middle of the bed, making

sure there's no way either of us can accidentally roll over. Satisfied with my little barricade, I settle in and lay the bag of meatballs on my face.

"Can you breathe alright with that on your face?" Lily asks.

"Yes." I laugh. "

"Ok, goodnight," Lily says as she turns on a true crime podcast and sets it on a timer before she turns to sleep.

I'm not saying I'm glad Lily punched me in the face, but I am glad the pain isn't letting me think about the fact that I'm in bed with her or pay much attention to whatever fucked up episode is blasting through her phone.

Before I know it, sleep takes over.

19

LILY

I wake up to a tangle of limbs draped over me.

When I turn my head, my gaze lands on Isabella, still sleeping peacefully beside me. Her dark hair spilled across the pillow, the bag of meatballs lying under her crazy hair, and her face relaxed in sleep. She looks so serene, so beautiful. It's almost too much to take in first thing in the morning.

Carefully, I slip out of bed, trying not to wake her. I need space to think, organize my head, and make sense of everything I'm feeling. I put a sweater over my pajamas, pad downstairs, and step out onto the porch. The cool morning air hits me—a welcome shock to my system—and I take a deep breath. The only sounds out here this early are the distant chirping of birds and the soft rustling of leaves outside.

A hand lands on my shoulder and I turn, thinking it's Isabella, but it's Alejandra.

"Morning," she mumbles.

"Morning."

"How was the rest of last night?"

"Good, Isabella fell right to sleep with the bag of meatballs on her face. When I looked at her this morning, it didn't look swollen."

"Good, I'm glad," she replies, giving me a sleepy smile. "Was she mad at you?"

"No, she was actually really sweet about it, which makes me feel worse. Leave it to me to try to fix our friendship by making her roll down a hill and punching her in the face." I say, letting out a little laugh, still feeling a bit embarrassed.

Alejandra sits next to me. "Oh, I don't know. You guys seem to be doing just fine."

"But are we really? Because half the time, I think Isabella is just doing this to appease you guys and will stop talking to me the second this is all over."

I look down at my hands and start picking Pickle's hair off of my pajama pants.

Alejandra sighs. "I can't tell you what she's thinking Lily, but there's definitely something there. I would just keep at it until you guys can fix whatever is keeping you apart. It's obvious you care about each other. Maybe it's time to loosen your grip on the fear you're holding so close. If you expect Isabella to hurt you, that's exactly what'll happen if you don't give her the chance not to."

I know she's right, of course, she's right. But letting go of ten years of hurt and that feeling of never being good enough for her to want to keep me around—it's not something I can just let go of. But I know I need to. I know I have to. If I want Isabella to trust me, I have to trust her, too. This can't be a one-way street.

"Morning," a voice calls from behind me. I turn and it's Isabella, looking even cuter than she did this morning—if you can believe it.

"Morning," Alejandra and I say at the same time.

"I'm about to start making breakfast if you guys want to come in," she says before turning around and heading back in.

Alejandra and I stand. I reach over to Alejandra and give her a tight hug.

"Thank you," I say.

"Anytime," Alejandra says as she leans into the hug.

Once we make it inside, I spot Clara making mimosas. Valeria and Brooke are nowhere to be found, and Isabella is standing over a bowl, mixing furiously.

"Need any help?" I ask walking towards Isabella.

"Nah, I'm fine." She says, turning to look at me with a sleepy smile.

"How's your nose?"

"A little sore, but nothing a few mimosas can't fix."

"Good."

"So, what should we do today?" Clara says as she hands Isabella a glass of what I'm sure will be her first of many mimosas.

"I saw hot springs signs on our way up," I say. "Maybe we can go to one?"

"Yes! I haven't been to one in years!" Alejandra says.

"What haven't you done in years?" Valeria asks as she turns into the kitchen.

"Hot springs, you guys down?"

Valeria turns to look at Brooke and she nods.

Alejandra claps excitedly.

The rest of the morning is quiet. Isabella makes us all eggs and bacon with pancakes for breakfast. Which is delicious. I didn't know Isabella could cook, so it was a welcome surprise.

Is there anything this girl can't do?

———— ♥ ♥ ♥ ————

When we finally reach the hot springs, we eagerly begin undressing and I have to remind myself to keep my eyes to myself but Isabella's black bikini fits her so perfectly and the way it hugs her curves has my mind spinning, and I'm completely lost in the sight of her.

Isabella catches my eye and winks, and it feels like the air has been knocked out of my lungs. My heart stumbles over itself as I quickly look away, my face burns. I fumble with the string of my pants, my fingers clumsy and desperate for something—anything—to focus on, trying in vain to pull myself together.

One by one, we slowly lower ourselves into the steaming water, letting out content sighs as the warmth envelops us.

I watch as Isabella melts into the water. Her breathing is slow and steady. The steam from the hot springs swirls around her, catching the sunlight and casting a dreamy glow on her face. She looks utterly relaxed, with a content smile playing on her lips as if the world outside has vanished. When she opens her eyes, her relaxed gaze lands on me before she closes them again, and a smile creeps up my lips.

I watch the rise and fall of her chest, my own falling in line with it. A sudden wave of panic hits me, and I look around to make sure no one sees me, but everyone has their eyes closed, leaning against the edge of the springs, noses pointed toward the sky, enjoying the sounds of the birds serenading us.

We've been here for about an hour when Brooke tells Valeria she wants to go back to the cabin.

"I'm ready to go too," Alejandra says, and Clara nods.

All four get out of the water, shivering as the cold air hits their skin.

"Are you guys ready to go too?" Alejandra asks as she wraps a towel around herself.

I look over at Isabella, hoping she'll want to stay a little longer.

"I kind of want to stay," she says, looking at me. "Do you want to go?"

"No, I want to stay too. Are you guys ok with that?"

"Of course." Alejandra smiles.

"Brooke, can you get Ale and me back to the cabin?" Clara asks.

"Sure," Brooke replies with a shrug before turning on her heel and heading toward the car.

Clara and Alejandra shoot each other an exasperated look but follow Brooke and Valeria. As they walk away, Alejandra calls back over her shoulder, "Love you! Don't stay in there too long; it's not good for you!"

"We won't!" I shout after them, as they disappear into the woods.

And then, just like that, it's just Isabella and me in the warm water. Steam curling around us.

Isabella reaches for her bag pulling out a bottle of wine. She hands it to me so she can fish out the corkscrew. Once she's got it in hand, I hand the bottle back to her, and she freezes.

She looks at the bottle, then at me, then back at the bottle.

"It's a fucking twist off," she laughs as she unscrews the cap.

She takes a big swig, and I watch the wine glide down her throat. Droplets of spring water glisten on her neck, making my pulse race. I swallow hard, fighting the urge to lean in and press my lips to her damp skin.

Isabella glances over at me, a daring look in her eyes as she holds out the bottle. I grab it from her, taking the biggest swig I can manage, letting the rich, smooth wine warm me up from the inside.

"So, what do you think is on the agenda for today?"

"Knowing Alejandra, we're probably in for another ten rounds of UNO or drink or dare," I say, laughing.

Isabella laughs. "God, I hope not," she says as she takes another sip of the wine before handing it back to me.

"So, how's your book coming along?"

I try not to look too surprised, but it's hard. I never really thought that was a question Isabella would ask.

"It's fine. I'm almost done, just waiting on last notes from my editor," I reply.

"Nice, that's cool. You're writing the sequel to your last book, right?" She asks, and I freeze.

"Yeah, I am. How... how do you know that?"

Isabella shrugs. "I've kind of, sort of read all your books," she admits, her cheeks turning the cutest shade of pink. A rare sight. In the twelve years we were best friends, I think I only saw her blush twice. Isabella's blushing catches me so off guard I nearly miss her saying she has read all my books.

"You've read all of my books?" I ask in disbelief.

She nods, biting her lip. "Yeah..." she says, taking another swig of wine. "Alejandra dragged us all to a bookstore when your debut novel published and bought each of us a copy. I wasn't going to read it because I was mad at you, but curiosity got the best of me. And by the end... I needed more. They're good." She shrugs, her cheeks flushing again. "So, every time you published a new book, I went out and bought it. They're all in my office at the gallery. I don't think the girls know about this."

I blink at her, stunned. "Wait, seriously?"

"Yeah," she laughs.

My chest feels impossibly full, like my heart might burst. I wasn't expecting this, and it leaves me completely unprepared and speechless, which is saying a lot. Because I'm not usually speechless.

"I hope that's not weird," Isabella says as she rubs the back of her neck.

"No, no... no... not at all. I just... I just don't know what to say. I'm... surprised is all," I say, grabbing the bottle of wine from her. "You know I've learned how to read palms because of my latest series," I say. It's a detail I didn't need to add, but I do because I'm nervous and I say random things when I'm nervous.

Isabella turns, her eyebrows knit together. A tiny smile threatening to break through. "Please explain," she says, turning her body towards me.

I chuckle, feeling a bit embarrassed, but I try to play it off.

"Well, as you know, the series is all about magic. And in this next book, the main character is a witch. At one point, she gets her palm read, and then she tries to outsmart fate. So, I ended up reading a lot about palmistry while researching, and... it just sort of stuck in my head. You can tell a lot about someone's personality and future by the lines on their hands."

Isabella raises an eyebrow. "Are you saying you can read my future?" she asks as she leans in closer.

I hesitate, feeling a bit self-conscious. "I mean, I've never actually tried it on a real person. But I guess I could."

"Read my palm then," she says as she offers me her

hand. I gently take her hand, brushing my thumb over her slightly pruney palm, savoring the warmth of her skin against mine. I trace the lines on her palm with my finger as I try to remember everything I've read but my thoughts are a bit scrambled.

"This is your heart line..." I say as my finger slowly traces the curved line between her index and pinky finger. "And it suggests you're a passionate person."

She raises an eyebrow. Her smirk growing. "Is that so?" she says, her eyes fixed on mine. I nod and do my best to ignore the way her gaze makes my chest flutter.

I clear my throat and try to sound more confident. "Well, you have a short head line, which I think means you're a little stubborn."

"Tell me something I don't know." She laughs. "How about you tell me about the future," she says, leaning in, her face inches from mine. Her breath is warm and her dark eyes lock on to mine with an intensity that makes it impossible to look away.

"Anything... exciting coming my way?" she asks as she leans in closer.

I try to answer, but I can't think. My eyes fixated on the curve of her lips. She notices and her smirk grows even more.

"I'm waiting," she whispers, her voice low and teasing, almost like she's daring me to make the next move. My heart pounds in my chest as the space between us shrinks and I fight the urge to close the distance.

I clear my throat and try to ignore how close her face is to mine. "I'd say... there's definitely something exciting in your fate line," I finally manage. Unsure of what that's even supposed to mean because that's not how the fate line works, but I can't think straight right now, and that's the best I can do.

Isabella's eyes darken, and her lips part slightly as she leans in closer.

"Something exciting, huh?" she breathes, her voice sultry. "Care to be more specific?"

I gulp trying to compose myself but I can't take my eyes off her. The teasing look in her eyes draws me in deeper. My hand holds hers, and the warmth of her skin, with her fingers gently curling around mine, sets my pulse racing and makes my breath quicken. Everything Isabella does captivates me and my world narrows down to her closeness, her breath, her eyes. I tell myself I shouldn't be doing this, but I'm so sick of fighting myself. I want her, I want to kiss her.

And then, as if pulled by an invisible force, I lean in, and our lips meet, my heart races with panic, but just as I'm about to pull away and apologize, Isabella kisses me back, her hands coming up to cradle my face, and all those doubts melt away.

The kiss deepens, growing more urgent and more intense as our bodies press closer together. I let myself get lost in the sensation—the warmth of Isabella's lips, the way her hands trail down my back, her breath mingling with mine. It's overwhelming in the best way possible.

The taste of wine on her tongue mixed with the sweat pooling on her upper lip is intoxicating. I've never felt so desperate to get closer to anyone. I climb on top of her, straddling her legs as I bury my hands in her curls, Isabellas eyes roll back and I pull her closer to me as I press my lips against hers.

Isabella digs her nails into my skin as her hands move up my thighs, over my hips and up my back leaving behind an electric trail. One of her hands finds it's way into my hair and when she pulls, my head falls back exposing my neck. She kisses the base of my throat, sucking and kissing her way down my chest.

Isabella looks up at me and grins. Her eyes go dark as she slowly pulls at the front string of my bikini top and slides it down my arms.

Without taking her eyes of mine she sucks one of my nipples into her mouth and I moan. Her tongue gently laps over my hardened nipple, making desire pool in my clit. Isabella's thumb traces the hem of my bathing suit near the dip of my inner thigh. Making my stomach flutter wildly. Her thumb slowly inches its way toward my clit as my heart pounds so intensely it drowns out everything, the rhythmic thudding echoing in my ears as her thumb finds its way to where I need it. Isabella rubs slow circles as the pressure between my thighs builds. I love what her mouth is doing to my nipple, but I need her lips on mine, to taste my new favorite combination of sweat and wine on her tongue.

"Kiss me." I say almost pleading.

Isabella smiles and gently bites down on my nipple as she lets go. My pussy tightens and I moan just as her mouth meets mine. She bites my bottom lip, making me moan even louder as she intensifies the pressure on my clit.

My body moves on its own, demanding more from her as it tightens, eager for release. Her fingertips tease my slit, sending shivers of pure, exhilarating ecstasy coursing through me, and all I want at this moment is to come undone.

I'm about to give into pleasure when Isabella stops and pulls her hand away. A sly smile creeping up her lips. I whimper at the loss, dropping my head.

"Why?" I say against her shoulder before I look up. "I was right there."

Isabella bites her lip "I know," She says as she kisses my breast.

"Don't do this," I say, grabbing her hand and guiding it towards my pussy.

Isabella smiles and shakes her head no. "Later," she says as she kisses her way from the bottom of my throat to the nape of my ear. "I promise."

But the promise does nothing to quell the fire raging inside me, a heat that's threatening to consume me if I don't get what I need right now. I slide my hand down my bathing suit bottoms, ready to finish this myself, when Isabella grabs ahold of my hand.

"No," Is all she says, and it only makes me want to do it even more. God, this is going to drive me crazy all day, but I know that's exactly what she wants.

"Isabella, please," I beg as I kiss her, trying to get her to feel the need I have for her but she doesn't budge.

"You've always been so impatient," she smirks. "I promise I'll make it worth it," she whispers against my ear before standing.

I'm still on top of her, so as she gets to her feet, I slide off, standing up too.

"You're the worst," I say she throws me a towel.

Isabella laughs and I'm glad she's having a good time. I on the other hand could kill her right now.

"We should go anyways," she says. "Before the girls start to worry and drive back up here."

"Yeah, I guess we should," I say, feeling a pang of disappointment.

We quickly get dressed, and before we head down to her car Isabella pulls me in closer and kisses me again, reigniting the fiery need in my body. I don't know what this means, I don't know what comes next, and I don't care. I don't want to think about it right now. I just want to enjoy it.

The drive back to the cabin is quiet. Isabella plays some deep-focus Lo-Fi music from her phone and I absentmindedly trace the lines of her palm as she drives letting myself enjoy this before one of us backs out.

When we finally pull up to the cabin and make our way inside, we hear our friends laughing and the sound of ice hitting glass. Isabella and I peek into the kitchen and they're all sitting at the island passing around shot glasses.

"Welcome back!" Clara says, clearly a little drunk.

"You guys need to catch up!" Alejandra says as she hands me a shot of tequila.

I take it without protest, hoping it'll calm the heat cursing through my body. My worries momentarily drowned out by the music and the warmth of the tequila. I see Isabella across the room, her eyes meet mine for a brief, electric second as she lifts her glass to me and winks, making my mind spiral.

"How were the springs?" Clara asks.

"Oh... um... good. We had some wine, talked... nothing too crazy," I stammer, feeling the heat creep up my neck, and I instantly regret saying, "Nothing too crazy." Because that sounds like something someone who did something crazy would say.

Isabella catches my eye and smiles, shaking her head slightly.

"Good," Clara says. "You guys got back just in time. We were just about to go outside and make some s'mores"

"Yum... okay, I'll meet you guys in a bit, I need to go shower," I say, trying to sound really excited about smores, but all I can think about eating right now is Isabella.

Isabella follows Clara into the backyard, and I run

upstairs to take the quickest shower I can, change into a sweater and jeans and run back downstairs, not wanting to be away from Isabella for another second.

When I step outside, the smell of woodsmoke hits me. I sit around the bonfire and stretch my hands close to the fire, trying to warm up. Isabella hands me a thick blanket, and I wrap it tightly around myself.

"Thanks," I say, looking up at her, and she winks. God, I love it when she winks at me.

Her hair is wet, and she's in new clothes, so she must have showered in Valeria and Brookes's bathroom, and the thought makes me sad. She could have just joined me, but then I realize how silly that sounds. The girls would have known.

With the fire going, we roast marshmallows and make s'mores. The girls tell scary stories, most of them about a group of girls alone in a cabin in the woods—very original.

As I turn to roast my fifth marshmallow, I catch sight of Isabella, and I can't help but watch her. She's laughing at something Brooke said. Her smile's bright as she playfully nudges Valeria with her elbow, sticky marshmallows clinging to her fingers. My eyes stay glued to her as she scrapes the gooey mess off with her teeth. She must feel me staring because, just as Valeria turns to Brooke, Isabella's gaze snaps to mine as she slowly slips her thumb into her mouth, sucking the remaining marshmallow from her finger. Her eyes fixated on me. My throat suddenly dry as I try to rein in the wave of heat rushing through me. But I can't. My brain's telling me to look away, to pull it together, but my eyes refuse to listen. And then, like nothing, Isabella turns back to Valeria. I really, really, *really* hate her right now...

Luckily, Alejandra pulls me into a conversation about her latest photoshoot, giving me a much-needed distraction.

She dives into it with detail—ISO settings, aperture, and a bunch of other photography jargon I no longer remember. I nod along, grateful for the chance to focus on something other than the heartbeat between my thighs.

"Oh shoot," Valeria says and we all turn towards her. "We need more wood or the fire's gonna go out."

"I can go get some sticks. Would that work?" Valeria nods.

"I'll come with you," Isabella says.

I wrap the blanket tighter around me and follow Isabella. No one seems to pay attention as we veer off the well-lit area by the fire and into the shadowed woods nearby. The sound of crackling branches underfoot is the only thing breaking the silence as we walk in deeper.

The light of the bonfire is further now, barely visible through the trees, but we can still hear Clara's laugh. Isabella stops abruptly and turns to face me, her breath visible in the chilly air. She steps closer and tugs at the blanket wrapped around me. She slips inside, pulling it around both of us. She wraps her arms around my waist. My heart's pounding so hard I'm sure she can feel it as she steps in even closer. Her lips crash into mine with a sudden, fiery intensity and I melt into it. Her fingers curl into my sides, and her touch sends sparks through me as I pull her closer, feeling the warmth of her body against mine in the cool night.

Isabella smiles into the kiss, and a slow, satisfied grin creeps up her lips. "I don't know what I'm doing," she murmurs against my lips.

"Me either," I whisper back, my heart still pounding.

I pull her in and kiss her, not wanting doubt to creep in. Wanting us both to let ourselves lose control. Isabella's hand finds its way to the nape of my neck, her fingers gently curling in my hair when Clara's voice cuts through the silence.

"Are you two ever coming back, or do we need to send a search party?"

Isabella breaks into a soft laugh, pulling away slightly but staying close enough for our foreheads to touch.

"I guess time's up," she whispers before biting her lip.

"Yeah," I agree.

But I don't want it to be. Because I don't know when reality will crash back in and ruin this perfect little bubble. And I hate not knowing which kiss, which touch, which warm stare from Isabella will be the last. I want to make every single moment last forever so it never ends.

Isabella smiles, giving me a quick kiss before stepping back and slipping out of the blanket. With a little shiver, she turns toward the cabin.

On the way back, Isabella and I stop to grab every stick we see until we're both struggling to hold everything, twigs poking out at odd angles. At least we'll have enough to keep the girls from asking why it took us so long.

When we get back, everyone's already heading inside, laughing and chatting. The fire went out, so they didn't even look at the ridiculous pile of sticks we lugged back. Isabella and I drop our piles near the firepit before following everyone else inside. *All that work for nothing.*

"What now?" I ask as I sit on the couch next to Isabella. Overthinking being next to her. Will the girls wonder why I'm sitting here? Should I move? I try to think of every time we've all hung out and every single seating arrangement, and I realize Isabella and I are almost always next to each other. And something about that makes me happy. It's like we're somehow drawn to each other.

"Oh, yeah! I'll make some popcorn," Clara screams from the kitchen, startling me.

"I'll grab us all some wine," Alejandra offers, standing and stretching.

"Red for me, please," Isabella says.

"Of course. I know, I know," Alejandra replies with a playful roll of her eyes.

I look around, confused, realizing I missed a whole conversation.

"What did I miss?" I whisper to Isabella.

She laughs. "We're watching a movie."

"Ah, ok."

"What were you thinking about?" She smirks, and I bite my lip.

"Nothing special," I say because it's true, but now all I can think about is the hot springs.

"Mhm." Isabella shakes her head and smiles.

Isabella moves closer and drapes a clean blanket over us. A giddy nervousness washes over me and I feel like kicking my feet because Isabella's so close to me.

Alejandra and Clara come back, Clara holding a huge bowl of popcorn and Alejandra carrying our wine glasses.

"Alright, here you go!" Clara says, setting the bowl down on the coffee table, while Alejandra hands out the glasses to everyone.

The couch is set up in a big U, and we all take a section. To my right, Valeria and Brooke are curled up together, while on the other side of Isabella, Clara, and Alejandra are in the middle of a popcorn toss, each of them trying to catch flying kernels with their mouths, laughing when they miss.

I inch closer to Isabella, and the heat of her arm against me sends a shiver through every inch of my body. Her hand wraps around my leg with a teasing touch that makes my heart race and my breath hitch. She turns to me with a mischievous smirk, fully aware of the effect she's having on me.

I can't tear my eyes away from her, my breath coming in ragged gasps, my chest heaving with every heartbeat. Clara calls my name, snapping me out of my intense focus on Isabella's fingers gliding up and down my inner thigh.

"Huh?" I mumble, barely registering the question. I grab Isabella's fingers, forcing her to stop so I can focus on what Clara's saying.

"Are you okay?" Clara asks, narrowing her eyes, looking back and forth between Isabella and me.

"Yeah, fine," I say, trying hard to keep my cool.

"Okay," Clara says, dragging out the 'A'.

"Clara was just asking if you're alright with watching a scary movie. We know they're not really your thing," Valeria chimes in.

"Oh, um, yeah, that's fine," I reply quickly. I'd usually opt out. But with Isabella's touch making it impossible to concentrate, I'm sure my attention will be elsewhere anyway.

"Cool," Clara says, not taking her eyes off Isabella and me. Her eyes narrowed.

The second I let go of her fingers they start, exploring my inner thigh with a feather-light touch that makes my breaths come in quick, uneven bursts.

The movie starts, but my mind is tangled up in the warmth of Isabella's touch to follow along. Her presence dominates my senses, and every touch and every look from her is like an electric charge, leaving me completely distracted and utterly captivated. Her thumb rubs small gentle circles around my inner thigh as she slides her thumb just under the hem of my underwear, rubbing back and forth. This has been going on for at least an hour and no matter how much I shift and adjust, trying to give her all the access she needs, she doesn't take it and it's driving me crazy.

She leans in closer, her breath warm against my ear as she murmurs, "I can't wait to take you upstairs."

Her proximity sends my heart racing. I'm already struggling to keep up with the movie, and now my mind is consumed with imagining what will happen later, praying the movie ends soon before Isabella's teasing pushes me over the edge or she changes her mind.

After what feels like an eternity, the credits finally start to roll. Thank God—because I couldn't take much more of this.

Clara stretches and yawns. "That was a great movie," she says.

I look over at Isabella, and of course, she's got a smug smirk plastered on her face. "Yeah, it was... definitely something," I reply.

Clara grabs a handful of popcorn and turns to me. "I'm surprised you didn't scream as much as I thought you would."

Isabella laughs.

"It wasn't that scary," I lie.

"Yeah, I guess it wasn't," Clara says as she stretches again. "Okay, what's next? Something funny?"

Isabella's hand finds mine, and she squeezes it.

"I'm going to bed," Isabella says, standing up and stretching. "The springs wore me out."

"Oh no, already?" Alejandra screams out from the kitchen.

"Yeah, I'm exhausted," she continues.

"Actually, me too," I say. Standing just a little too quickly, I make myself dizzy and sit on the couch.

I watch as Isabella does her best to contain a laugh while Alejandra and Clara exchange a look from across the room but neither of them says a word. Valeria stares at them, probably trying to figure out what they're thinking. I kind of want to know too, but going upstairs with Isabella is all I can think of right now.

We slip out and kiss everyone goodnight as Clara makes thirty jokes about me not punching Isabella in the nose again.

Just as we're out of sight, Isabella's fingers intertwine with mine and she guides us toward the stairs. Isabella takes them two at a time and I do my best to contain a giggle as I try to keep up. The soft murmur of Alejandra's voice fades as we go up the stairs, the anticipation in my belly building with each step. When we finally make it to our door, we step into the room, and I press my back against the door. Leaning into it, Isabella's eyes lock on mine as she disappears into the darkness.

I've been waiting for this all day, but now that it's seconds from happening, I'm nervous and as much as I want to give in, something is holding me back. I think back on how losing Isabella felt and the fear of it happening again is too overwhelming. I can't lose her again. I've been trying for years to get her to talk to me, to get her to try to rebuild our friendship, and this could ruin it all. But the thought of walking away from this moment doesn't feel right either.

I chew on the inside of my bottom lip, thinking up a quick pro/con list. Pro: you both want this, con: you shouldn't want this. Pro: Sex with Isabella is amazing, con: sex with Isabella is amazing.

I've feel like I've been standing here for hours, and the

tallies are even. And then my mom's voice pops into my head.—a voice I would rather not pop into my head right now, but it's too late. *Listen to your gut.* I hear her say. I close my eyes and try to figure it out, but all I feel is my clit throbbing, so I decide that's close enough.

I take a big breath and let it out as I release my grip on the doorknob, following after her.

When we finally meet in the center of the room, the big windows let in moonlight, lighting Isabella from behind, making her look ethereal. All the blood in my body rushes to my head, and my heart pounds in my ears.

"Are you nervous?" Isabella asks with a wide, flirty smile.

"A little," I say as I step closer to her, trying not to look down at the floor.

Isabella steps forward, her teeth sinking into her bottom lip. "We don't have to do this, you know? We can just go to bed."

Nervously, I take another step towards her and wrap my fingers around her waist, fisting her sweater in my hands. A heated pulse tingles in my fingertips craving the warmth of her skin against mine.

"But I want to," I say, my voice shaky.

Isabella's fingers weave gently through my hair and she pulls me in closer. Her lips gently meet mine, and I melt. All the cons from earlier disappear and this feels like the only right answer.

Her fingers wander beneath the hem of my sweater, finding my skin. The contact makes my breath hitch, and she smiles against my lips. Every ounce of desire I felt at the hot springs comes roaring back as our kiss intensifies, and now there's a fierce urgency that sets my body on fire. Every cell in my body aching to feel her touch.

Her fingers trace up my torso as her thumbs move in slow circular motions until they're tracing the curve of my bra.

"Lift your arms," she says.

My hands shake slightly, but I do as I'm told, I am too turned on not to.

Isabella's hands find their way to the bottom of my shirt and she pulls it over my head until only my black lace bra is showing. A bra I was really hoping she'd see.

Isabella bites her lip and gives me a knowing smile. Like she knows I put this on just for her.

Isabella's hands come up and cup my breast. Her thumbs sweep over my hardened nipples and I suck in a breath. Her touch is too much to handle, even over the fabric. She pulls me in closer and presses her mouth against my neck. A shiver runs down my body and I let my head fall back, as Isabella kisses the top of my breast, biting and kissing her way down my chest.

My stomach flutters as desire pools below my belly button, hot and insistent.

"I've been wanting to do this all night," she murmurs, sinking her teeth gently into my breast.

"Yeah?" I say with a moan.

"Yes," she replies as I pull her close to me.

She unhooks my bra and lets it fall to the floor next to us.

"God, you have perfect tits," she says, and a blush creeps up my neck.

Isabella's hands cup my breast as her thumb and index finger pinch my nipples and I moan. I've never been a fan or nipple play but right now Isabella is driving me wild. She still knows my body so well and knows exactly what to do. I arch my back and lean into her. Craving the slight pain.

Isabella kneels, kissing her way down my torso until she's at the dip of my hips. Her hands tug at the waistband of my jeans as she unbuttons them.

"Take these off," she says as she tugs them down.

I blush even more but begin to pull my pants down my legs. I manage to free one of my feet, but the other is stuck. If this happens to me one more time this week, I will throw away all of my skinny jeans.

"Let me," Isabella says, holding back a laugh.

She tugs at the bottom of my jeans, freeing my foot. Once they are off and on the floor, Isabella's fingers trace up my leg, leaving a fiery path behind. She lifts one of my legs and rests it on her shoulder. Isabella's tongue teases the crease where my leg meets my hip. I suck in a sharp breath and tip my head back. "Fuck" I moan loudly, and Isabella suddenly stops.

I nearly whimper at the loss of her mouth on me. I look down and watch as a slow grin appears across her lips.

She presses a finger to her lips, her eyes locking onto mine. "Be a good girl," she murmurs, "and try not to let our friends know what we're up to," she says as a sly smirk tugs at the corners of her mouth. Her gaze suffocating.

I nod.

"Good girl," she says as her lips brush softly against my skin, continuing their tortuous path down my thigh. Each kiss sends a shiver through me, making it nearly impossible to hold myself up. My clit is swollen and throbbing, desperate for contact, but Isabella seems to be in no hurry.

"Please," I beg, threading my fingers through Isabella's hair and lifting my hips towards her mouth. Anticipation pooling.

She smiles against my skin as she hooks a finger through the top of my underwear, pulling them down my thighs and off my feet. Isabella grabs my hand and kisses me hard as she leads us toward the bed. She miscalculates and falls on the bed. I trip over her, falling, and we both land on the bed laughing. I get on top of her and realize she has entirely too many clothes on.

"I need you to undress," I say.

Isabella smirks and shifts around as she pulls her pants and underwear down. Her eyes never leave mine. I reach down and help her out of her sweater. And I am thankful for her never wearing a bra. When she's finally naked, I look down and take in the sight of her. The soft curve of her waist. Her lush hips. Somehow, she looks even more beautiful with nothing on, and her hair is splayed out around her. I place my legs between her thighs, and Isabella lets out a soft moan. A bolt of arousal courses through me as I feel Isabella's wetness. My mouth waters at the thought of her on my tongue.

I lean down and kiss her. I lean deeper into the kiss, hungrier. God, I want her. I want my mouth on every single part of her. The kiss was bruising, wanting, desperate. Isabella's thumb stroking the dip at the base of my throat. One of her hands hooks around me as she rolls on top of me. Her mouth leaves mine as she buries her head on my neck. Her mouth biting and sucking, kissing its way down to my core. Isabella kisses just below my belly button, kissing her way down until she's hovering just above my swollen clit. She places a light kiss, and my breath hitches.

"Isabella, please don't tease me," I groan in frustration.

She slides a finger over my warm wet center, circling my clit, flicking and rubbing.

"Tell me what you want," she says before dragging her tongue slowly from my center. Isabella's feral eyes locked onto mine.

"I want you to make me cum" I say, feeling myself blush all over.

Isabella smiles and slowly drags her tongue down my center. Her mouth closes around me as she sucks and licks. A delicious shiver coursed through my body. I press harder into her, and she licks and sucks faster. Moaning into me. She slips a finger inside me, curling around until she finds my G-spot. My pussy swells, and I feel myself wrap around her finger as she pushes harder and deeper into me.

"Fuck Isabella," I moan, tilting my head towards the ceiling, trying to be as quiet as possible.

"More," I demand, and she adds another finger, thrusting them in and out, teasing her tongue slowly. A moan escapes me again. Isabella's hands cover my mouth as she thrusts into me harder. I moan even harder, unable to keep myself quiet. So I stick my tongue out and suck her fingers into my mouth. I feel Isabella moan into me, her mouth agape. So I sucked on her fingers harder. Isabella grins up at me, her eyes blown out.

Isabella thrusts her fingers in and out of me, and I gasp as her tongue sucks at my clit harder. My hands wrap around the bed sheets. As her fingers go deeper into me I succumb to her completely.

Isabella watches me twitch until my body settles, a self-satisfied grin on her face. Once I've regained full function of my body, I pull Isabella on top of me. And flip her on her back. I sit up and straddle Isabella's hips.

"Good?" she asks looking up at me her pupils blown. A smirk on her lips.

"It was ok," I tease. But good, is an understatement. I could do this every second of every day until I die and never get enough.

"Rude," she says with a smile her breath ragged.

I lean down and kiss her. Isabella wraps her arms around my waist and pulls me in closer. A rush of desire pools at my center again and I kiss her. The kiss is bruising, wanting, desperate, and hungry. God, I want her. I want my mouth on every single part of her.

"Scoot up," I demand. Isabella smirks at me but does as she's told.

I nuzzle the side of her neck and begin kissing my way down to her core and flick my tongue against her.

"Fuck," Isabella mutters towards the ceiling.

My tongue darting between her clit and her entrance. I wrap my lips around her and slowly lick circles over her sucking harder and harder. Isabella rolls her body upwards seeking more pressure.

Isabella's fingers slide gently into my hair, curling around the strands at the nape of my neck.

I wrap around her clit harder and faster against her.

Isabella's grip tightens. Her palm presses firmly against the back of my head, pulling me closer to her body clenching tighter.

"Fuck," Isabella mumbles before shuddering. Her body going limp. I stay still for a few minutes entangled between her legs.

"Come here," Isabella murmurs, gently tugging at my waist. I settle beside her and she brings my hand to her lips, pressing a soft, kiss against my knuckles.

She doesn't say anything. She just wraps her arms around me, and I lean into the quiet warmth of this perfect moment.

20

ISABELLA

I feel the light pressure of lips on mine, and it pulls me out of sleep, slow and warm. My eyes flutter open, and I see Lily. What a perfect way to be woken up.

"Morning," she whispers, her voice still thick with sleep. Her hand gently caresses my cheek as I turn to kiss her wrist.

"Morning," I say as I lean over her and press a soft kiss on her lips before moving to kiss down her neck, a low moan leaving Lily's lips. "Sleep well?" I ask, still nuzzling my mouth and nose onto the side of her neck. My nose is still a little sore but I don't care. The smell of her skin is heaven.

"Mmm," she hums as she wraps herself around me.

Immediately, my mind plays a movie of last night. Lily cuming on my fingers, the taste of her on my tongue. My mouth goes dry. A familiar want creeps up inside me. Fuck... I want her more than ever. I had a taste, and now I'm hooked, and I'm afraid I'll never be able to get enough, which is the exact opposite of what I thought would happen. How'd I bamboozle myself into thinking I could just fuck Lily out of my system? Lust-fueled decisions can not and should not be trusted...

I trace my hand down Lily's torso. Lily shivers and her legs part.

"Fuck," I say into Lily's neck as my hand runs down her center, and I realize just how wet she is. Maybe if we do it one more time, I'll get over it. Yeah, one isn't enough, two will do the trick. For sure.

My hand moves to Lily's clit and her legs tremble. Her breath speeds up as her back arches.

"Yes," Lily moans, panting softly.

I lift my head, locking eyes with Lily, wanting to see the exact moment I make her cum.

"Please don't stop," Lily begs.

I slip two fingers inside her, and her pussy wraps around my fingers tighter and tighter. I curve my finger inside her, and just as I feel Lily is about to give in to plea-sure, a knock at the door startles us. I freeze. I blink at Lily, who reaches for a pillow and throws it on her face. A second knock follows, louder this time.

I groan and untangle myself from under her.

"Coming," I say as I grab the nearest sweater from the floor. I open the door to find a red-eyed Valeria standing in the hallway, looking like she's been awake all night. No doubt from her late-night fight with Brooke.

"Oh, uh, sorry," she mumbles, her eyes darting awkwardly over me. "Did I wake you guys?"

"No, I was just scrolling on my phone. What's up?" I say, doing my best to block Valeria from peeking inside at a very naked Lily.

"Can I ride home with you guys?" she asks, her voice small. And my heart shrivels up. I hate seeing her like this. "Brooke broke up with me last night and left. I was hoping you wouldn't mind dropping me off at home since Clara and Ale have to stay for a check-out inspection."

"Of course, yes, whatever you need," I say looking back at Lily, who is now dressed and standing behind me, nodding faster than I thought humanly possible. I stifle a laugh and turn back to Valeria.

"Thanks," she whispers.

I pull Valeria into a tight hug, hoping that somehow, it can make all the pain Brooke caused her to disappear. She leans into me, her body softening as a quiet sigh escapes her. I feel her tears on my shoulder, and I know she's finally letting herself feel it all, finally letting herself break.

"Want me to kill her?" I joke.

Valeria laughs and pulls away from the hug. "Only if you can guarantee you won't get caught."

"I don't know Lily's got me listening to a bunch of true crime. I'm sure I can figure it out."

Valeria shakes her head and smiles "I should go pack," she mumbles before kissing my cheek and walking toward her room, her steps slow and heavy.

When I close the door behind me, Lily is already in the bathroom and I can hear the water flowing. I have half a mind to go in there and shower with her, but I figure I should just start to clean up our room and pack my things.

I start organizing my bag, picking up the scattered clothes on the floor, and checking under the bed for anything that might've rolled under. I pack up most of my things, and when I'm done, I starfish on the bed, listening to the soft trickle of water in the bathroom. I close my eyes and get lost in thoughts of Lily and last night—the warmth of her touch, the taste of her, the sounds she made—it all keeps replaying in my mind in a wonderful, delicious loop.

Honestly, I thought I'd be more freaked out this morning, but I'm not. Maybe I'm still riding the post-orgasm high. I'm sure I'll find time later to overthink, overanalyze, and retreat into my keep Lily away cocoon. But right now, I'm enjoying what it's like to be outside of it.

I'm so lost in thought that I don't hear the bathroom door open or notice when Lily steps back into the room. But when I open my eyes again, Lily is holding a towel around herself, looking down at me with a smile.

"Hey," I say, looking up at her. I blink away the blur and slowly sit up, running a hand through my tangled hair.

"Hi," Lily says as she sits next to me, towel still wrapped snugly around her. She studies me quietly before letting out a big sigh. Lily shifts around, tucking a damp strand of hair behind her ear, her expression turning more serious.

"Do you think we should talk about last night?" she mumbles.

"Yeah, probably," I say, as my chest tightens.

"I just want you to know I'm not expecting anything from this. This can be just a one-night thing if that's what you want."

I blink, caught off guard. I haven't thought about what came next. "Is that what you want?" I ask.

"No, I'd like to keep doing... this... but I also don't want to risk things getting weird and you never talking to me again," she says as she intertwines her fingers in mine.

"I don't want things to get weird again either," I say, feeling the teensiest bit of relief. "I think we can try, we clearly want to keep fucking each other, so maybe having some rules would help as long as you're fine with this being insanely casual."

"Yeah, that's ok. And if something changes, we can talk about it, right?" she says, giving my hand a gentle kiss.

"They won't change on my end, but if they change on yours yeah, we can talk."

"Good," Lily says before leaning in to kiss me.

"Wait is this ok?" she asks backing out quickly.

I laugh. "Yeah, the only rule here is don't fall in love with me... and maybe let's not tell the girls. Not yet, at least. They're going to try and marry us off if they know we're sleeping together."

"No falling in love, no telling the girls," Lily repeats. "Easy enough," she chirps before standing.

I don't know what I thought would come after all this, so knowing things are good and won't get awkward is great. I'm glad Lily and I had this talk. It feels like we're finally doing things the right way. It's more than we ever managed ten years ago, and whatever's going on between us now just seems so much more stable. When the time comes to let it end in a couple of weeks, it won't be messy or dramatic. Hell, maybe we'll even be able to move on as friends. I don't know if it's because we're older or because we're actually on the same page this time, but whatever the reason, I'm glad we're here now.

I grab my bag and throw on a sweater before heading downstairs, feeling like I'm flying.

In the kitchen, Clara and Alejandra are cleaning up and cussing out Brooke for leaving a mess. Valeria is in the living room, going through every couch cushion, making sure no one leaves anything behind.

Lily comes down the stairs struggling with her bag in one hand and waving the list in the other.

"We need to check off the cabin from the list," she says, looking around at all of us. "I guess I could've done it at home, but I wanted to do it with you all."

Alejandra grins and claps her hands together. "Oh, yes! Let's do it!"

Lily hands her the list and a pen and Alejandra checks it off.

"Now all that's left is the art show and we'll officially be done," Alejandra squeals as she bounces in a circle.

We all say bye to each other and promise to text the group chat as soon as we each make it home. Valeria, Lily, and I pile into my car and start the three-hour drive back. With Valeria in the car, the ride back is quiet as she sits in the backseat, lost in thought, earbuds in, staring out the window.

Halfway through the drive, Lily and Valeria fall asleep, leaving me alone in my thoughts. And I think about Lily and me ten years ago. Still wondering what made Lily disappear on me. Part of me wants to know, but the other part doesn't care anymore. It feels like a lifetime ago, and honestly, it's not like it changes anything now. Lily and I are fine. More than fine, and whatever happened back then doesn't seem to matter as much anymore.

I pull into Valeria's driveway and park, turning to give her a gentle shake to wake her up.

"Are we here?" she asks, rubbing the side of her neck as she stirs awake.

"Yeah."

"Thanks for the ride."

"Of course," I reply.

"If you need anything, text me, okay?" Lily adds.

"Thank you both," Valeria says, leaning over to give us both a quick kiss on the cheek before she steps out of the car.

Lily and I watch her go, making sure she makes it inside safely. Brooke's car noticeably missing from the driveway.

I pull away from Valeria's house and head toward Lily's.

"Will you come over later?" I ask.

Her lips curl up slightly. "I'm only going home 'cause you're taking me," she replies as her fingers fiddle nervously with the hem of her sleeve.

"Is that so?" I joke. "Well... in that case," I say, my voice low and playful, "I'll just take you to my place instead."

She looks at me, a small, shy smile tugging at the corners of her lips.

"If you insist," she jokes before leaning over to give me a quick peck.

Once we make it to my house, we step inside and when I flick on the lights, I immediately regret bringing Lily over. My house is a mess. Papers are scattered across the coffee table, curling at the edges from the coffee mugs I've left sitting on top of them. There are paintbrushes all over the place, some crusted with dried paint, I must have left some paint tubes half-open because paint oozed out onto the floor.

"I promise it isn't always this messy in here," I lie. It almost always is, except for the rare moments when I manage to tidy up. But even when I do, it doesn't last very long.

"It's not even that bad," Lily says, walking in past me. "I'll help you clean up," she says.

"Thanks, but you don't have to," I say quickly, waving her off. "I just hired someone to help me clean. She should be here in a few days. I should probably clean up the paint on the floor before it dries though." I say as I head into the kitchen to grab some paper towels.

"Want some wine?" I ask, hoping to distract her.

"Yes, please," she says.

I grab a bottle of red from the pantry and pour us each a

glass. I tuck the paper towel roll under my arm and head back into the living room. I hand Lily one of the glasses and then drop down onto my knees to tackle the paint on the floor.

"Thanks," she says, taking the glass and sitting down on the couch nearby.

Thankfully, the paint is coming off pretty easily.

From the corner of my eye, I can see Lily's eyes have landed on a half-finished canvas propped up in the corner of the living room. It's a painting of two women kissing— intimate, raw. Only one of the women is fully painted, her face detailed, soft, and vulnerable. And now, with Lily here next to it, I can't ignore the uncomfortable realization that the woman I've finished painting kind of looks like her.

My stomach drops to hell, and I silently pray to every God I can think of that she won't notice. I try to ignore the nervousness in my chest, hoping the dim lighting hides the slight flush creeping up my neck. I need to stop doing this...

"This is really beautiful," Lily says as she takes a sip of her wine.

"Thanks," I reply, forcing a smile, wanting to steer the conversation anywhere but here. "It's not finished yet."

She scoots closer to the painting, her head tilting slightly as she studies it. My heart pounds in my chest as I wait for her to make the connection. But she doesn't, and if she does, she doesn't say anything, which is just fine with me.

"Well, it looks great," she says before turning to look at another half-finished painting. I let out a big breath before taking a massive gulp of wine.

"Thanks," I manage to say.

"So, what's on the agenda?" she says.

"How do you feel about frozen pizza and a movie?"

"Sounds perfect."

As I clean the mess of paint on the floor, I make Lily find us a movie. She scrolls through the endless sea of streaming apps, our choices ranging from horror, overhyped dramas, and even a documentary about competitive butter sculpting. Finally, She settles on a rom-com that boasts a sparkling 30% approval rating.

When I'm finally done scraping the paint off my floors, we make our way to the kitchen, and I rummage through the freezer. Lily hops up onto the counter, her legs swinging slightly.

I pull out a pepperoni pizza, still encased in its frosty plastic cocoon. I pop it in the oven and set the timer for twenty minutes. I turn around and lean against the counter, facing her, mirroring her posture. She sits there, looking way too comfortable, sipping her wine with a cute little grin.

"Come here," she says.

I push off the counter and stand between her legs. She shifts closer to the edge of the counter and wraps her legs around my waist, my heart races, and my breath catches as she locks her feet behind me, and before I can catch the breath I just lost, she leans in to kiss me. Her lips brush against mine softly, and already I feel a pulse throbbing between my legs. I grip her thighs to steady myself as our kiss intensifies. The taste of wine on her lips is intoxicating, making me want to live on the tip of her tongue forever.

I instinctively pull away, my mind shouting danger, but it isn't, not anymore, there are rules, and I can lose control and fuck her on the counter if I want to. And I do, God, I really fucking do. I quickly scan the counter, making sure there's nothing I need to move out of the way, and for the first time—probably ever—there's nothing. *Bless.*

I lean in to kiss her again my hands already untying the string of her sweatpants.

Lily smiles against my lips before lying down. I pull her sweats down her thighs, accidentally pulling her underwear down with it. She lets out a yelp as her skin touches the cold of the counter and resist the urge to apologize for the counter being cold.

I climb on top of her, burying my mouth in her neck. Lily's hands find their way inside my sweater. Her hands move up my torso until they cup around my breast.

"You're not wearing a bra?" Lily asks, her voice breathy.

"I never do," I say before crossing my arms over my sweater and pulling it off. I accidentally hit the pot rack that's hanging on the ceiling above me and we both freeze bracing for impact. But when nothing falls Lily's fingers start to trace over the soft of my stomach, her thumb brushes over the top of my shorts making my skin tingle as she pulls them down my legs.

I reach down to the hem of Lily's sweatshirt and pull it off her head, tossing it onto the floor. A lacey white bra greets me, and my mouth waters. Lily's dark nipples are showing through, and suddenly, being shirtless isn't enough. I need her completely naked.

I hook my finger on one of Lily's bra straps and pull it. Hearing it snap back against her skin. "Take it off."

Lily grins up at me and unhooks her bra, pulling it down her arms.

I kiss my way down from her neck down to her nipples and suck one of them into my mouth. Lily moans as her back arches, pushing me further into her.

I run two fingers down Lily's center. "You're dripping," I say as I drag my lips up Lily's throat.

I let my thumb strum around Lily's swollen clit. Hearing her whimper every time I move my thumb away.

Lily grabs my hand and moves it where she needs it, but I move it back not wanting her to cum yet.

"Please, Isabella."

"Please, what?" I grin at her.

Lily groans in frustration, letting go of my hand and running her own below her belly button. I stop her and hear a growl come from Lily's throat.

"Just tell me what you want," I say, kissing my way down her inner thigh.

"Touch me," Lily says, arching herself into me.

I wrap my mouth around her clit, kissing and licking in and out of Lily's center.

"Yes, Isabella" Lily pants.

And the way my name sounds in her mouth drives me wild.

I slide two fingers inside her. Lily's walls instantly clutching around me. Her thighs tremble as she lifts her hips pushing against my hand, matching my rhythm. Her clit swells on my tongue. Until Lily finally breaks, and her legs tighten around my head.

Fuck, the taste of her on my tongue is my new favorite thing.

An alarm beeps loudly above us, startling me. I sit up too fast and hit my head on the pot rack.

"Fuck," I whisper as I rub the back of my head.

"Something's burning," Lily says as she props herself up on her elbows.

I look around and see smoke coming out of the oven. I jump off of counter and shout. "No, no, no."

When I pull the pizza out, it's completely charred. I accidentally set it to broil instead of bake.

Why am I like this?

21

LILY

I tiptoe across Isabella's floor, my bare feet brushing against the cool wood as I make my way to the kitchen.

Isabella fell asleep a few hours ago. But I haven't been able to get my mind to shut off and I don't know why. I was fine all night, we had amazing sex on the kitchen island, and then we ordered Chinese food, and watched two scary movies. But I've been restless since we got in bed thinking of everything that's happened with Isabella and me since I walked in on her and Myra.

I lean against the kitchen counter, letting the quiet of the night calm my racing thoughts. I feel overwhelmed and crazy—crazy for still wanting someone who hurt me, for still wanting her ten years after. I don't know what made me think I could do this casually. We're twenty-four hours into it, and it's already more than I can handle. I want to be with Isabella. The thought of all this ending makes my chest tighten, and the air in my lungs feels dense and heavy. Everything about her feels so right.

I can't do this. I can't lie to myself or her. I need to talk to her, to tell her we can't do this anymore because I already want—no, need—more. But the thought of her not wanting the same makes me want to just let it play on to keep this going until Isabella changes her mind and tells me or until she breaks my heart without even knowing.

I stand there, lost in thought, when I hear the soft padding of footsteps behind me. I turn to find Isabella, her hair tousled, her face sleepy. She pauses in the doorway, her eyes meeting mine.

"Couldn't sleep?" she asks quietly, her voice soft and drowsy.

I shake my head, managing a small smile. "Just needed some water."

Isabella crosses the room and comes up beside me, wrapping her arms around my waist. Pulling me into a soft kiss. The warmth of her touch easing the tension all over my body.

"Come back to bed," she whispers, nuzzling her nose into my neck, sending a shiver down my body.

Without hesitation, I follow her lead. We walk to the bedroom, the soft rustle of sheets filling the quiet as we settle beneath them again. Isabella curls up next to me, her head resting on my chest, her breath warm and steady against my skin. This—this intimacy—is everything I've ever wanted and in a few hours, I might never have it again.

I wrap my arms around her, pulling her closer, trying to anchor her here to keep her from slipping through my fingers. I close my eyes tightly, willing myself to please let this be enough, but I can't... whatever this is, won't ever be enough. And I was an idiot to think it would be. The closeness of her, the way her body molds to mine so easily, makes my heart ache. What if I lose this? I try not to think about it, and instead, focus on the weight of her head on my chest. But doubts linger just on the edges of my mind, like shadows waiting for a chance to creep back in. But at this moment, with Isabella in my arms, I let myself believe maybe this isn't just temporary.

———— ♥ ♥ ♥ ————

When I wake up again, I'm wrapped up in Isabella's arms and the soft comfort of her sheets. For a moment, I just lie there, taking in my surroundings. Her bedroom is quiet. All I hear is the gentle creak of her house settling in. But the quiet doesn't last very long. Every thought I ignored last night starts creeping back in, strangling my brain, and it feels like they're cutting off all my air supply. I need to move. To go somewhere else. I need coffee, so I carefully slide out of bed, making sure I don't wake Isabella.

I grab all my clothes, putting them on as I head toward my car. Grabbing Isabella's keys before stepping outside, and that's when I realize my car isn't here. *Shoot.* I look down at Isabella's keys and decide to take her car—a decision I probably wouldn't make any other time, but I need to get away from here right now. I get in her car and lean my forehead against the steering wheel. Trying to figure out why my heart insists on complicating whatever good thing I've managed to build with Isabella, but my brain doesn't think of a thing, not a single word, because it smells like her in here and it feels like a hug.

My heart tightens, and my sinuses sting as tears start gathering in my eyes. I shake my head, sigh, and put Isabella's car in reverse, backing out of her driveway. I need to go. I need to put some distance even if it's just a few minutes.

22

ISABELLA

S he's gone... When I woke up this morning, I was expecting to find Lily next to me—but instead, I found cold, empty sheets. The pillow beside me still had the faintest outline of her head. Stupidly, the first thing I did when I didn't see her was scan the room, hoping I'd spot her, but she was nowhere to be found. Her clothes, her shoes—everything, gone.

Now, here I am, staring at the empty spot on my bed where she's supposed to be, wondering why the fuck I let myself believe this time would be any different. I should've seen it coming. It's her thing, after all, to vanish—no message, no note, no explanation. I hate that her being gone is messing with me this much. Myra came and went for months, and I didn't care. Hell, I was almost glad when I woke up to her gone. But this is different... It's Lily... And as much as I wish her being gone didn't trigger me, all I can think about is the first time she left me. And how much it fucked me up. The day she left, something in me cracked, and no matter how much time passes, that crack's still there.

I drag myself out of bed and head towards the bathroom. The cold splash of water doesn't exactly do wonders for my mood, but at least it wakes me up enough to shuffle into the living room.

I slump onto the couch, the weight of Lily's absence pressing down on me. This isn't how it's supposed to be. This isn't how I work. This doesn't feel casual, and casual is what it needs to be.

I throw on a random show and just as I start to zone out, the sound of the door unlocking catches my attention. My heart races, and I sit up, confused, thinking someone might be breaking in. But then I see her—Lily—walking in, holding two cups of coffee in her hands. And I wish it didn't, but hope creeps back in—that sneaky bitch...

"Morning," she says with a sheepish grin. "I woke up early and... I hope it's okay, but I took your car. Thought you could use some coffee."

I blink at her, still processing the fact that she's here. She steps over to the couch and hands me one of the cups, her warm smile cutting through some of the heaviness in my chest.

"Thanks," I say, managing a small smile as I take the coffee from her.

She sits down beside me, pulling her legs up onto the couch. "You okay?" she asks softly, her eyes studying me.

"Yeah," I murmur, taking a sip of the coffee she brought me. It's a honey lavender latte, and I can't help the way my heart flutters. She remembered my order—the same one I got the morning after the party at Alejandra and Claras. "I just... wasn't expecting you to come back."

Her brows lift slightly, and she tilts her head. "You thought I'd leave without saying goodbye?"

"Yeah, kinda," I admit with a laugh, but it comes out a little shaky.

"Ouch. No faith in me, huh?" she says as she nudges my arm.

I shrug as I rub my finger along the edge of the coffee lid. "History isn't exactly on your side," I say.

"Fair enough," she says quietly as she takes a sip of her coffee.

We sit in silence, sipping our drinks. After a few minutes, Lily sets her cup down and turns to me, "I want to talk to you about something," she says, her voice trembling slightly. "It's about us."

"Oh?" I say confused. "What about us?"

She takes a deep breath, looking a little nervous. "Well, I don't think this casual thing is going to work for me,"

"Oh?" I say, feeling a little disappointed. "Why?"

"Because I don't think I can do casual with you, I know. I said I could, but I think I somehow deluded myself into thinking that when, deep down, I knew I couldn't."

I stare at her, shocked. Not sure what to say or what to think.

"I know we never really talked about what happened between us, and I don't know if we can fix it now, but I want to try because I think we have the chance to have something good. Something we should have always had."

"Okay," I say, sitting up. "Talk."

I've been ignoring this conversation for far too long, and I can't keep doing that. Not when I kind of agree that Lily and I are on the verge of something good.

"I don't know where to start," Lily says.

"Why don't you start by telling me why you left," I manage to say calmly, but my chest is already tightening.

"Because you lied to me," Lily says as she nervously picks at a hangnail on her thumb.

I blink, thrown off for a second, trying to figure out what

she could possibly be talking about, but I come up with nothing. "What the fuck are you talking about? When did I lie to you?" I say defensively because how dare she blame me?

"Oh, come on Isabella, I overheard you and Valeria talking by the bleachers the day before your art show. That's why I wasn't there," she says, and I can see the glimmer of tears threatening to spill from her eyes.

"What?" Is all I manage to say. Because what she's saying makes no fucking sense. My mind racing as I try to piece together that conversation with Valeria.

"I thought we were building something real," she says as she shakes her head slowly, her knee bouncing up and down.

"Lily, I don't know what you're talking about," I say, trying to keep my voice steady, but I want to pull my hair out.

"You told Valeria you wanted to give Resy another shot because you saw her, and you felt conflicted about your feelings for her." Lily's face softens as she drops her head, her eyes fixed on the same hangnail she was messing with earlier. "You lied when you told me you were over her. Was I just a distraction while you figured out how to get back with her?" she says as she pulls the hangnail. She winces, and blood starts rushing out.

"Yeah, I ran into Resy at a club with Clara, and yeah, I mentioned it to Valeria—but I never said I wanted to get back with her," I say, trying to keep my voice steady, but I want to scream, cry, laugh because this is so fucking stupid. "I think you misunderstood what you overheard," I say, as all the empathy and understanding I was willing to give this conversation leaves my body.

"What?" Lily says, her voice almost a whisper as her

brows knit together, and her confusion only annoys me more. I take a deep breath, trying to calm myself so I can explain this clearly.

"Look, that day, Valeria was talking about getting back to this girl she'd been hooking up with all summer. She'd stopped seeing her because Valeria was starting to like her, but this girl didn't want to commit, she wanted to keep fucking around with other people, but she kept texting Valeria to meet up, telling her maybe she'd change her mind to stick around and to just give her time to grow out of her hoe phase until she was ready to commit to her but that she never would if she didn't stick it out 'cause then that meant she didn't like her enough, it was all a fucking mess and Vale didn't know what to do. So I told her the same thing you told me when I was thinking about going back to Resy— how dumb I'd look if I went back to her just because I was worried I'd missed out on something. And then I asked her what she'd tell me if I told her I saw Resy and wanted to be with her again, you know, like when you realize something's not good for you, but you still kinda want it? I was just trying to talk Valeria out of meeting up with this girl again by using my mess with Resy as an example. I wasn't going back to her, Lily. I loved you. I wanted to be with you," I say, my voice cracking. "I had already started planning out how we could make long-distance work. I mapped out the drive from Seattle to Portland and figured out when I could visit. Hell, I even looked into bus fares for a bus that goes back and forth between the two cities. I was crazy about you." I say as I crack my knuckles. It's not something I usually do, but the tension is all over my body, and I need a release.

I pause for a second, making sure she hears me. "In that very same conversation, I even told Valeria about this amazing girl I was dating, someone I didn't think I deserved but was happy with. That was you. You, Lily. But maybe you didn't hear that." I watch her shoulders tense, and before I can stop myself, I add, "You clearly didn't eavesdrop properly." I let out a small, nervous laugh thinking it might ease the tension but Lily gives me a flat stare—maybe now isn't the time for a joke.

I quickly clear my throat, trying to shift the tone. "You have to believe me. I loved you, Lily. You were everything to me." But as soon as the words leave my mouth, I can see the doubt in her eyes. It's like she's trying to figure out how what I'm saying now fits into what she thought she knew.

"I..." she whispers, her voice trembling. "I thought you'd made your choice, and I knew hearing you say you couldn't be with me would break me even further, so I didn't want to give you the chance to hurt me, so I left before you could. I should have talked to you about what I heard... I'm sorry."

"Yeah, you should have," I say with a bit more bite than I mean to. "We could have made it work."

"I don't know what to say," Lily says, her gaze drifting away "Do you think we still could?" she asks hesitantly.

I stare at her, conflicted. Part of me wants to jump in with her, to believe that we could pick up the pieces and rebuild something from the wreckage of what we once had I mean, we're halfway there. But the other part of me—the part that has been sitting in pain and anger for the past decade—replays every painful memory and tells me to stay away. And right now, that's the part that's right.

"Lily, I've spent ten fucking years waiting to hear what the hell went so horribly wrong between us that you felt you had to disappear and now you're telling me it's because you misheard a conversation and didn't bother to talk to me? How could I ever be with you if that's your default?" I'm screaming at this point and I don't know how to rein my anger in.

"Isabella, I was eighteen! And how can you not get it? You went back to Resy every single chance you got, no matter how much time had passed since you broke up, even if you were seeing someone else. You left three girls for Resy! How the hell was I supposed to know you wouldn't do the same to me when that was always *your* default? I was protecting myself from you."

I lose my breath all at once and it feels like I just got kicked in the stomach. Fuck... When she lays it out like that it makes perfect fucking sense. And I hate it because I don't want it to.

I run a hand through my hair. "Look Lily, you're right, I can't say I would have trusted me either, but we were best friends. You knew you could talk to me, that's why we worked so fucking well. Because we trusted each other with everything."

"Isabella, you weren't just my best friend anymore, you were someone I was in love with, I couldn't just turn to you as friends anymore, my heart was too deep into it."

"Yeah, but you shouldn't have just walked away without a word either."

"I know," she whispers as she reaches for my hand her touch is gentle and hesitant, like she's waiting for me to pull away. But I don't. Instead, I sigh and run my free hand through my hair. "That will forever be the biggest mistake of my life."

I look up at her, trying to choose my words carefully, "I like you, Lily. I'm being honest I don't think I ever stopped, but no matter how much I want to, I can't just gloss over what happened. You left me hanging, no explanation, nothing—for ten years. I know you thought you had a good reason, and now that I know why, I can almost understand it. But it's fucked with me for so long, I think maybe it always will, and I don't think that's fair to you or me. When I woke up this morning, and you weren't in bed, my first thought was, 'Oh great, she's going to ghost me again.' And I don't want to feel like that every time you need to rush out of bed and don't say goodbye. I want to give whatever this is a chance, I do, but... I'm scared to trust you, and I don't think I can offer you any more than I already am."

"I know I messed up, and I'm sorry," she says, her voice soft, almost pleading. "This whole time, I thought you were in the wrong, but it was me. And I know there isn't anything I can do to fix the damage I caused, but I want to try because I want to be with you."

"Lily, you're throwing too much at me right now," I say, running a hand through my hair again. The weight of everything she's saying is starting to pile up, and I'm not sure how to carry it all at once. "I just... I don't know right now, Lily. This whole casual, amazing sex, no-strings-attached thing worked so well because I didn't have to figure out my feelings for you. I could just enjoy being with you."

"We don't have to figure it all out right now," she says quietly. "I'm not asking us to go back to how things used to be. I just want a chance to show you that you can trust me now—that I'm not the same impulsive eighteen-year-old who left without talking to you. I know I broke your trust, and I'm really sorry, but I can earn it back."

I want so badly to let go of the fear and just let it happen. Let myself be consumed by Lily the way I had been when we were teenagers—wild and all-in, without a second thought. To believe everything will fall into place as long as we are together. But I can't, Lily's hurt me too much.

"I don't have an answer for you right now," I finally say,

my voice barely above a whisper. "I need some time. Is that okay?"

Lily's eyes glass over, and her lip quivers. "Of course," she says as she brings my hands to her lips, pressing a kiss to my knuckles.

A tear lands on my hand, and I want so badly to bring her close and soothe the pain she's feeling, but I don't... because right now, I need to take care of myself.

"I'll go," she says as she wipes away her tears, and she stands, her hands slipping from mine, leaving behind the warmth of her touch.

I nod, unable to say a word as I watch her walk out the door.

I spent months replaying every moment Lily and I shared, trying to figure out where I went wrong, and what I had done to make Lily vanish. And now that I know... I'm even more angry because it wasn't anything I did. I'm mad at Lily for breaking my heart into pieces over nothing, and I'm mad at myself for wanting to put it back together just to hand it back over.

23

LILY

I stare out at the quiet street, wishing—begging—for something to distract me from the guilt that tightens with every breath.

The soft rustle of leaves in the breeze barely registers as yesterday's conversation plays in my head on an endless loop, like one of those scratchy old vinyl records I can't stop from spinning, no matter how badly I want to. For ten years, I took a half-heard conversation and twisted it into this grand betrayal, building it up in my mind until I had convinced myself she wanted to leave me because I wasn't good enough, our friendship didn't mean as much to her, and she regretted everything that happened between us that summer and worse yet, that she didn't love me the way I loved her. But yesterday, she told me that wasn't the case, that she had loved me, that she had wanted to be with me. The moment those words left her mouth, regret settled even deeper in my chest.

Each moment is sharper and more vivid as if my brain is determined to make sure I don't miss a single detail of my massive screw-up. I'd been too wrapped up in my insecurities and too quick to jump to conclusions. I blew it over nothing.

I rub my forehead, feeling the dull throb of tension creeping in right behind my eyes. My eyes start to sting as tears well up and blur my vision, but I don't let them fall. I can't even figure out if I deserve to cry—because, really, how did I manage to mess things up so badly?

The porch creaks softly as I shift my weight, my legs stiff from sitting in the same position for hours. I set the empty coffee mug down next to the thermos. The world is waking up—birds chirping in the trees, a neighbor's car sputtering to life—but I'm stuck, watching the same stretch of sky brighten.

My mom's house sits quiet and dark across the way, her windows like blank eyes staring back at me. I've been waiting for a sign—a light flickering on, her shadow passing by—anything to tell me she's awake. Anything to give me an excuse to go to her and fold myself into her. But it's a little past 7 a.m., and there's still nothing. Finally, I give up on waiting and text her.

> Lily 7:15 a.m.: Hey, are you home?

> Mom 7:16 a.m.: Hi honey, yes! In the front garden, come.

I walk down the narrow driveway from my cottage to the front yard, the crunch of gravel under my boots calming me just a little. The front yard is neatly trimmed. Climbing vines draping over the porch, their tendrils weaving around the railing, their colors bursting forth in a riot of reds, yellows, and purples, all thanks to my mom's "let nature do its thing" philosophy.

I turn the corner expecting to find her lost in her

garden, her hands covered in soil, humming softly to herself, but instead, I find her sitting on the front porch drinking tea.

"Morning," I call out. She looks up, her face lighting up with that easy smile she always wears when she sees me.

"Hi honey!" she says, waving me over.

I walk over, pulling her into a hug, the scent of fresh earth and flowers clinging to her clothes. It's a smell that always feels like home. I cling to her letting the comfort of being in her arms wash over me. This won't fix anything, but right now, being here with her is exactly what I need.

"I thought, you'd be gardening," I say.

"I'm just about to get started, but I needed some tea first," she says, setting her tea down on the small table beside her. "You want to help me out for a bit?"

"It's freezing out," I reply, shoving my hands into my pockets. Hoping that's enough to signal I don't want to. She chuckles and hands me a pair of gloves.

"Fine," I sigh and grab them. "What do you need me to do?"

She tilts her head toward a patch of empty beds near the edge of the yard. "Let's start clearing out the dead stuff or anything that looks like it's about to die."

We work side by side, pulling up brittle stems and dry leaves. We don't talk much. Mom occasionally points out which flowers bloomed better than expected or laughs at how some stubborn plant refuses to behave. There's something calming about working in the dirt, just like when I was a kid. It's grounding, literally and figuratively.

The sun climbs higher as we move from one flower bed to the next. After a few hours, in the sun Mom finally stands up.

"I think that's enough for today," she says and I get up

so quickly I make myself dizzy. "Why don't we go inside and get something to eat?" Mom laughs as she watches me lean on the flower bed.

I nod, grateful to be done. My forearms are starting to burn and my stomach is growling.

We wash up and make sandwiches in the kitchen.

"So, what's going on bug?" Mom asks, her voice gentle. "You've been awfully quiet today. Something on your mind?"

I stare down at my sandwich, my appetite fading. I know I can't keep it to myself much longer, not here with her, where everything's safe.

"I messed up, Mom," I say, picking at the lettuce peaking through the side of my sandwich.

"With?" She asks as she takes a bite of her sandwich.

"With Isabella."

She raises her eyebrows but doesn't say anything she just waits for me to continue. That's how she's always been—patient, never pushing, allowing me the space I need.

I take a deep breath and start telling her everything— our short-lived relationship, the years of misunderstanding, our conversation yesterday morning, the heavy cloak of regret I've been dragging around. I tell her how I let my insecurities take control, how I wasn't there for Isabella when she needed me the most, and how I'm not sure if I can ever fix what I've broken. Tears roll down my face as she rubs my back. When I finish, I feel drained.

Mom sits quietly, her hands wrapped around me as she processes everything I just told her.

"You know, honey," she begins. "We all mess up. It's part of being human. But the real question is—what are you going to do about it?"

"I don't even know where to start," I say, fighting through the tears that won't stop coming.

"Let her process everything in her own time and give her space. She will reach out when she's ready. But more importantly, honey, you need to figure out how to forgive yourself."

"Forgive myself?" I say, looking up at her like she's just said the most ridiculous thing I've ever heard. Because it sounds like it, how do I forgive myself for being an idiot when I don't think I deserve it?

She nods. "If you want to fix things with Isabella, you have to start by forgiving yourself for the past. Holding onto guilt won't help either of you."

I nod slowly, letting the idea settle in my mind, but the thought sounds crazy.

"You know, it's like gardening," she says. "You can't rush the flowers to bloom. They need time, patience, care, and a lot of love. And even after they've bloomed, you need to tend to them, make sure they get what they need to thrive."

I chuckle softly, shaking my head because, of course, her analogy kind of makes sense. And, of course, it's about gardening. "Thanks, Mom."

She squeezes me closer and kisses the side of my head.

"You guys will be okay. Just give her time."

I nod, trying to believe it's true. I need to believe it's true. The weight in my chest feels a little lighter, like I can finally take a full breath.

We finish our sandwiches, and I help her with the dishes.

"Thanks for the sandwich and for talking to me. I love you," I say, leaning down to give her cheek a peck.

"Of course, honey. I'm here whenever you need me."

"Do you want to do some clipping with me?"

I laugh. "No. I should probably head home and do some work."

"Alright, then," she says as she grabs her gardening sheers.

I walk out the door and head back to my office. I'm not feeling that much better, but it's enough to try to get some work done. There's nothing I can do about Isabella now. I told her everything I could. I apologized, and now I'm going to give her space. The ball is absolutely in her court. All I can do now is make sure I focus on what I can control. My book.

I sent my editor my manuscript last week and have been chipping away at the edits while also querying literary agents. So far, I think I've sent out about fifty queries. Most of them have either been rejected or are still sitting in the queue, buried under thousands of other amazing stories. I thought the process would be easier, honestly. I've published seven books already, and I'm working on my eight...why am I such a hard sell?

Impostor syndrome is hitting hard lately. Maybe lesbian fantasy is just not what I should be writing...

I open my laptop and go through all my emails—I have four, one I've had since I was eight that I refuse to close because it's still connected to my old Myspace account, the second is my trash email, the one I use to subscribe to things and will probably never read, the third is my adult email, where my bills and anything important goes to, and the fourth is my author email where all my book orders and communications with my editor go—I've been sending my queries out through my author email, so I keep a close eye on the last one. But as expected, I don't have a single thing.

I guess no new emails are better than rejection emails.

I check my spam, and that's when I see it... I have an email from a literary agent named Natalie.

My hands start to shake, and my heart starts to beat like crazy as I open it and read it.

Subject: Excited about your work

Dear Lily,

I hope this email finds you well! I recently had the pleasure of reading the first three chapters of your new book, and I must tell you— I'm hooked. Your storytelling is captivating, and your voice is fresh and compelling.

To be honest, I'm already a fan of your work; I've read some of your earlier books and was thrilled to see your query land in my inbox. It's not often I come across an author whose work resonates with me this strongly.

I would love to discuss your manuscript and your career further. I'm going to be in Portland in a couple of days, and if you're available, I'd be thrilled to meet in person. I think we could make a fantastic team and take your work to the next level.

If you're interested please send me your first six chapters and let me know when might be convenient for you to meet. I'm flexible and happy to adjust my schedule to accommodate yours.

Looking forward to hearing from you soon!

Warm regards,

Natalie Black
Literary Agent
Harbor Light Literary Agency
natblack@harborlight.co | 555-555-5555

I read the email about ten times making sure I read it right. This is exactly what I've been waiting for.

I email her back immediately, letting her know I can be in Portland tomorrow if need be.

After some back and forth, we agree to meet on Thursday, which gives me just enough time to prepare. Today and tomorrow, I'll dive into some research about her agency and polish my manuscript before sending it to her. I'll drive up on Thursday and drive back down on Friday just in time for Isabella's exhibit!

Holy crap... I can't believe this is happening!

24

ISABELLA

I was supposed to go to my office yesterday since I was out Monday, but I just couldn't focus on much, so I spent the majority of the day working on the centerpiece for the installation and spent the rest of the day trying to figure out what to do about Lily.

This whole thing with her has completely fucked up my schedule these past few days, but today, I absolutely can't let myself get sucked in. Clarke flies in later to start working on her part of the installation, and I still have a few paintings to finish up. I push myself off the couch, finish the rest of my coffee, and drag myself to the bathroom. There's too much to do, and not enough time to lie around thinking about Lily.

Once I've showered, tamed my hair, and dried off, I head to my closet and throw on dark jeans, a simple black button-up, and some white and yellow tennis shoes. I grab my phone, jump in my car, and head towards the gallery.

———— ♥ ♥ ♥ ————

While I wait for Clarke, I head to the back room and grab a few older pieces I want to showcase during the installation, hoping they will sell. Once I've picked them, I set them aside and grab some paint to finish anything I might want to change. As I work on that, my phone pings. I grab it and it's Clarke—right on time. When I open the door, Clarke's arms are filled with bags, grinning from ear to ear.

"Hey! I made it!" she shouts, letting her bags drop to the floor as she pulls me into a hug.

"Welcome! I'm so glad you're here," I reply, hugging her back tightly. "Come inside—it's chilly out here." I grab one of her bags from the floor and step back, leading her through the door.

Her eyes go wide as she looks around the gallery. "Dude, this is amazing," she says, turning in place. "I love how you've set everything up."

"Thanks," I say with a smile. Trying to see what she sees. I've gotten so used to the gallery that sometimes it loses its magic. But when I look around now, I'm reminded of how lucky I am. And how crazy this all is. There's a whole store dedicated to me and my art. It's not grand by any means, but it's mine.

"Where should I put these down?" Clark asks as she adjusts the strap on her bag.

"Here, let's put your bags down over here, and I'll show you where we're setting up."

Clark nods, dropping her bags next to the front desk before falling into step behind me.

"Okay, this is where you'll set up," I say, pointing to an empty spot near the gallery's front window. People won't be able to see the installation from the outside, but you'll have a great view of the crowd, and according to Sarah, that's what'll make people want to walk inside.

"Alright, well, I'll start getting everything out of my bag and I'll start to set it up. It's almost done. I just need to put it back together and solder a few pieces," She says.

"Perfect."

Her centerpiece is an intricately designed anatomical heart sculpture made of twisted metal and glass. The shape is natural and flowing, with the curves of the heart and veins wrapped in a way that looks both delicate and strong. When I asked her about it she said it's meant to represent the fragile but strong nature of love. The glass panels are tinted soft pinks, purples, and oranges.

Around the sculpture, I set up a series of my paintings. Some are abstract paintings of women hugging—some are more cubism than abstract—and I also included a few of the realism female body paintings I tend to keep to myself. I'm a little nervous about putting those out because I've never showcased my realism paintings before, and even though my paintings almost always have some sapphic aspect to them, I'm worried these will feel too in people's faces. But I can't back out now, so they're going up whether I like it or not.

For a little extra touch, Clarke and I decide to string up tiny twinkling lights through the sculpture and paintings. So when the lights are dimmed, the whole installation takes on this soft glow that makes it feel like something out of a dream.

As we work, I focus on the way the light plays off everything, adjusting each piece to make sure it all flows together. This installation is meant to capture the beauty, strength, and tenderness of sapphic love. Getting lost in the process and watching it all come together is such a good distraction, a way for me to channel everything I'm feeling into something beautiful and meaningful. I let my mind drift away, focusing on the textures, the colors, and the way each element fits together.

We've been working for hours, so Clarke and I decide it's time to rest.

I pull a hotel key from my back pocket and hand it to her. "Here's a key to your hotel room up the street. Go rest, we can pick this back up tomorrow."

"Thank you! That's perfect," she says as she takes the key.

"Do you want me to show you where it is?"

"Nah, thanks. Your assistant sent me the deets. I already looked it up."

"Alright then, see you tomorrow."

Clarke grabs her bags and heads out. I'm about to follow her out the door when I realize I didn't grab the painting I need to work on. I head back to my office, grab the painting, and head to the supply room to grab some extra paint tubes and brushes since most of the ones I had at home dried up when I went to the cabin.

The supply room is a cluttered treasure trove of old canvases, forgotten projects, and art supplies. I push aside a stack of boxes trying to find the box with all the new brush sets when I catch sight of a partially covered canvas leaning against the wall. I pull off the dusty sheet and uncover an old painting—one I haven't seen in years. It's of Lily, asleep, with this soft smile on her lips. I can picture the nights I worked on it so clearly. Lily and I were having sleepovers almost every night the summer before college, trying to squeeze in time before we'd be apart.

I trace my fingers lightly over the surface of the painting, feeling the texture of the brushstrokes beneath my skin. Remembering the hours I spent pouring my heart into this.

Lily always fell asleep first, and on those nights when I

couldn't sleep, I'd stay up and paint her. I was planning to give it to her as a goodbye gift, but I never got the chance. I tried throwing it out a few times, but I could never bring myself to do it, so when I opened the gallery, I hid it back here, hoping I'd never find it again.

I look at the painting, and a wave of nostalgia hits me. It's like staring at a snapshot of my past self—the Isabella who painted this was hopelessly, madly in love with Lily. A reminder that I'm back to square one, caught in the same dizzying mix of hope and love.

I can almost hear my teenage self sighing dramatically, wondering if I'll ever escape the emotional rollercoaster that comes with loving Lily. Because even if I can't admit it to her... I love her, I think I always have, but loving her isn't enough. She destroyed so much of me and now I can't see past it.

Not every love story has a happy ending and maybe ours is one of those. Still, there's a part of me that wants to reach through time and touch that version of myself, the one with the soft smile and open heart, and let her take over because I don't think I'll ever be the same person who painted this—wide-eyed, hopeful, willing to give my heart without hesitation.

I tuck the painting back where I found it, covering it with the dusty sheet. This painting is best left in the past, where it belongs right alongside what Lily and I were. Right alongside what we probably can't ever be again.

I grab the supplies I came in here for and head back towards my car.

I think about the painting the entire drive home. And even as I settle into work, I can't shake the thought that, no matter how much time passes, no matter how much pain

Lily's caused, part of me will always be tethered to Lily, and I wish I could put that part of my brain on mute.

25

LILY

I step out of Natalie's office, and my mind is still spinning from the meeting. Natalie—the literary agent who reached out to me—was everything I'd hoped for. Warm, professional, and, most importantly, genuinely excited about my work, or at least, I think she was.

Her words replay in my head as I walk down the street, clutching my coat tighter against the wind.

"You have such a unique voice," she'd said, her eyes lighting up as she talked about my characters and the story. That should've made me feel on top of the world, right? But then she asked about my plans for revisions, and I stumbled through my answer. Hopefully, she just attributes it to nerves and not to me not being prepared.

I stop at a crosswalk, waiting for the light to change, and pull out my phone to check the email thread where we first talked. It's silly—I already know what it says I read it a million times—but seeing her initial excitement makes me feel a tiny bit better.

The walk back to my hotel feels longer than it should have. Every step filled with overthinking: Did I talk too much? Did I sell myself enough? Should I have brought a more polished revision? Am I good enough?

When I reach my room, I slump onto the bed, fish my notebook out of my bag, and jot down every detail I can remember from our meeting, hoping that writing it out will keep my brain from spiraling. When I'm done, I flip through the pages, now filled with frantic notes. Reading it back, the meeting sounds... good.

She smiled a lot, laughed at my weird jokes, knew so much about my previous books, and said she was impressed with the sales I had, considering I did no marketing.

That's good, right?

I let out a heavy sigh and toss my notebook back into my bag. I pull out my phone and stare at our email thread for the hundredth time today.

Should I send her a follow-up, thanking her again? Or would that make me look desperate? Thankfully, Clara texts me, and I can think about something else.

Clara 11:00 a.m.: Thursday night game night! are we still on?

Shoot... I completely forgot to let the girls know I was coming to Portland... now that I think about it, I don't even think I told my mom.

Lily 11:01 a.m.: Hey, I forgot to tell you guys, but I'm meeting with a literary agent in Portland. I'll be back tomorrow morning!

Alejandra 11:01 a.m: OMG! how exciting! good luck!

Valeria 11:01 a.m: Good luck!

Clara 11:01 a.m.: You got this! you'll have to tell us all about it when you get back! the rest of you, I expect to see you tonight!

I throw my phone into my bag and try to settle my mind. I'll either hear from Natalie in a few days with good news—or I won't, and I'll have to figure something out. Until then, all I can do is try not to let my nerves drive me crazy.

There's nothing I want more than to reach out to Isabella and tell her about all of this, but we haven't talked since our argument at her house.

I can't decide if reaching out is completely wrong because she asked for space or if I should be the one making the first move since I was the one who messed up in the first place.

I grab my phone, ready to text her, but I can't bring myself to do it. I shouldn't text her, she's probably busy and most likely doesn't want to hear from me anyway.

26

ISABELLA

It's been four days since I talked to Lily, and I should be consumed with prepping the gallery, but instead, my brain has decided to go on a Lily bender. Thanks to her text message in the group chat this morning, all I can think about now is how hurt I'll be if she doesn't show up.

I only do these installations once a year, and they're only up for a few short weeks, but man, do they draw a crowd. Sales from the first few days alone are enough to keep both the gallery and me floating comfortably for the entire year. So, yeah, no fucking pressure, right? This has to go off without a hitch, but I can't focus on it for more than five minutes without Lily or the memory of my high school art show popping into my head.

"Isa, should this be here? The Feng Shui is totally off!" Alejandra says jokingly—or at least I hope she's joking.

I look up to see what the hell she's talking about, and she's looking at Clarke and my very elaborate installation. I can't help but laugh.

"Are you crazy? Do you see how many things are hanging from the ceiling? I can't move the installation."

Alejandra looks at me and smiles, then looks back up at the installation. "I know you just looked somewhere far away, and that felt like the only thing that would bring you back. Are you all set for tomorrow?"

"Yeah, I'll be done as soon as I figure out which piece should go in the center of this wall," I say, pointing at the three paintings leaning against the back wall.

Alejandra walks over, eyeing the three paintings critically. "Tough choice," she muses, tapping her chin. "They're all amazing Bel, whichever you choose will be great."

I sigh, crossing my arms as I study them again. "I know they're amazing, that's why I picked them, but which one screams 'Look at me, I'm the star' without actually screaming?"

Alejandra laughs. "That one," she says, pointing at a painting across the room.

I look at her, deadpan. "You're not helping."

She shrugs, unbothered. "I'm not the artist here."

I groan, walking closer to the paintings.

The first one is of a woman with her arms stretched high above her head, feet planted firmly apart. Her hair sweeps back in these bold, wild strokes that make it look like she's dancing. Deep reds and oranges bring the whole painting to life.

In the second painting, the woman is in a more relaxed pose, sitting on the ground with one leg tucked beneath her. Her back is arched slightly, and her head is tilted to the side, giving her an air of tranquility. The soft curves of her body are highlighted with gentle pastels of pink and lavender, while her hands rest lightly on her knees.

The third painting merges both, with a woman caught mid-motion. She's in the middle of a twirl, with one arm extended outward and the other bent at the elbow, fingers pointed. Her body is slightly twisted. She's painted in greens and gold. It's beautiful, but does it belong in the center? Do any of these? I should have just grabbed the painting I had at home but one of the girls looks too much like Lily and that would have been weird.

Alejandra leans against the wall, watching me silently debate with myself.

"Honestly, Bel, whichever one you choose will be fine, just eeny, meeny, miny, moe it, and call it a day," she says as she comes up behind me. She wraps her arms around my waist and hugs me, resting her chin lightly on my shoulder.

"Will you just pick one? My brain isn't working right now... there's too much in there." I say, rubbing my eyes until I see splashes of color behind my eyelids.

"You mean Lily?" she says softly.

I freeze. "How... how do you know it's about Lily?" I ask as I turn to face her.

"Please, I'm not an idiot. I've seen the way you look at each other. Plus, the cabin walls were insanely thin." she says as she wags her eyebrows at me. "At first, Clara and I thought it was Valeria and Brooke, but then we heard them arguing. You should've seen Clara's face when she finally put it together." Alejandra smirks.

"Well, that's not embarrassing at all," I mutter, running a hand through my hair.

"Clara and I had a feeling though. We've been talking about this forever," she says with a grin. "Did you really think Clara, of all people, would accidentally book a cabin wrong? We thought forcing you two to share a room would make you work things out. And, well... I guess it worked... and then some," she adds with a laugh.

"Honestly, I was way too distracted to think about it at

the time, but now that I am... yeah, that doesn't sound like Clara at all."

Alejandra chuckles. "How did this even start?" she asks as she leans in.

"Which time?" I say.

Alejandra's eyes go wide. "What? this has happened before?"

I nod. "Yeah, in high school."

"No fucking way."

"Way. That's why she and I stopped talking to each other."

"You sneaky bitches. I need more, tell me everything."

So I do. From our first kiss to our first time hooking up, to Lily being a dumb ass.

"I can't believe this. Now I feel like an asshole for pressuring you to talk to Lily. If I had known all this, I promise you I wouldn't have done half the things I did."

"It's fine, I think, maybe I let you do it for so long cause I'd hoped one day it would work out. I could have told you, I knew you'd stop but I never did."

"So, what now?"

"Now? I don't know... I want to work things out with her, but I'm scared of getting hurt again."

"Do you think this is something you can live with never have explored?

"I don't think so, I feel like if I run from it, I won't ever forgive myself. I want to see if it can work this time. Even if we just end up back where we were a couple of weeks ago. But I also like hanging out with Lily and all of you, so I don't know if it's worth risking it again. This thing between us might not work."

Alejandra's grin turns into a warm smile as she nudges

my shoulder. "That's growth, Isa. Scary, complicated, messy growth—but growth."

"Thanks, Dr," I say, nudging back into her.

Alejandra watches me carefully. "Do you trust her?"

"No," I laugh. "But I want to," I say.

And I mean it. I've been debating with myself for days, thinking nonstop about everything, and I can't blame her for what happened. I don't know what I would have done if I thought I heard her talking about her wanting to be with her ex, especially if it was such a messy on-and-off relationship like the one I had with Resy. I hate that she didn't talk to me back then, but considering my history with Resy up to that point, I can see why she thought I'd just go back to her— because I always had. And we hadn't talked about what we meant to each other either, so she didn't know how much I loved her and how badly I wanted to be with her.

"You owe it to yourself to see where it goes, even if it goes nowhere," Alejandra says.

I take a deep breath, letting her words sink in. "I know... It's just hard to let go of our past."

"Of course it is, but you can't let fear hold you back. You deserve a chance at happiness, even if it comes with a little risk."

"Yeah, well, easier said than done," I mutter, staring at the floor.

"Look, Isa, this thing with Lily will get sorted out. She'll be here tomorrow, and maybe you guys can start talking about it then"

"Will she be here, though?"

"Of course! And if she isn't, well, that's an answer too. If Lily doesn't show, that means you shouldn't be putting your heart in her hands. But you need to give her the benefit of the doubt. You can't just decide she won't show and close yourself up. Not trying isn't the right answer either."

I nod.

Whatever happens tomorrow will decide what happens next. Right now, though, there's nothing I can do but make sure I put on an amazing show tomorrow. My art has always been my safe space, the thing that grounds me when life gets messy, and I can't let it or myself down. I need to focus on tomorrow's show and nothing else right now because I can't control what Lily will do.

I turn toward the paintings again and pick the second one—the one with the softer, dreamlike feel—and carefully place it at the center. It doesn't scream for attention, but it whispers, and sometimes, that's louder.

Alejandra gives me a thumbs-up. "Perfect choice."

Now, let's hope everyone else thinks so, too

27

LILY

Today's the day of Isabella's installation debut, and I'm not sure if I'm even welcome.

She still hasn't reached out, which isn't a good sign.

I kind of want to skip the whole thing, so I don't make this awkward for Isabella—in case she doesn't want me there—but I keep thinking of the regret I still hold on to for not being there for her during her high school art show.

Do I really wanna pile it on?

Plus, Isabella doesn't deserve me doing this to her again. She will never forgive me if I don't show up, and honestly, I might not forgive myself either. I have to go. I have to be there even if it's just for Isabella to throw me out—which, if I'm being honest, is what I deserve.

I need to show her that she can trust me and that I am worthy of her trust again.

The opening is at 6 p.m., and according to Clara, we should all be at the gallery at 5 p.m. to help Isabella with whatever we can.

It's almost 11:00 a.m., and I still need to drive back and get ready. Check-out is at 11:30 a.m., so I have about thirty minutes to get all my things and pick out an outfit for tonight. Thankfully, I thought about bringing my two favorite dresses from home.

Option one is a deep red silky dress with spaghetti straps. It hugs my curves just right and has a leg slit that's a little too dangerous for a girl that never sits on a chair properly. Option number two is a black strapless dress that's a little more flowy and has a back leg slit that's just as dangerous. I try them both on, but I can't decide. So instead, I text the group chat with Clara, Valeria, and Alejandra pictures of me in them to have them help me choose.

> Lily 12:15 p.m.: Attachment: 2 Images
>
> I need help deciding what to wear tonight!
>
> Clara 12:16 p.m.: Okay... hot... I like the black, but I LOVE the red
>
> Alejandra 12:16 p.m.: Oh yeah! Vote #2 for red!
>
> Valeria 12:17 p.m.: Ditto
>
> Lily 12:18 p.m.: Red it is! Thanks, guys.

I throw the red dress back on and take a look at myself in the mirror. The silky fabric clings perfectly to my body in all the right places, and I can't help but smile at myself—this dress looks like trouble, but in the best possible way.

I slip out of the dress and hang it behind the bathroom door. I take a quick shower before heading to the front desk to check out. Once I've given my key card back, I get all my things into my car, ready to start the three-hour drive back. But, of course, when I turn the key, the car doesn't start. *Great...*

I sit in my car for a second, my forehead resting against

the steering wheel, letting out a groan. I glance at the dashboard and immediately realize I left the headlights on all night, and now the battery is completely dead. Just my luck.

I dig into my purse, looking for my phone. I need to call my insurance and get roadside assistance asap. My fingers close around my phone, and for a second, I feel a spark of relief—until I press the power button. The screen stays black. Dead. Perfect. Just perfect.

I grab my bag, head back into the hotel, and approach the woman at the front desk, trying to muster up a polite smile despite the frustration bubbling inside me.

"Hi," I say, resting my hands on the counter. "My car battery's dead, and my phone is, too. Do you happen to have jumper cables or have someone who could help?"

The receptionist—a kind-looking older woman with glasses perched on her nose— looks up from her computer.

"Oh no! That's never fun," she says. "Let me check if we have any jumper cables. If not, I can call someone for you."

"Thank you so much," I reply, relief already starting to creep in.

She disappears into the back, and I look around the lobby, tapping my fingers against the counter, trying to keep myself from spiraling. A few minutes later, she comes back shaking her head.

"Sorry hun, we don't have any jumper cables," she says apologetically. "But I can call roadside assistance for you. They'll be able to jump your car or get you sorted."

"That'd be great," I say with a sigh, trying not to sound as frazzled as I feel. Because of course, this would happen today of all days.

I look over at the clock hung behind the front desk and

it's somehow already 11:45 a.m., not ideal but I still have time.

She picks up the phone and starts making calls to everyone she can think of, glancing at me as she speaks. A few minutes later, she hangs up.

"Okay, they'll send someone out, but it might take a little while. They're saying about an hour or so."

An hour? I can hear the clock ticking in my head, and I want to scream. I force myself to nod. "Thanks. I really appreciate it."

"No problem. Feel free to hang out in the lobby while you wait. We've got coffee over there if you need it."

"Thanks," I mutter, walking toward the coffee station. I pour myself a cup and try to push down the frustration threatening to bubble over. It's fine. I've got time. Sort of...

I sit in a chair near the main entrance to the hotel, my leg bouncing up and down nonstop as I quickly run the math in my head.

They'll be here in one hour, which puts me leaving here around 1 p.m. If I don't hit traffic, I can be there by 4:30 p.m. at the earliest. That's with no traffic, and hoping they actually get here in an hour.

Why today, Universe?

28

ISABELLA

Today is the fucking day!

It's almost 4 p.m., and the girls should be here soon—thank God—because there's still so much to do. Clarke and I have been at the gallery since 7 a.m., making sure everything is ready for tonight. And, for the most part, it is, all that's left is setting up the bar area for the bartender I hired and making sure every piece up for sale has a QR code for the auction. This is something new I'm trying this year. Instead of each art piece having set prices, anyone who's interested in buying it will need to place a bid online. No one will know what anyone else is bidding—you simply bid what the painting is worth to you, and the highest bidder takes it home at the end of the night. I wish I could say it was my idea—because it's kind of genius—but it was Sarah's.

I look around the gallery one last time, double-checking the lights for what feels like the hundredth time before heading home to get myself ready.

Clarke walks over with a bottle of water in hand and a raised eyebrow. Probably wondering what the hell I'm still doing here. I've said goodbye to her at least thirty times in the last hour.

"Alright, I'm gonna head home for real this time. I'll be back in like thirty minutes," I say, grabbing my jacket from the counter. "Need anything before I go?"

"No, I'm good," she replies, waving me off.

I nod and run to my car.

When I make it home, I run to the bathroom and take the fastest shower known to man. I step out and slip into a black dress—I wanted to wear a fitted black suit, but when I tried it on yesterday, it didn't fit the way I wanted it to. It was a little too boxy, and the measurements were all wrong. But that's what I get for waiting until the day before to try it on. But now that I'm looking at myself in the mirror, I clean up nicely in a dress. Lily will love it.

My heart sinks as I realize what I just thought about... I haven't thought about Lily once today. I've been too busy making sure the gallery is ready for tonight, but of course, the moment I'm alone, she takes over my thoughts.

I don't know if I'll see her today. I haven't heard from her in days. Not that I was expecting to—I told her not to reach out—but immaturely, I thought she would have by now. I can't fault her for not, though. She's respecting my wishes and I'm kind of glad. Last time, she blew up my phone for weeks, even when I told her not to, and it drove me crazy.

I should text her, though... It's last minute, and she probably won't be able to come anymore, but I should tell her she's welcome.

I pull my phone out and text her. Hoping against hope, she'll see it in time. I should have texted her sooner, but I didn't want to. I didn't want her to show up just because she thought we were ok but because she decided to put herself out there for me. But the more I thought about it, the dumber I felt because there's no way in fucking hell I would show up if she wasn't talking to me, so why would she?

Ball's in her corner now, if Lily doesn't show up by the time we do the unveiling I'm done with her, for good.

I set my phone down, and I try to push all thoughts of Lily to the side and do my makeup. If I take any longer, Sarah might kill me, so I keep my makeup nice and simple: foundation, blush, mascara, and eyeliner for my signature wing.

I look down at my phone to check the time and realize I'm running a little behind. There's also a string of messages waiting for me.

I immediately unlock my phone, hoping there's a message from Lily, but there's nothing. There are, however, a few from my mom, letting me know she's on her way to the gallery. Some from Sarah, making sure I'm on my way back to the gallery soon, and a few more from the girls.

I swipe over to the group chat and scroll through the messages.

> Clara 4:45 p.m.: Ale and I are ready. does anyone want us to pick them up?

> Valeria 4:45 p.m.: Yeah would you grab me? I was going to drive but since you're offering!

> Clara 4:45 p.m.: We'll be there soon. Lily?

> Valeria 4:45 p.m.: Lily isn't replying to any of my messages. Have any of you talked to her since this morning?

> Alejandra 4:46 p.m.: not since we all did…

> Valeria 4:46 p.m.: you think she's ok?

Clara 4:46 p.m.: yeah, her reception is probably bad on the passes. I'm sure she'll be there soon

Fuck... Now, all I can think about is how she probably won't show up, and it'll play out just like it did before—where she disappeared and stopped talking to me. And no matter how hard I try to trust she'll show up this time, all I can think about is that deep, nagging fear of being let down again. Just when I was ready to open up to her again. I already feel myself slowly shutting that part of me off.

I couldn't be a bigger idiot if I tried.

29

LILY

I stumble through the front door, crashing into a table on my way in. It's already 5:45 p.m., and I'm late—too late to even think about the bruise that's probably forming on my thigh. I run upstairs and plug my phone into the charger.

I slip into my red dress and run into the bathroom, doing my best to tame my hair, which is now a frizzy mess. Last night, I tried a TikTok hack—wrapping socks around my head to style it—but instead of neat waves. I ended up with frizzy hair. I was going to straighten it once I got home, but I'm out of time. With no other option, I throw it into a messy bun, quickly run a straightener over my bangs to give them some shape, and move on.

I put my makeup on haphazardly and throw on my dress, smoothing it down for the hundredth time as if that's going to magically fix the knots twisting in my stomach. I look at myself in the full-length mirror in my closet one last time and decide it'll have to do. I'm already running so late. Thanks to what happened this morning. What should've taken an hour at most somehow turned into a two-hour ordeal. When the roadside guy finally showed up, he couldn't get my car started, so it had to be towed to a shop, and I had to rent a car, which proved to be a lot more complicated than I thought. I had to go to four different places just to find an available car to rent that wasn't insanely expensive.

I was supposed to be at the gallery about an hour ago. Isabella must be thinking, I won't show up. I've never wanted super powers, but telepathy would be a great one to have right now, so I could let her know I'm on my way.

I grab my phone, hoping it's got some juice so I can text Isabella, but no matter how many times I press the power button, it won't turn on. I grab the portable charger from my nightstand, plug my phone in, rush downstairs to grab my keys, and head out the door.

———— ♥ ♥ ♥ ————

When I make it to the gallery, it's a little past six, so I rush inside, scanning the room for Isabella. The gallery is packed. I can't walk more than a few feet without running into someone. Servers move through the crowd with trays of champagne while people chat—some about the paintings, others about the big installation reveal happening in a few minutes. Even with the chaos in my head, I can't help but feel the excitement in the air. The anticipation is almost electric.

I think of calling Isabella but there's no way she'll be on her phone right now, so I keep moving through the sea of people, hoping I'll spot her. My heart races as I weave frantically through the crowd. But from every angle, people seem to be trapping me, blocking my way through no matter how many "excuse me" I mutter or how many "accidental" elbows to the ribs I throw to clear a path.

"Excuse me," I say and who turns around? Myra... *Great. Love that for me.*

She looks me up and down, and I have this irrational urge to throw a big blanket over myself, her eyes a little too icy for my liking.

"Lily," she says.

"Would you excuse me?" I say as I step to the right, trying to ignore her, but she steps right alongside me and blocks my way.

"She's not going to settle down with you, you know that right?"

I roll my eyes, trying to show her that what she's saying doesn't bother me, but man does it...

"That's for her to decide, don't you think?" I say as I step back to the left, but she steps with me again. I close my fists trying to suppress the need to punch her. I'm not usually an aggressive person, but she's really digging it out of me right now.

"She won't choose you. Not after what you did."

My blood runs cold, and all the warmth drains from my body as a thousand questions overflow my mind. *How does she know? Did Isabella tell her about our talk? When? When did she see her? Are they back together?*

But only one thought sticks out among the noise... Isabella made up her mind and didn't tell me.

Tears spring into my eyes, and I blink furiously, trying to hold them back. I can't be here anymore, so I roll my shoulders, muster up every ounce of composure I can, and look straight at Myra.

"Just because she didn't want you, doesn't mean that it

will be the same with me," I say even though I don't believe it.

I don't wait for her response. Instead, I shove past her and run to the bathroom. I open the door, and thankfully, it's empty. I rush into one of the stalls and sit on the toilet. I pinch the bridge of my nose and try to focus on the ceiling. Still trying to hold back the tears pooling in my eyes.

Myra's words are messing with my head and I don't think I can handle rejection from Isabella right now. I should go, talk to her another day. There's no shame in waiting, right? But then I think about disappointing her again. The whole reason I came here was to prove to her that she can trust me, but is proving that worth me getting hurt? I don't know what to do, but the more I think about this, the more I think I should go home. I pull my phone out in a last-ditch attempt at staying.

Maybe if I can find the girls, I can stay and get heartbroken knowing my support system is there. I try to turn my phone on, but it still hasn't charged. I follow the cord down to the charger only to see it's disconnected, and It's like the universe decided for me.

Home. I should go home.

I throw my phone back in my purse and walk out of the stall, wash my hands, and step out of the bathroom. I turn right and head towards the front door. Each step feeling like relief and regret tangled together.

I'm about to push the front door open and leave when I hear a laugh... her laugh. And I stop dead in my tracks. That laugh... God, it's worth getting your heart broken a thousand times just for a chance to hear it.

And now I have to make a choice.

Do I keep going and leave, or do I turn around and find her? Give her and us a chance. The knot in my chest tightens as I try to decide. Myra said Isabella's going to walk away. I already know how this ends. Who could blame me for protecting my heart? But I should be brave this time. I should show up for her, not because I want to be with her—even though I very much do—but because she deserves the kind of friend I failed to be ten years ago. Someone who shows up no matter what...

I don't know what to do.

30

ISABELLA

I take my place in the middle of the room, right next to the covered-up installation. Thankfully, I don't need to corral everyone this way. As soon as I stand next to it, everyone notices and starts walking towards the center of the room.

I look around, unfamiliar faces everywhere, all of them excited to see me, but the one I'm looking for is missing. *Where are you, Lily?*

I spot Clara in the crowd, and I mouth, "Lily?" she shakes her head. No one has seen her, which means she's not here.

She must not be coming because she hasn't answered any of our texts.

I try not to let the sinking feeling in my chest drag me down, but it's hard. My throat tightens, and I almost wonder if I'll be able to speak at all. I look down, close my eyes, and try to focus on my speech, a speech that now will be even harder to get through. I let out a big sigh, and when I look up, Myra is in the front row, looking at me with such adoration it makes my chest tight. Why can Myra put our past aside and be here, but Lily is nowhere to be found? She asked for another chance, and this is what she does? The same fucking thing she did last time? I feel like I'm about to lose my mind, but I can't because Sarah is done with her introduction, and I need to take over.

"Ladies and gentlemen, thank you all so much for coming today. I'm so excited to present this year's installation. As you can tell from the artwork up around the gallery, this year's theme celebrates sapphic romance through a unique fusion of abstract, realist, and intimate elements. As the curtains draw back, you'll see one of many centerpieces. Closest to you stands a heart sculpture, meticulously crafted from intertwined metal and glass, symbolizing the delicate yet enduring nature of love made by the very talented Clarke Cameron. Suspended from the ceiling are panels of tinted glass in soft, iridescent shades of pink, purple, and blue. These panels are designed to catch and refract the light, creating a play of colors that evokes the feeling of first love—vivid, chaotic, and all-consuming. It's like stepping into a world where everything is in technicolor, and the intensity of it surrounds you, falling like rain and enveloping you entirely."

The crowd gasps in awe as the installation comes into full view.

"I encourage you to focus on the center of the installation, where you'll find something deeply personal." I close my eyes, trying to figure out how to change this fucking speech, but when I look up, I think I'm dreaming... Lily is in front of me with a big smile on her face.

A wave of self-doubt makes my stomach churn at the sight of her, but seeing Lily look so calm and relaxed makes my racing heart settle, my brain quiet down, and the tension in my body melt away. The knot that was building in my throat earlier is completely gone, and the sight of her fills me with a warmth I hadn't felt in days. She looks so beautiful that, I forget how to breathe.

She's here, fuck... she's here, she's actually here. I want to run to her to wrap myself around her and ignore the hundreds of people here now, but I can't because Sarah's standing next to me whispering, "Isabella, finish your speech"

I tear my gaze from Lily and clear my throat, but as I look around, I can't settle my eyes on anything. My eyes keep wanting to find Lily, so I let them. And when I do, I focus on her and anchor myself to her, to this moment. Finding a spark of comfort in her eyes.

"This piece is one of my earliest works, created when I was still figuring out what love meant to me, trying to break free of destructive patterns, and allowing myself to believe I deserved happiness. All while trying to make sense of some very complicated feelings for my best friend. Feelings that consumed my very being, feelings that monopolized my thoughts and made me feel giddy and safe. Feelings that made me want to be all the amazing things I never thought I could be."

Lily's eyes widen. She takes an unsteady step back but her eyes never leave mine. The vein in her neck pulsing harder matching my own.

A nervous laugh slips out of my mouth before I've even started the last of my speech. I take in a big breath and continue.

"What you're looking at is a portrait of my first and only love. I felt it was only fair to lay myself bare since I'm asking all of you to connect with this installation and bear your own feelings. This piece represents not just my artistic journey, but also a tribute to my journey of self-discovery. It's not just about romantic love, but about understanding who I am through the lens of love's complexity and beauty. I invite you to immerse yourselves in this work, to revel in its presence, and to reflect on the multifaceted experience of love it represents. Thank you."

The tension that has been coiled in my chest since I saw Lily in the crowd. Turns into a flutter of nerves as I watch Lily frozen in place.

Fuck... maybe it was too much.

31

LILY

I stare at the painting in the center, completely taken aback and frozen in place. A wave of emotions hits me. It's a portrait of me—eyes closed, looking so peaceful, like I'm in the middle of some blissful dream floating on a cloud. Isabella's voice echoes in my head, repeating over and over: "This is a portrait of my first and only love."

Tears prick at the corner of my eyes, desperate to break free, and a lump starts forming in my throat. Just as I think my knees are about to buckle, someone places a hand on my shoulder, grounding me. I turn back, and it's Clara, a gentle smile tugging at the corner of her lips. Valeria and Alejandra appear behind her, each one of them grabbing, one of my hands rubbing small, soothing circles on the back of it.

"Are you okay?" Valeria asks.

I nod, a smile starting to break through my initial surprise. "Yeah, I'm just... this is..." My voice falters, and the tears that had started to well up before spill over, as the weight of everything hits me all at once.

Isabella walks over to me, her eyes searching and

worried. She's worried? Worried I hated it, maybe? But I didn't, I loved it.

"Lily I'm so so—" I lunge at her because what's about to come out of her mouth is not what I want her to say, so instead I do exactly what I've been wanting to do all week and kiss her.

I kiss her as if it's our last day on earth, pouring out all the love, excitement, and yearning I've felt over the past decade. Despite the anger and frustration that's been part of our story, I've always loved her and longed to be with her. In this moment, all those feelings come together in a kiss that speaks more than words ever could. *Or at least, I hope it does.*

When I finally pull away, a wave of clarity hits me, and I remember—we're still very much at her gallery, surrounded by strangers. The room is silent, and I swear I can almost hear the collective gasp of the crowd as they process what just happened.

My eyes start darting around, looking for a way out, but all I see are curious faces and the soft flicker of the gallery lights.

I want to say I'm sorry, but nothing comes out because I'm not sorry, and I don't care that there's a thousand eyes on us. I lunge into her again and kiss her. The entire world could be judging me, but I don't care because I am so happy nothing could ever bring me down. She wants to be with me, and knowing that lift, some of the tension gathered in my shoulders, and a wave of relief and happiness washes over me. The gallery and everyone in it fade into the background as we stand there, caught in this perfect moment. A moment that doesn't last nearly as long as I want it to, though.

"I hate to do this Isabella, but I need you to talk to

someone about a painting," Sarah says and Isabella pulls away.

"Stay after the show?" Isabella asks, her voice almost pleading.

"Of course," I say, pressing a quick kiss to her cheek. I wrap my arms around her just as Myra looks at us. I turn Isabella lightly so I'm eye to eye with Myra, and I flip her off. I don't think I've even flipped someone off before and the motion feels so foreign on my hands I don't think I will ever again, but she deserved it, so I'm glad I did it.

Myra rolls her eyes and walks out the door and I feel on top of the moon—*yes moon, it's higher than Earth.*

When I let go of Isabella, Sarah swoops in to whisk her away. I watch her walk off, and despite all the hurt and chaos of these past few years, I know without a doubt this is exactly where I'm meant to be.

32

ISABELLA

The debut of the gallery's newest installation went off without a hitch, and, to my massive relief, this year's auction surpassed last year's in every way.

When my assistant gave me the news, I almost fainted on the spot.

Now, the gallery is quiet. Everyone has left, and it's just Lily and me.

I flip the 'open' sign to 'closed' and take a deep breath before turning back around. Lily's standing in front of the installation, taking it all in again like I just unveiled it. The glass panels catch the dim light, reflecting it across her face. I've never seen anything more beautiful, and I silently beg my brain to hold on to this moment forever.

Adding the painting I made of her when we were teens was a last-minute decision, but from the moment I decided to do it, I knew it was the right choice. I'd been planning to talk to Lily about us and tell her I wanted to try again. But somewhere during a restless night, in one of my insomnia-fueled moments of clarity, I realized a grand gesture might make my feelings clearer.

I had half a mind to swap it out and change my speech when I thought she wasn't going to show up, but I decided to trust her and stick to it. But it would have been very embarrassing for me if I had gone through the whole speech and she hadn't shown up. Not that anyone would know, but I would've, and that's enough.

I take a slow step toward her, my heart pounding in my chest.

"Lily?" I whisper, and she turns to me, her eyes soft.

"Yeah?"

I gulp as I inch closer to her. Suddenly, all the nerves from earlier are back in my system.

"You're here," I say, still not fully believing it. "I didn't think you'd come. You never replied to my text."

"Oh, um... my phone is dead. It has been all day."

The second those words leave her mouth, everything in my body tingles, and the butterflies in my stomach flutter wildly. She came without knowing I wanted her here... fuck... that feels amazing. Maybe it wasn't crazy to want this from her. For years I wished she'd chosen me, and now she has, and everything feels safe.

Her eyes hold mine and I can't breathe. She steps closer, reaching for my hand. Her touch is gentle, but it's everything I need.

"This is beautiful," Lily says as she wraps my arms around her.

"I meant every stroke of that painting... you're still the one and will always be," I say as I kiss her shoulder. And before I can finish my sentence, my heart starts racing, and for the first time—ever in my life—my hands are sweaty. I swallow the knot in my throat and finally choke out, "I want us to try again, for real this time."

"I've been waiting for you to say that," Lily whispers as

she turns to face me. "I've always been waiting," she adds, wrapping her arms around me. I pull her close, resting my forehead against hers. Neither of us speaks as if words will somehow break the magic of the moment—gross I know, but I'm happy, let me be.

"I'm sorry it took me so long," I murmur. "I was scared. Scared of getting hurt again, scared of losing you, and scared of losing myself."

Lily's hand cups my cheek. I turn and kiss her palm.

"We were both scared," she says as her thumb brushes against my skin. "But maybe we needed that time. Maybe we had to grow before we could find our way back to each other."

I nod because it's true. The years apart weren't for nothing. I learned so much about myself—what I like, what I don't, how to communicate better, and how to set boundaries—something I didn't understand as a teen. But more than that, I learned what it was like to live without Lily, and I never ever want to do it again.

"Oh shoot, we didn't check off the last item with the girls!" Lily randomly shouts.

"I'm trying to profess my love for you, and you're thinking about the list?" I laugh caught off guard.

"I'm sorry, it just popped into my head," she says, picking at something on my dress.

"We'll see them in a few days we can check it off then," I say, trying to get the conversation back on track.

"Or...well... we can do it ourselves," she says. "Technically... I was at your high school art show years ago."

I blink, trying to figure out what she means because I remember that day vividly, and there's no chance she was there, and I didn't see her. She must be confused.

"What do you mean?" I finally ask.

Lily exhales slowly, her voice quiet "I was outside the gym the entire time. I saw some of your paintings, and I saw you talking to people about them. I just... didn't go inside."

"Why?" I ask as my chest tightens.

"I wasn't sure if I should. After I overheard you talking to Val, I kind of assumed you'd invite Resy, and I didn't think I could handle seeing her there."

"I can't believe you were there." I don't know what I'm feeling if I'm sad because she was there and didn't come in, or if I'm sad because she let me believe she didn't come, but I guess it doesn't matter now. She was here today, and that's exactly what I needed. But just knowing she was there... it heals something inside me.

I press a soft kiss to her forehead, and she sighs, leaning into me like she belongs there, like she always has. And for the first time in years, everything feels right.

EPILOGUE

"I love you," I shout to Isabella as I run out the front door. "I'll see you at the bookstore!" I don't wait for her to respond. I'm so late, I don't even have time to stop for coffee and that is the saddest part of today. But absolutely nothing can dampen my great mood today. It's publishing day! And I have an author signing at this cute queer bookstore in Seattle.

It's been six months since my meeting with Natalie—and Isabella's art show—and I never did hear back from her, which is still a bit of a bummer. I wish she'd just said no and let me move on with my life. But I guess that's what I get for putting all my eggs in one basket.

So, I decided that instead of leaving my fate in someone else hands, I'd take control of it myself and continue to self-publish—this decision was also a lot easier to make because my super amazing best friend, who's a marketing genius, agreed to help me market myself and this book. Thank the universe for Clara. I don't know why I didn't think of this sooner.

I get into my car and start to peel out of Isabella's

driveway—which, I guess, is my driveway now, too. So, I guess I pull out of our driveway. Ah, just the thought makes me want to scream with excitement. I moved into Isabella's house last week and there are still boxes everywhere. But man, was it the right choice.

I mean, Isabella and I haven't been apart since the gallery, and moving in together just made sense with how crazy life is getting. Her commissions have exploded since her art show, and they have only picked up pace as we inch closer to pride. Meanwhile, I've been running all over Washington trying to get every bookstore within a hundred-mile radius to stock my book. Plus, we missed out on being together for ten years, so any moment apart now feels like entirely too much.

I put my car in reverse and just as I'm about to hit the accelerator, Isabella walks out the door. She flags me down and rushes down the stairs. She opens the passenger door and slides in, buckling herself in.

"I thought you were gonna go with Alejandra and Valeria," I say

"Yeah, I was, but sitting in the car with you for an hour sounds like a much better plan," she says as she grabs my hand and kisses my palm. And it makes me blush. Everything she does still makes me feel nervous and shy.

"As it should," I joke, pressing my cold hands against her warm cheeks. Isabella laughs.

I go to grab her hand and spot something in between her hands. A book... my book.

"What are you doing with that?" I laugh.

She looks down and smiles. "The author's pretty cute. Gonna have her sign this and I'm going to ask for her number," Isabella says, wagging her eyebrows.

"Are you now?" I say as I shake my head, feigning hurt.

Isabella leans in closer until our shoulders brush. "Duh, you think she'll say yes?"

I laugh, rolling my eyes as I turn towards the road. "She might. She's a bit of a softie for romantic gestures."

"Oh, lucky me," Isabella teases.

Her lips meet mine in a sweet kiss that melts into warmth, spreading through my chest. And for the umpteenth time today, I feel like the luckiest girl alive to love and be with my last & first love.

ACKNOWLEDGMENTS

Wow, where do I even start?

Thanks to my wonderful wife, Angelica, for reading and loving every single iteration of this book (even the ones I'm convinced she only loved because she loves me). You are so much more than I deserve, and I cannot get enough of you. Te amo.

Thanks to my furbabies for doing their very best during long writing days and not driving me—totally—insane. You made the best writing partners a girl could ask for. Thank you, Porter, Pickles, and Shadow, for your slobbery love, and to Mulder, thank you for the calming purs on days I was stressed. I know you only did it because your favorite mom wasn't around, but I appreciate it anyway.

Anna, Cass, Neika, Meikko, Rose, and Bri, thank you for being my first readers! I'm kind of embarrassed I sent that first draft to you, but this book wouldn't be what it is now without your notes, questions, and flat-out confusion. I don't know what I would have done without ya'll.

Rebecca, I really cannot express how much your developmental notes helped me with my book. You are the best editor I could ask for, and I'm so so thankful to you for your input and notes. You helped me bring this book to life. Thank you.

Last but—absolutely—not least, thank you, the reader. I cannot express how fucking thankful I am for you. You took a chance on me and my debut novel and are helping my dreams come true, and I don't think I could ever express all that means to me. I hope you loved Isabella and Lily just a fraction of how much I loved writing them and sharing them with you. Thank you, thank you, thank you!

Made in United States
Troutdale, OR
02/21/2025

29214246R00166